PRAISE FOR NICK

"*Where the Bones Lie* isn't just Nick Kolakowski's strongest novel yet, it's a helluva page-turner, loaded with sinister humor, a twisty plot, and the kind of complicated characters readers deserve. Don't miss this one."

Alex Segura, author of
Secret Identity and *Alter Ego*

"Sharp, gritty, and knowing, *Where the Bones Lie* is a road trip into California's gleaming, seething underbelly. Movie stars, mobsters, wildfires – buckle up and hold on for a heady ride."

Meg Gardiner, #1 *New York Times* bestselling author

"*Where the Bones Lie* crackles and burns like the wildfires chasing its cagey characters from one deathtrap to the next. Nick Kolakowski has dragged the California noir out of the ashes and into the 21st century."

Scott Von Doviak, author of
Lowdown Road

"Although noir wasn't born on the sun-scorched streets of LA, it took to them like a natural. Now the seas are rising and the hills are burning but Hollywood continues on, more in need of its cleaners and fixers than ever. Nick Kolakowski slots his beautifully-drawn characters deftly into the dark mechanism on the flip side of fame. A propulsive pace, first-class dialog, and a setting so hot you can feel it made this a book I couldn't put down. Highly recommended."

SJ Rozan, bestselling author of
The Mayors of New York

"Nick Kolakowski's *Where the Bones Lie* starts off in fifth gear and never slows down. This is the best detective novel I've read in years."

Steve Weddle, author of
The County Line

Nick Kolakowski

WHERE THE BONES LIE

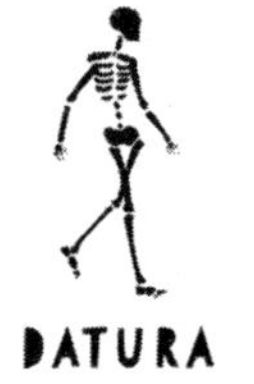

DATURA

DATURA BOOKS
An imprint of Watkins Media Ltd

Unit 11, Shepperton House
89-93 Shepperton Road
London N1 3DF
UK

daturabooks.com
twitter.com/daturabooks
Hold them over a barrel

A Datura Books paperback original, 2025

Edited by Daniel Culver and Alice Abrams
Cover by Rebecca Wright
Set in Meridien

ISBN 978 1 91552 349 5
Ebook ISBN 978 1 91552 350 1

Printed and bound in the United Kingdom by CPI Group (UK) Ltd, Croydon CR0 4YY

9 8 7 6 5 4 3 2 1

For Medora

"The city burning is Los Angeles's deepest image of itself."
Joan Didion, "The Santa Anas"

1.

Manny found me after my set on the *Giggle Lounge*'s second stage, the smaller one where they dump the newbies and terminally unfunny. I was working on new material but nobody in the audience laughed until I made jokes about traffic. When all else fails, you can always joke about traffic and Angelenos will at least give you a chuckle, even the hipsters from Silver Lake who work from home and travel around on electric scooters.

"You really bombed," Manny said. He had followed me from the stage to the far end of the bar, where he cornered me against the wall – one of his classic moves, allowing him to use his massive girth to its most intimidating effect. "They pay you for that?"

"They pay me in alcohol," I said, shoving a free drink ticket at the bartender, who retaliated with a watered-down rum and Coke. "Why are you here, Manny? You finally develop a sense of humor?"

"I got a sense of humor. I hired you, remember?" He jabbed a finger at my neon-orange Hawaiian shirt. "I also remember when you, the great Dash Fuller, the terror of paparazzi everywhere, used to wear lovely suits instead of that abomination."

"Helps me blend with this crowd," I said, noting how

Manny's two-piece Tom Ford suit was impeccable as usual, but his dress shirt was wrinkled around the collar. Given his intense dedication to always looking faultless – *my image is the job*, he liked to say – it was a startling flaw. Something big was distracting him.

"Maybe it's time for you to unleash the bespoke," he said. "I have an urgent quest for you."

"I quit, remember? I'd rather dunk my head in a barrel of fire ants."

"Oh, stop being dramatic. We need someone who's not on the payroll. The scumbags are all over this one."

"Not interested," I said, draining the drink. Onstage, a shaggy dude in a Scooby-Doo t-shirt launched into his first joke of the night, about the ghost of Marlon Brando watching a Marvel movie. He was unfunny enough to make me feel better about my own performance.

"Yeah, like your standup career is going so well," Manny snorted. "Come on, we both know you could use the cash. And you won't have to hurt anyone this time. Promise."

I considered it. It was five days until the end of the month, and I was down to a couple hundred dollars in my bank account. I had originally planned to re-download the usual gig apps and spend fifteen hours a day delivering food and driving people around until I could cover my rent. I preferred gigging for ZoomFood, a local app that paid a great rate but forced its drivers to wear a purple vest and baseball cap stamped with its yellow 'Z' logo, a humiliating costume I kept wadded in the corner of my car trunk. A job with Manny could spare me that exhausting fate.

I didn't want to dip a toe back into his swamp.

But I didn't want to end up on Skid Row, either.

"Half in advance," I said, already hating myself. "And if I

don't like where the job is going, I'm keeping the cash and walking away. Can you live with that?"

Manny nodded. "It'll have to do. I'm not explaining the job here. Come outside with me."

"Why? It's a hundred degrees out."

"More like eighty. Don't tell me you've gone soft like all these twits in here."

"Careful," I said, gesturing for him to lead the way to the doors. "They're very sensitive."

We exited the *Giggle Lounge*. The air smelled faintly of smoke and the night sky had an orange tint. There was a fire in the rolling hills near the Getty Center, three hundred acres burned and counting, powered by the Santa Ana winds. As we stepped beyond the club's bubble of air conditioning, the heat was like a feverish hand over my face.

Manny's blue Mercedes SUV sat at the far end of the parking lot. He unlocked it to disable the alarm before leaning against the driver's side door and pulling a vape from his suit pocket and sucking on it. "I get the comedy thing. It's the girls, right?" he said, blowing a cloud of apple-scented vapor. "You're still relatively young. You can score those hipster chicks, they're fit from all that Pilates, they'll do anything to show they're marriage material. It's got to be that. It's sure as hell not the money. How much does the average comedian make? A buck-ninety?"

"Instead of exposing me to your grodiest fantasies," I said, "how about you tell me what the wonderful world of Hollywood PR needs tonight?"

"Okay." He blew a cloud of apple-scented vapor. "You follow Karl Quaid on social media?"

"I don't do social media, remember?"

"Oh yeah, you're one of the few smart people on that

front, I forget. But even in your precious bubble, you know about the Karl Quaid situation, right?"

I nodded. How could I not? Karl Quaid was the front-page story on every tabloid website from here to Karachi. The studio had structured a superhero franchise around his performance as Doppler, a heroic vampire with the powers of eco-location and flight, and the first two movies had racked up almost two billion dollars at the box office. Of course, that was before Quaid went nuts.

"As of now, Karl's officially crossed the line from weirdo to dangerous," Manny said, taking another hit of nicotine. "Filming on the next movie starts in three weeks, and nobody can find the guy. One of the biggest stars in the world, and he disappears, poof. What makes it even worse is–"

"News said he's got that actress with him, right?" I said. "The parents are upset?"

"Amber Rodney, yeah, and the shooting on her new show kicks off in a month. Thank everything holy she's a couple years too old to be jailbait, but her parents are threatening to sue the studio, and so's the streamer producing her show. That's not even the worst of it. Karl's posting about crazy Jonestown stuff – demons run the world, everyone needs to commit suicide at the same time, one big adios to save the environment. Police are getting a little too interested."

"And you can't find him?" I grinned, enjoying Manny's discomfort. "Even with all his posting?"

"No. He's smart enough to never post a photo of a place we recognize. It's not a criminal investigation, technically, so we can't get a court order for the location metadata. I got people sitting outside his houses – he's got three, if you're wondering. We're watching his mom in Utah, his sister in

Colorado, anyone else he usually hangs out with. Nothing."

"And you think I can do something."

The front doors of the *Giggle Lounge* crashed open, ejecting a crowd of drunken twentysomethings into the parking lot. Manny quieted until they stumbled past. "You were my best guy," he said, not quite meeting my eyes. "Look, I'm sorry how it ended. I shouldn't have asked you to do certain things. But I appreciated it, and I know the studios did, as well. This situation with Karl, it won't be like the old days. We need fresh eyes on it."

"Ten thousand," I said.

"You don't come cheap," he said.

"You're well aware of what I can do."

"Sure, but I can't do that amount. How about four?" He nodded at my ancient Nissan Altima in the far corner of the lot, beyond the flickering edge of the *Giggle Lounge*'s neon lights, where I'd parked it in the forlorn hope that the shadows would cloak its rusted panels, the dented driver's door, the sky-blue paint bleached in odd patterns by years of fierce sun.

"I can't believe you're driving that," he said, "instead of that beautiful Benz you used to have."

"I couldn't deal with the Benz," I said.

"Then upgrade to something that doesn't burn as much oil as gas, mother of God. Please tell me it's got more power than a Prius," he said, and winked.

"Ten grand," I said again, before dropping into a passable Liam Neeson imitation: "You need my very particular set of skills."

We regarded each other. Manny's gaze was like a laser heating flesh, and the longer I stayed within its focus, the harder it was to keep my face stony and my eyes neutral.

Except I was tough enough to win this round. He notched his head to the left, his laser drifting to the front of the club, and said, "Fine."

"Half in advance."

He patted his jacket. "Got it right here. Figured you'd drive a hard bargain."

"Plus expenses." Maybe I couldn't tell a joke that brought down the house, but I could leverage a desperate soul.

He raised a hand. "Just a couple hundred bucks at most. I won't give you more leash than that. You know what you'd do with it."

Yes, something unbearably stupid. Deep in the tailspin of my former life, I'd tried to expense a bad weekend in Vegas. Studio accounting is a wiggly game, and its high priests ensure even the biggest blockbuster never earns a profit on paper, and yet they'd objected to my attempt to pass on several thousand dollars in liquor and gambling expenses. Nor had Manny appreciated my joke about itemizing Krystal (the champagne) and Krystal (the stripper).

"Fine," I said. "But I'm not signing anything. No NDAs, no non-disparage agreements. I'll never talk."

"Yes, yes, okay. I love how you get more annoying with age."

"Making sure we're clear."

Manny puffed again, tilting his head to follow the roaring lights of a 747 descending toward LAX. I wondered if he regretted his choice of profession. I could have told him that quitting feels liberating at first, but the memories never leave. I had cracked the heads of hangers-on who'd leaked to the press, stolen phones and laptops from expensive villas, rescued kidnapped dogs, and escorted pregnant girlfriends onto buses bound for Omaha, all so the studios could keep their stars untarnished and the money rolling in. How do you ever scrub clean of that?

And now they wanted me back in.

I hated how that idea made my stomach tingle, but I couldn't deny a part of me had always loved the hunt.

Manny prodded my elbow with a thick envelope. "Here's the first payment," he said. "You know the drill: absolute discretion. You find Karl, you call me immediately, and only me. You got it? Silence, cunning, and deceit."

2.

After Manny left, I returned to the *Giggle Lounge*'s second stage. The shaggy dude was still working the microphone, telling a long and convoluted story about how he ended up in the emergency room with a beer bottle stuck on his thumb. The audience was silent as deep space. I ascended to the stage and the dude – I vaguely remembered his name was Trevor – trailed off, squinting in confusion.

"Give me the mic," I said, snapping my fingers.

Trevor handed it over, proving yet again the maxim I'd learned as a fixer and bagman for Hollywood's finest: do anything with confidence, and people will follow your lead without hesitation. We all have a reflexive need to obey someone in clear command. I took the sweaty microphone and turned to the crowd, figuring the club's management would ban me from the premises after performing this stunt, but I was never going to become the next Robin Williams anyway.

"I have money," I said, holding up the fat envelope from Manny. "If anyone can give me any information on where I can find Amber Rodney and Karl Quaid, I will give you a thousand bucks. Potentially a lot more. But the information needs to be good, you understand? I'll be waiting in the parking lot if any of you want to take me up on it."

Someone at the bar broke into hysterical laughter.

"This isn't a bit," I said. "Everyone in this room is an actor or knows an actor, even you D-list reality show wannabes. I know how all of you talk. I'm not interested in harming Amber or Karl, but I do need to find them. You know where I'll be."

Someone to my left giggled. Maybe I should have built my comedy routine around my old job. There's always humor in doing horrible things, right? Trevor stared at me with big puppy eyes as I handed the microphone back and whispered, "Good luck."

Outside the club, I took position in the most well-lit portion of the parking lot, within sight of the bouncers, and waited to see who bit at my lure. Discretion and silence are all well and good, but I've learned you sometimes need to go loud if you want results.

Trevor's set must have ended, because a sizable crowd pushed through the doors, some of them hollering and pointing at me. I waited. If anyone wanted to volunteer information, they would hold back until the bystanders thinned out. There was a slim chance that someone in a crowd of fifty would have what I needed, but I had to start somewhere.

Fifteen minutes later, as I was debating whether to leave, a thin blonde girl in a tank top crept toward me. She had a spider tattoo on her left shoulder and a ring through her nose. She stopped well beyond my reach and crossed her bony arms over her chest.

"A thousand, huh?" she asked.

"If you got something good."

She waggled a hand. "I might. What are you? Reporter? Paparazzi?"

"Private detective." That was a lie, of course, but it felt like the right thing to say.

"You got a license, something like that?"

"Working toward it. You need three years of investigative work." I'd read that in a magazine once.

She tilted her head. "Okay, well, I'm not telling you my name. Show me the money first."

I pulled the envelope out of my pocket and opened it enough for her to see the crisp hundred-dollar bills inside. "If the info's good, ten of these bills are yours. What is it?"

"ZenKittenThree, no spaces. It's a profile on Instagram."

"Whose profile?"

"A friend of Amber's. She's got, like, three followers. Doesn't use tags, hashtags, anything like that."

"A friend of Amber Rodney."

"Yeah."

"And Amber's in her posts?"

"Yeah, but she's all disguised. Big hat, sunglasses, scarves. Karl Quaid is with her, too, but he's wearing a mask in all her shots, like a cloth one with an octopus design on it, plus sunglasses."

I pulled out my phone and opened Instagram. I'd half-fibbed to Manny about social media: I didn't maintain any accounts under my own name, but I had a few ghost profiles sprinkled around, just in case. I tapped 'ZenKittenThree' into the search bar. "And the posts are all recent?"

"Within the last day or two."

As the profile popped into view, I flicked through the images. The most recent ones were snapped in what was clearly West Hollywood: a stretch of Laurel Avenue, a popular brunch place with a line of angel-headed hipsters stretching out the front door, the public entrance of the

Chateau Marmont. Against this glitzy-gritty backdrop paraded young people dressed in hip, expensive clothes, their faces covered by hats and sunglasses and cloth masks – but their clothing couldn't fully cloak the profiles of two of the world's most famous people. I noted Karl Quaid's razor-sharp cheekbones poking above the edges of his colorful mask, and the galaxy-dark eyes of Amber Rodney below a wide-brimmed cowboy hat.

The next few images were bleak: baggies of pills on a table, alongside a gold-plated 9mm handgun. A thin forearm with a nasty bruise near the wrist. A gleaming white sink smeared with blood.

"Is your friend in trouble?" I asked.

The girl shifted from foot to foot. "She's been friends with Amber since they were kids. Maybe 'friends' is too strong a word – she's more like a follower? Amber lets her post if she doesn't tag anyone, mention the location, whatever."

I tilted my phone so she could see the image of the sink. "Whether or not this blood is real, it's a call for help."

"You think I don't know that?" she snarled. "I been telling her to get away, but she says she needs to protect Amber. Karl's got a whole lot of girls around him. There are guns, pills, plus he's making them fast for, like, three days at a time to boost their chi–"

I put my phone away and slipped ten bills from the envelope. "Before I give this to you, I have one last question: where are they?"

"I don't know, okay? If I did, I would tell you. Was that good enough? Do I get my money?"

"Sure," I said, holding out the bills. "Don't tell anybody about this, okay?"

"I swear." She snatched the money and backed away. "You'll make sure they're all okay?"

I didn't answer her. I'd seen too many bad things to promise anything to anyone.

3.

After the blonde girl disappeared into the night, I sat in my car and turned on the air conditioning and examined the Instagram feed again. Amber Rodney and Karl Quaid lurking around town was a good sign – they weren't in Antarctica, at least. I started by Googling Karl Quaid's known houses. The only one in California was his three-bedroom bungalow on Tianna Road in Laurel Canyon, but if Manny was telling the truth, it was surveilled by scary guys like me.

Searching a famous person's online presence for anything useful is like trying to find a valuable coin in a mound of elephant dung: the shit-to-gold ratio is always too damn high. As I flicked through the images, my frustration rose, a pressure building behind my eyes. I was too rusty at this. How would I track down this freak if I had no idea where to start?

It was so tempting to call Manny and tell him I was keeping the cash and walking away. I had better things to do with whatever time I had left in this burning world. Except the professional in me, the one who'd once cruised these streets like a shark, refused to stop.

I kept cycling back to the photo of the brunch place in West Hollywood. It was named *Voodoo Carb*, and I'd been there before: I recognized the wooden columns strung with holiday lights, the scrawny desert plants in garish clay pots, the plates stacked high with slices of fruit and wedges of the joint's signature purple pancakes. Karl and Amber wore masks and sunglasses, but the staff would have guessed their identities instantly, because you don't spend years slinging meals in a high-end place without developing a keen ability to guess stars by their voices, especially after the pandemic.

I found *Voodoo Carb*'s main number on its website and dialed.

"Voodoo Carb," answered a bored voice, loud over the chaos in the background.

"Jimmy working tonight?" I asked.

"Jimmy who?"

"That stringy guy behind the bar."

"Oh, our mixologist. Yes, he's currently on shift. Would you–"

"Thanks," I said, and ended the call.

I shifted into drive and aimed my rattling Nissan toward Sunset Boulevard. The sky was melting, blurring neon and steel and concrete and glass into a throb of color, and I remembered too many nights like this one, driving home exhausted after another secret mission, the radio cranked to a sad song so I'd feel something, anything.

I needed to do better this time.

4.

Voodoo Carb was stuffed with beautiful people picking over its new dinner menu. To most of the world, it was a hot West Hollywood spot known for its kimchi pancakes and pierogis, the latter supposedly made by the chef's grandmother. I knew it as the place where I'd once pulled an overdosing pop star named Riley Valentine out of the bathroom after blasting a double dose of naloxone up her nostril. As I entered, I wished I was wearing one of my old suits, perhaps the black two-piece with the narrow lapels that made me look like an owner or a gangster.

Jimmy the Bartender was pouring drinks for a long line of customers along the bar, bobbing his head to the electronic thump from the expensive sound system. I positioned myself at the far end, closest to the double doors leading to the kitchen, and draped a hand on the bar, a twenty-dollar bill folded between my fingers. He never looked in my direction, but like all good bartenders, I knew he sensed me.

While he worked his way down, I read the menu beside my elbow. The drinks cost as much as a full tank of gas, elaborate concoctions of rum and dry vermouth and egg whites and sherry and oregano. I'm sure they all tasted sublime, but I preferred drinks that smashed my brain to nonsense as quickly as possible. A couple straight-up shots of whiskey were better than therapy.

"Hello," Jimmy said, arriving before me. Then he recognized my face, and his wide smile shriveled and died like a worm on hot pavement.

"You remember me," I said. Not a question.

"Want to get rid of that gray?" He gestured at his neo-hillbilly sideburns. "I got a guy for that."

"I'm not worried about the gray in my hair." I beckoned for him to lean closer. When he did, I said as softly as possible over the pounding music: "I'm worried about finding Karl Quaid. I know he was in here a couple days ago."

"I don't know anything about that," he said, leaning back – and I snagged his wrist, holding it lightly with my thumb and forefinger.

"No, you do," I said. "The staff always talks. Even if you weren't on shift."

He tried pulling away again, and I squeezed harder, right on the pressure point, sparing a quarter-second glance at the restaurant's open front door, where an enormous bouncer sat on a stool, facing the sidewalk.

"I remember that night here with Riley," I said, jutting my head toward the bathrooms to our left. "You're the one who sold to her. Tell me what you know, and I'll leave, I swear."

"I can't help you." He swallowed. "I won't help you." In his straining eyes I could see the whole sorry hierarchy of Hollywood, where bottom-feeders like him forever lived in fear of the leviathans in their mansions. The fear of never seeing your sorry dreams fulfilled. The fear of ending up in a plastic bag in a canyon grave.

I could have tried for a bribe. A thousand dollars has a

way of loosening lips. But I would have no way of knowing whether he was telling the truth, not until it was too late. My fingers clenched again, grinding his bones, and I wondered how much pain I could deliver before someone at the bar noticed and made a scene. Back in the day, I had a solid grip, more than enough to crack a bone open.

The thought made my stomach clench.

I wasn't that guy anymore.

Manny had hired a ghost.

I released Jimmy and leaned back. "Fine," I said, as he winced and rubbed his wrist. "I thought we were friends."

I stood, bracing my hand against the bar as my guts flipped again, and slipped through the double doors to the kitchen, ignoring the line cooks' shouts as I exited through the rear door to the alley. Back in my car, I leaned forward and rested my head against the steering wheel until I felt a little more solid.

Emphasis on the word 'little'.

What could I do now?

5.

With my options fading away, I flicked through ZenKittenThree's photos again. Another one caught my eye. I reverse-pinched the screen, zooming in on Amber Rodney standing in a gravel driveway hemmed by palm trees. Her head was tilted to the left, and her sunglasses reflected a swirl of black on white.

I pinched again, and the swirl resolved into the letters 'H' and 'u' in loopy script, above '23'.

I hadn't noticed it the first time.

Or maybe my brain had refused to see it.

My throat tightened, trapping my breath in burning lungs.

To seven billion other people, that pixelated reflection would have meant nothing, but I knew exactly what Amber was viewing: a pillar beside a mansion's front door with iron lettering bolted to it. The lettering read 'Huell House 2394', and I knew that because a long time ago, I had to execute a stunningly dirty deed in that house to save a fading movie star from public shame.

I willed my throat to relax. Breathed out slowly, then sucked air. You're fine, I told myself. You're fine.

I wasn't fine. The universe had just extended a stiff middle finger in my face.

A quick web search informed me that Huell House was available for rental for thousands of dollars per week. It was a Spanish Colonial pile with a heated saltwater pool on the back terrace, four bedrooms on the second floor, and a screening room in the basement. There was also a three-bay garage, but none of the web pages mentioned its concrete floor and large drains, which made it easy to scrub away any spilled oil. Or poisoned vomit.

Hell House, Manny once called it.

The place where I'd failed someone who needed help.

I wanted to run as fast as I could in the other direction.

But I also wanted my money. I needed to know if Amber and Karl Quaid were inside.

Traffic had thinned out at this late hour, and it took me only a few minutes to motor up to the address on Cole Crest Drive. I kept the Nissan in as good condition as I could afford, but the steep inclines made its engine whine like a starving dog. Of all my everyday fears, I dreaded the prospect of a car breakdown the most: life in L.A. without a vehicle was like trying to survive on a shrinking ice floe in the Arctic.

I'd lived in L.A. for twenty years and the chaos of architectural styles in the Hills always bothered me: tile-roofed Spanish Colonials fighting for space along the crumbling cliffsides with ultra-modernist blocks of glass and white concrete, interspersed with smaller ranch houses out of an old sitcom. You needed a fortune to live in these heights, and I suppose that also fueled my simmering resentment against this part of town: despite doing so many bad things, I couldn't afford an outhouse here. So much for the American Dream.

Cole Crest Drive was a narrow road, and it was trash day, so I had to slalom around recycling and garbage cans wheeled too far from the curb. I passed Hell House's beige wall, split in the middle by a narrow iron gate, through which I caught a sliver of gravel driveway. I shuddered as I drove past the house and stopped at the curve fifty yards downhill, parking on a sandy shoulder with a sweeping view of the hills.

Before I flicked my headlights off, I checked the nearby walls and poles for surveillance cameras, seeing none. I noted how the nearest trees were scorched black, along with patches of the dry grass below. It was expensive to live at this altitude, but the fires didn't care about the residents' net worth or their latest deals.

Memories of days-long stakeouts made me wish I'd stopped for a coffee before driving up here. Part of me wanted to call Manny with an update. No, that was a bad idea. Manny was an okay guy when he was off the clock but an absolute nightmare when he smelled prey, and I didn't want him calling me back every five minutes for news.

I opened the music app on my phone, which was connected to the car's stereo, and selected an ambient chill playlist. Soaring fjord music filled the space. I settled back, imagining black water and majestic icebergs beneath a gray sky. I was prepared to wait.

I didn't have to wait long.

Headlights swept across the hilltop. A cherry red convertible stopped in front of the gate, and a gaunt man in a snakeskin jacket climbed out, a black backpack in his right hand. He buzzed at the gate, bent to say something into the speaker grille, and leaned against the wall.

I activated the camera app on my phone, zoomed in on him, and snapped a few images. The man's head swiveled in my direction, but I couldn't tell if he saw me in the dark. In the driveway beyond the gate, lights popped to life, framing a moving silhouette. Even in the dimness, this new person's hair and jawline belonged unmistakably to Amber Rodney.

The gate opened, and the man opened the backpack and passed her a small package wrapped in plastic. She nodded and closed the gate again before disappearing up the driveway. The lights snapped out.

The man stared daggers in my direction before returning to his car. His headlights flicked on, followed by the deep roar of his engine. He slowed down as he passed me, his black eyes meeting mine. Then he was gone. I knew a high-end drug dealer when I saw one.

I resisted the urge to call Manny. Locating Amber would solve some of the studio's problems but not all of them. I needed eyes on Karl.

As I sat there, wondering what to do and trying to ignore the worry gnawing at my gut, red and blue lights flickered in my rearview mirror. An LAPD cruiser pulled close to my rear bumper, its spotlight playing over my license plate. I turned off my music and lowered my window and took out my driver's license and registration, resisting the urge to laugh as I did so, because surely it was the dealer who'd called the police on me. What kind of self-respecting criminal ratted someone out?

The shadows of two officers approached. The one on my left flicked a flashlight across my front and back seats, then tapped on the front passenger window. When I buzzed that window down, he said, "My partner here is gonna help you out."

The other cop was already beside me, his flashlight beam in my eyes. "Good evening," he said. "License and registration?"

"Sure." I handed those over. Yet again, I wished I was wearing one of my beautiful suits. Cops relax when they see a man in a tailored two-piece.

"Dash Fuller, that's actually your name?" he asked as he scanned my information. "What brings you out here at this time of night?"

"Enjoying the evening," I said, pointing toward the glittering lights of the city. "It's a real fantasia once the smog lifts."

"I'm going to need you to move on," he said, passing back my documents. "We've received some complaints from residents about you loitering."

"This is a public road, right?" I asked.

"Hey, partner?" the other cop said, his light playing over my face. "You said Dash Fuller?"

"That's right," the first cop replied. "You know this guy?"

The other cop chuckled. "By reputation. Hey, Dash, how's it going? You remember Brian Pinto, deputy chief out of West Bureau?"

"Yeah," I said, unsure of where this was going. I had a quid pro quo thing with Pinto for a couple of years, mostly the kind of friendly information exchange that takes place nightly between cops and creatures like me. His people also did me a favor once – the kind of favor you kept secret for the rest of your life.

"Excellent. Because he remembers you good," the other cop said, lowering his light. I had a clearer view of his face, round and hairless as the full moon, but I didn't recognize him. The reflective nametag on his chest said: 'M. SANDERSON'.

"I heard you quit the gig," Sanderson said into my silence,

leaning closer. "Pinto's mentioned you a bunch of times. You did some *wild* stuff, I heard."

"I did," I said. "But I just do standup these days. You should come by, catch a show."

Sanderson froze. Maybe he wondered if I was messing with him. In that ticking silence my nostrils flared with the acrid scent of smoke. It smelled like burning wires and drywall, like a house was burning to the foundations.

"I'll tell him I saw you," Sanderson said.

"You do that," I said.

"Let's go," Sanderson told his partner. "This guy's okay."

His partner grunted deep in his throat. "Have a good evening," he said, before walking away. As their cruiser shot past me, its lights flashing, I flicked my music back on, hoping the gentle electronica would calm my nerves, slow my heartbeat. *He remembers you well.* Was that a threat? How was it not?

Another few minutes of droning synth did nothing to soothe me, so I cut off the music again and exited the car. The sun had set hours ago and yet the breeze felt hotter than a dog's breath. I stepped to the crumbling edge of the precipice, wondering what would happen if I tumbled over. The fall would probably break my neck. How long would they need to search the brush and rocks below for the stinking, bloated thing that had once been me? A day? A week?

Who would bother calling the cops if I went missing?

It wasn't worth thinking this way. I retreated from the cliff, toward the Hell House where I was sure a pair of stars were trying to start up their own cult. From the rear of the house, hidden beyond the wall and a line of scraggly palm trees, a monotonous drum pulsed, and the wind carried a tinge of prime weed.

I scanned the outer wall. It was too high and smooth to climb. The house residents, amidst their secret debauchery, had still remembered to move their trash and recycling barrels to the curb for pickup. I lifted the lid of the recycling, which was filled with carboard takeout containers of identical size and shape, 'JOJO KOREAN FRIED CHICKEN' stamped on the flaps.

I returned to the car and blasted the air conditioning until my sweaty shirt dried. I couldn't stay out here all night. Sooner or later, a resident would notice my car and dial the cops again. Maybe I could drive home, get some shuteye, and start fresh tomorrow – with even fewer hours to gather the cash for rent, credit card payments, electric bills.

I also needed food. The sight of all those empty JoJo Korean Fried Chicken containers had triggered a ravenous hunger. When I was a gig worker, I delivered food for them regularly. They had the best chicken tenders for miles around, in my humble opinion, and their special sauce was more addictive than heroin. It was the perfect food to order when you were so stoned you thought the cat was communicating with you telepathically. No wonder the people inside the house had eaten so much of it…

I had an idea. It wasn't a great one, and I might fail like I did at *Voodoo Carb*, but I had no choice.

On my phone, I opened the website for JoJo Korean Fried Chicken and placed a delivery order for a Big Pimpin' Chicken Bucket, an order of Banger Fries, and three kombuchas. In the notes section, I asked them to deliver it to the car outside the address. I didn't figure that would raise any eyebrows at the restaurant: this was the Hollywood Hills, where the local establishments were used to customers' odd requests. Once I paid, I started the car and drove up the hill, headlights off, until I was twenty feet from the front gate.

The delivery car turned the corner before my playlist finished the next song. I flashed my headlights and exited the vehicle. The driver cruised in my direction, lowering their window to reveal pink hair framing a cherubic face: Ellie James, with whom I'd crossed paths on a few occasions while delivering food. We'd bantered while waiting for kitchens to blast out customers' orders, so I knew she was into UFOs, video games, and running a blog about the Charles Starkweather murders.

She offered a gap-toothed grin. "Didn't know what I was heading into," she said. "Way up here, this time of night? You could've been a serial killer or one of those Instagram influencers. No idea which would've been worse."

"Definitely the influencer," I said, taking the oversized bag she stuck through the window. The smell of fried chicken was heavenly.

Her eyes flicked to the gate. "You staying there?"

"No."

"Good. I've delivered up here three times. They're not good people in there."

"Oh?" I tried to sound casual. "How so?"

"I was delivering up a couple of Big Pimpin' Buckets – it was two nights ago – and the girl who took 'em asked if I wanted to come inside and party. Now, I'm always down to party. But then she said something about sacrifice, and I noticed she had this, like, blood on her hands…"

"You think it was real?" You could never tell in this town.

"Smelled like it. I have a finely attuned sense of smell. Sorry, that sounded weird." She scrunched her nose. "Anyway, you still delivering? Haven't seen you in a long time."

"I don't know," I said. "I'm trying to do standup."

"You're funny?"

"Working on it," I said. "You ever want to try out a new career?"

"Nah. Ever since I was a little girl, my dream job was to drive around in a tiny car, listening to NPR." She started her engine. "I ever get low on cash, I can sell photos of my feet online. I got world-class feet."

"Whatever works."

"You're sure you're okay up here? You ever need protection, I can get you something. I know this chick, she sells these tasers, except they're shaped like cute cartoon characters."

"Not sure that goes with my look."

"Yeah, maybe not. You got this Venice Beach dirtbag thing going, but you make it look cool." Her voice dropped. "I could get you something heavier, maybe."

"No, I'm good. I appreciate it, though."

"Okay. Stay safe, please."

"I will." I waved again as she closed her window and rumbled down the hill toward the curve. Maybe I shouldn't have been surprised at her appearance. L.A. is a big city, a snarling beast trapped between the hills and the ocean, but if you stick to your patterns, you run into the same people again and again.

Setting the bag on the ground, I opened my trunk, extracted the ZoomFood cap and vest, and dressed like a delivery drone. For any acting role, you need to power past the embarrassment, embrace the character. Cradling the food in my arms, I advanced to the gate and pressed the buzzer.

The speaker crackled and hissed, followed by a high-pitched voice: "Yeah?"

"Delivery," I said in my most authoritative voice. "JoJo Chicken."

The speaker clicked off, followed by a pause that felt like minutes. The bag in my hands was hot, my palms sweating through the paper. Beyond the gate, Hell House's front door gleamed liquidly in the tiny lights lining the driveway. From my brain's basement, a memory floated up unbidden: *dragging a heavy bundle of torn bedsheets out that door and around the corner to the garage–*

The door opened and a woman emerged, shadowy despite the driveway lights reflecting off her, like a black hole swallowing everything around it. The house's music thumped, thumped, thumped, louder and louder as she strode across the gravel, whisking her long and expensive hair away from her face. She was maybe sixteen or seventeen, her skin smooth, her gaze haunted. She stopped at the gate and said, "We didn't order anything?"

I held up the bag. "The app doesn't lie. It's paid for, I just need someone to take it."

"God, that smells good." Her hand drifted toward the gate handle – and stopped. Her eyes flicked hard to the right, as if trying to see through the back of her skull toward the house. It might have been a trick of the night, but her lower lip appeared to tremble.

"It does smell good," I said. "And who doesn't love some Big Pimpin' Chicken?"

Her hand pushed down the handle, and the gate shuddered open an inch.

I resisted the urge to push it open, shove her aside, charge into the house.

Her hand snaked through the gap, fingers waggling for the bag's paper handles. As she twisted her hip, I spied the oversized phone jammed in her hip pocket, its white case studded with fake diamonds. I decided to bet big: "You're ZenKittenThree, right?"

Her eyes snapped wide. If she was going to slam the gate shut, now was the time. The music from the house pounded like my heart. I shifted my right foot, ready to jam it in the gap.

"How'd you know?" she asked. "Who are you?"

"I'm a friend of your friend, the blonde one with the tattoo? She says Amber's no good for you."

She bit her lower lip. "How do I know you're not lying?"

"You don't. But I found you, and I know what you're dealing with in there, and you know that it's better out here. This might be your only chance to leave before something terrible happens."

She chewed her lip like she meant to tear off a chunk. "Man, you have a *hard* aura," she said. "You're not a cop?"

"More like a private detective," I said, feeling more comfortable with the term. "And I brought you dinner, too. That, plus your safety. Good deal, huh?"

She opened the gate and slipped past me. I tore open the bag and passed her the bucket of fried chicken. "Thank you," she called over her shoulder, already picking up speed on the downhill, the bucket under her left arm. I stepped through the gate, hoping she would sprint back home with a full belly, a few good Instagram photos, and as little lifetime trauma as possible.

In the meantime, I had a job to do.

6.

The interior of the house was exactly as I remembered it, down to the blood-red tiles in the entryway and the gilt-framed paintings lining the stairway to the second floor. The last time I was here, its movie-star owner's staff had kept it so pristine you could see your reflection in the doorknobs. The current tenants had strewn trash along the hallway leading from the foyer to the kitchen, and the living room through the doorway to my right looked like the aftermath of an experiment involving oxen and quality amphetamines. On the tilted sideboard, a charred bong the size of a Chihuly sculpture wisped smoke.

My earlier nervousness threatened to transform into a full-on panic attack. You don't have to think about what happened here, I told myself. Finish the job and get the hell out.

I was too exposed in the foyer, with too many doors opening onto the unknown, but I stood there and focused on my breathing until I felt more in control. The music pulsing from the back of the house had a deep bass that vibrated my ribs. At least the air conditioning was set at meat-locker levels, preventing me from pouring copious amounts of sweat.

I folded the top of the delivery bag to disguise the tear and followed the sound, entering the massive kitchen, its every surface piled with debris. The sink overflowed with dishes and shattered glasses. Liquor and wine bottles lined every counter, the glass humming in faint symphony with the music. On the central island, a tower of crushed pizza boxes and fried chicken buckets threatened to topple. A man in a blue bathrobe stood at the far counter, staring through the windows at the rear terrace. I recognized him: the one and only Karl Quaid, in the flesh.

"Delivery?" I said, trying to breathe shallowly through my nose, because even the omnipresent stench of weed couldn't disguise the kitchen's epic funk. "Your friend let me in."

Karl turned. "Did we order food?"

"I guess," I said, raising my voice over the bass as I set the bag on the edge of the nearest counter. "It's already paid for, so have a good night, okay?"

I turned, ready to jog out the door and call Manny, when Karl said, "Have we met before?"

"No," I said, tilting my ZoomFood cap so the bill covered more of my face. "I got other deliveries tonight, but enjoy that food, okay?"

"Hold up," Karl said, and stepped toward me, the left side of his robe swinging low because there was something heavy in the pocket. I thought about Manny telling me about Karl's social postings, the ones about guns and revolution and suicide. If he drew down on me, I had my pick of random objects to throw at his head. Not that a bottle or plate can do squat against a bullet.

I stopped. "Yeah?"

"Look out there," he said, flapping a hand at the windows. "You like what you see? We're creating a new reality out here, one based on the Mythos of the Great Beast."

The terrace was black except for the luminous green of the pool. I took a half-step to the left, keeping Karl in view while peering past the kitchen lights reflecting off the glass. Movement in the night: what might have been a writhing arm, a squirming hip. Maybe a dozen people out there, no doubt locked in activities that would make a Baptist minister burst into flames.

Amidst that shadowy wriggling, I spied a pale oval spotted with black holes – a mask floating in the murk, swiveling slowly from right to left and back. Its shape reminded me of a skull, attached to a body I couldn't see. Like Death itself was hanging out at a Hollywood orgy.

I looked away. "Yeah, looks like a good time," I said, stepping toward the doorway. "No loads barred, and all that. But I haven't had all my shots."

Karl reached into his pocket and drew the gold-plated 9mm I'd seen in ZenKittenThree's Instagram feed. Speaking of shots – his wide eyes and trembling hand suggested he was ready to fire a few in my direction.

"Karl," someone said to my right. "Drop the gun."

I turned. Amber stood in the other doorway, leveling a silver pistol at Karl. "Who are you?" she asked me.

"Delivery guy," I said.

"He's down to party," Karl said, smiling, as if Amber pointed a gun at him on a regular basis. Maybe she did.

"No, he's not. He's leaving." Amber widened her stance and raised the pistol slightly, squinting down the barrel. She was too calm. It could have been chemicals in her blood – or something else. When you pushed some people too far past their limits, their personalities disappeared into an abyss, along with their guilt and inhibitions.

They became capable of anything.

"Actually, I'm not a delivery guy," I said, terrified and unsure of what to do. I knew I wouldn't have time to cross the kitchen before Karl pulled the trigger, and if I tried leaping at Amber, Karl might shoot us both. If she pulled the trigger and killed Karl, Manny would never pay me the money.

Karl's smile widened. "I knew it. There's something in your eyes, man. You're a real animal, aren't you?"

"Listen," I told Amber, struggling to keep my voice low and calm. "You don't need to shoot him."

"You have no idea what he's done to me," Amber said. "How many lives I'd save by doing this."

I needed to break the circuit, focus her attention on anything other than her finger tightening on the trigger. I swallowed and met her eyes and said, "I once watched someone die in this house. The guy who owned it was a big star, like you two. He punched a girl in the face, then poured a bottle of vodka down her throat. She wasn't getting in the right mood, he told me. The punch made her bleed, but it wasn't enough to kill her. She choked to death on the alcohol."

Amber lowered her pistol a few inches. "What star?"

"It doesn't matter. He's making movies, enjoying his life." I paused. "Back then, my job was to keep things quiet. But that time, I couldn't do it – something about the girl, maybe. Anyway, I called the cops. Can you guess what happened?"

Their attention was locked on me. Over the music I heard – or imagined I heard – the rhythmic thump of flesh on the terrace.

"The cops showed up and told the movie star that

everything was okay, they'd take care of it," I said. "These were cops who owed my boss a favor. They dragged this girl into the garage, where she died. Then they took the body away. They lied to her family about what happened. They left me to clean the–"

I placed a hand on the counter and dipped my head and forced myself to breathe, breathe, breathe. In my watery vision, the colorful blurs of Amber and Karl slumped, and amidst my fresh grief I felt an unexpected burst of joy: it was going to be okay. Karl and Amber would live, Manny would return them to their gilded cages, and I would walk away with the cash.

"So, please, no more killing in this house," I said, blinking my eyesight clear. "Whatever's happened, you can all come back from it. If you're alive, you can come ba–"

Amber raised the pistol and shot Karl three times. Her stint as a television star must have included time on a shooting range because all three shots hit his sternum in a cluster tight enough to cover with a quarter. Karl coughed blood and fell onto his knees before toppling onto his side, his eyes half-lidded.

Before he hit the floor, I scrambled behind the island, figuring it would buy me a few seconds if she decided to start firing at me. Instead, Amber stood in the doorway, her smoking pistol aimed at Karl's leaking corpse. I couldn't hear any screams over the ringing in my ears, and I wondered if the folks on the terrace had bothered to slow their debauchery.

"Can you hear me?" Amber asked.

I slipped free of the stupid ZoomFood vest, tossed away the cap. I had no urge to die wearing the logo of a delivery company.

"Yeah, you can," Amber said. "Listen, you think the past has any meaning? Nah. Here's your meaning: Karl was grooming and gaslighting and all the rest of that stuff. Nobody was going to stop him, so I stopped him. Go ahead, call your boss or the cops or whoever. I'm going to bed."

I stayed behind the island as her footsteps echoed up a stairway. A door slammed. I edged around the tower of pizza boxes to find the kitchen empty except for the dead star. No movement from the terrace, no creepy skull mask floating in the void. I grabbed my cap and vest and exited the mansion at a fast trot, pausing briefly to wipe any surfaces I'd touched.

Outside the gate, my stomach cramped harder than it had at *Voodoo Carb*. I bent over with my hands on my knees and willed myself not to vomit. Despite the nausea, I felt oddly free. I understood a truth known to murderers and traitors: confession is good for the soul. And the past is the past. None of this was the best outcome for my wallet, however.

With my phone in my hand, I debated whether to call the cops. No, that was the worst possible idea at this juncture. Amber had already dispensed enough justice, and I had zero interest in becoming an accessory to murder.

Manny answered on the first ring: "What you got for me?"

"The good news is, I found Karl," I said. "The bad news is, he's dead. Amber shot him."

"Is she alive?"

"Yeah." I scanned the dark windows of the mansion's second floor. "I think she might be sleeping it off."

"Good, text me the address. Don't call the cops, we'll

handle that part. And listen, don't worry about the money. You'll get it all."

"You're screwing with me."

"Oh, I am most assuredly not screwing with you. This is the best outcome for us. Karl killed himself, we'll say. What always happens to a celebrity who dies tragically? Their next movie is a blockbuster. We're talking Oscars, baby."

"Because that's the most important part in all this."

"Oh, spare me the sanctimony, man. You're a hardass with the best of them. In fact, you need to come back here and work for me. You were always meant for this job."

7.

I turned down Manny's offer of a full-time gig.

"You're making a big mistake," he said when I saw him a few hours later, in the parking lot of the *Giggle Lounge*, as he slapped the rest of my cash in my palm. "This would've been just a taste."

"I'll be okay," I said, sliding the cash into my pocket. "You take care."

"Yeah, take care." He snorted. "Half the studio will have a coke-induced coronary this morning. PR girls – you remember the latte brigade – throwing themselves off whatever roof they can find. It's probably the biggest mess since that thing with Jake and the ambulance, you remember that? My left knee remembers it on winter nights."

"I'm sure you can handle it." I gave his shoulder a companionable squeeze. "Keep up your sense of humor."

His cheeks reddened. "Listen, asshole," he said, leaning in. "This is the work you're meant to do. You might not want to hear that, but it's true. You're a meat-eating son of a bitch, and if that fact makes you feel bad, well, that's what the money is for. You'll never be anything different."

"Maybe I want to do something that's actually honest."

"Yeah, sure, standup is the Lord's work."

"See you around," I said, opening my car door.

"You've never said *anything funny in your life,*" he shouted, followed by a barrage of curses as I gunned the engine and peeled out.

It was barely dawn, the sky a bruised purple, the air cool enough to zip the window down and let the breeze dry my sweaty shirt. I found an old-style diner a few blocks down the boulevard with a reputation for great huevos rancheros. I sat in a rear booth and shoveled food into my mouth with all the passion of a dying robot while the television above the counter murmured about polar bears drowning in a warm arctic sea, a nuclear threat in Russia, the best dresses at the most recent Met Gala. Nothing yet about Karl's death.

I shifted my gaze out the window at the traffic clogging the boulevard, hundreds of people trapped in steel coffins on wheels. Karl would never see another dawn like this one. Maybe that was better for everyone. I felt cored out, as much a husk as a corpse lying on a kitchen floor.

You'll never be anything different.

Screw you, Manny.

I pushed my smeared plate away. Despite my exhaustion, I was suddenly seized by the urge to settle another piece of business, something I'd meant to do for years but always chickened out at the last moment. I paid the bill and left the restaurant, pausing outside for a few deep lungfuls of air that smelled like a dead battery. Yes, I could do this. Let's exorcise all my old ghosts today.

I decided to leave my car where it was parked and walk a few blocks over to an address on Fountain Avenue I'd memorized a long time ago. This was a part of West Hollywood I liked, quieter streets lined with small houses and tall hedges, a world away from the Strip with its flashy restaurants and bullshit. I stopped across the street from a small green bungalow tucked behind a white picket fence, taking another epic inhale and holding it until my lungs strained against my ribs. A light burned in the bungalow's front window and I figured it was early enough that someone was home.

Do it, I told myself. Just walk up and knock on the door. Do it. You owe it to yourself. You owe it to them.

I crossed the street, placed a numb hand on the gate set into the picket fence. The rising sun was hot on the back of my neck and yet my skin was cold, like I'd spent an hour in a walk-in freezer. Beside the bungalow's front door, a stubby palm tree's brown leaves rustled softly in the wind, reminding me of bones rattling in a box.

The door opened and a small blonde woman stood there, framed against the darkness. She wore slacks and a dark blue polo shirt with a hexagonal logo on the right breast. The name tag clipped beneath the logo read: 'NATALIA'. I'd clearly interrupted her on the way to her job. She startled when she saw me.

"I know you. What are you doing here?" she asked, her voice lightly accented. Her family had come from somewhere outside of Moscow, if I remembered correctly, and immigrated to the States when she was nine, too late to lose the accent completely.

I opened my mouth, finally ready to deploy the big speech I'd rehearsed in my head on so many nights, and nothing came out.

She blinked and her face hardened, her surprise replaced by volcanic fury. With her bright blue eyes and pageboy haircut and almost translucently pale skin, she looked like an avenging angel as she stormed down the walk, her finger jabbing at my face. "You have no right to be here, you understand?"

I was going to tell her everything, finally. How Hell House had killed her sister. The part I'd played in it. Except her blistering rage forced me back a step and blew out every circuit in my brain, and all I could say was, "I'm sorry."

"Sorry does nothing," she snapped, stopping at the gate, her finger an inch from my eye. "I want blood. Only blood will do."

"I would if I could," I said, retreating down the sidewalk, my hands raised. If I stayed in her presence any longer, I would collapse in a puddle of nerves. Maybe even burst into flames. How could I have thought this would go well? When I reached the end of the block, I spun on my heel and fled.

So much for purging all my sins.

I retrieved my car and drove home, which was a one-bedroom apartment in a bunker-style building on La Cienega. The radio reported another uptick in inflation and a flaming mattress blocking two lanes of the 101, but nothing on Karl. I was so fearful to avoid the media storm about to erupt that, after I arrived home and stuffed Manny's cash into my small safe, I found an old bottle of my ex's sleeping pills in my bathroom cabinet and downed one, expiration dates be damned. I didn't even bother to remove my shoes before lying down on the bed. As reality melted away at the edges of my vision, I thought:

I must be something different.

I woke up feeling like a black hole had pierced the core of my being, draining all hope and light. Not to get too dramatic about it or anything. It wasn't the black hole's first visit.

The air conditioner in the living room hacked and wheezed as it fought to keep the heat at bay. I moved from bed to couch, opened a fresh bottle of whiskey, and tried to summon up the energy to mull my life. Manny was right about one thing: the comedy thing was never going to work out – I was about as funny as a colonoscopy. Maybe I could do like so many other people in L.A. and hire a spiritual guru to guide me into my shiny future, a poreless woman from Beverly Hills who had a vision of a gun-toting Virgin Mary at Burning Man and thinks she can predict your fate based on tarot cards and whether she had a life-affirming poo that morning.

The television screen resembled a hollow eye-socket. I steeled myself and turned it on. Now it was nonstop Karl. His devastated fans had built a massive shrine of flowers, framed photographs, and teddy bears at the gate of Hell House. Tearful commentators claimed a beautiful light had left this cold, hard world. I'd seen two-dozen variations on this story before: when you're famous, death erases all sins.

All that faux uplift must not have drawn the ratings the networks wanted, because soon the tone darkened. Talking heads began yammering about suspicious circumstances, murder, and what did anyone else in the house have to hide?

A quiet apartment is the perfect place for the worst parts of yourself to grow stronger. I paced between the living room and kitchen, my pulse hammering my skull like a prisoner locked in a closet-sized cell. What if the cops decided Amber was a murder suspect and threw her in the box? What if she talked without a lawyer present? If the truth came out, they might charge me as an accessory, and a merry trip through the criminal justice system was the last thing I needed. Although it was probably what I deserved, if you believed what Natalia said.

I tilted the whiskey bottle to my lips and sucked air. Empty. How did that happen? Stumbling into the kitchen, I tossed the bottle into the recycling bin, where it joined a graveyard of crushed beer cans.

When had I finished off all that beer? I couldn't remember doing so. The room tilted on its axis, my stomach tying itself into a greasy knot. I opened the fridge, hoping for any kind of food to sop up the alcohol in my bloodstream, but only a bottle of hot sauce and an empty egg carton stood sentinel in the chilly wasteland.

Well, there was an app for that. I careened back to the living room, found my phone on the couch, opened ZoomFood, and flicked through the menus of the closest restaurants until my thumb paused over the one for JoJo Korean Fried Chicken.

My stomach squeezed tighter. Tossing the phone on the couch, I swallowed, too aware of my apartment's stench, the unbridled funk of a single man stewing in his own juices. I rolled up the blinds over the living room window and cracked it open, ushering in an oven blast of night air to help cleanse my funk, if not my sins.

My apartment overlooked a dingier stretch of La Cienega. Across the street stood a check-cashing place, a secondhand lingerie store, and a shuttered restaurant that had once done a solid business in late-night sushi of questionable origin. The windows of all three establishments were black, reflecting the streetlights as flickering stars.

Something moved behind the restaurant's windows. I squinted, trying to sharpen my vision, only for the world to blur more. Deep in the abyss, the gray smudge solidified into a familiar white circle –

I startled, almost tripping on my rug.

A skull mask pressed against the restaurant's glass.

The air stank of smoke.

I couldn't see the body attached to the mask, which was already fading back, dissolving into the nothingness that birthed it. The world was coming apart, blurring into streaks of orange and black and gray. I slammed the window shut and retreated into the living room. The backs of my knees bumped into the couch, and I flopped down, my hand scrambling across the end table for a weapon, anything heavy, anything sharp. That's how I fell asleep, clutching my ex's cat statue like a grenade.

8.

I awoke again at dawn. The television was still on, at low volume, the commentators murmuring about Karl, Karl, Karl. My head felt like someone had crunched a railroad spike through it. I sat up, choked back my nausea, and tossed the cat statue onto the couch beside me. It was an ugly thing, two balls of clay with triangles for ears and a squiggle for a tail. I always regretted how things ended with its maker, a very nice lady named Cynthia, back in the day.

There's a good person inside you, Cynthia had told me on her way out the door for the final time. *But I doubt you'll ever find him.*

Ouch. At least I'd kept her espresso machine. Small victories.

I rose and walked to the bathroom on quaking legs and dumped the rest of the sleeping pills in the toilet. I bet the pills were the source of my weird headspace, because I could down a bottle of whiskey or vodka like it was water. But I'd mixed last night's alcohol with a pill, and my overloaded brain had fired back a ludicrous vision of that man in the skull mask following me home.

I wasn't really followed. I would've spotted them.

Back in the living room, I tried dropping into a downward-facing dog, a yoga pose an ex had taught me. I sometimes melded it into my morning routine because the rush of blood to the skull helped clear out the toxins. My knees refused to cooperate, my arms trembling, and I lasted only a few seconds before pancaking onto my carpet, feeling sick and hating myself for it.

On the couch, my phone trilled.

I rose to my knees and squinted at the screen. I didn't recognize the number, so I did my best to ignore it. Whether it was a cop or a reporter or Manny trying to call me from a new phone, it meant nothing good.

On the television, a commentator with a tower of stiff blonde hair wondered whether Karl had been killed by the Illuminati.

"Actually, it was aliens," I said. "Visitors from Mars."

My phone beeped. I retrieved it. A text from the same number that tried to ring:

Are you the guy from the comedy club who was looking for Amber Rodney and Karl Quaid?

Okay, so not Manny and not a cop. Maybe it was a reporter. I stared at the phone's virtual keyboard, debating what to do. There wasn't any use in answering, and yet my fingers moved, curiosity getting the better of me. I typed:

Who're you?

Thirty seconds later, another ping:

I was in the audience that night. I'm looking for an investigator. I'll pay. Can I call again?

If this person was a reporter, their approach was a weird one. Apropos of nothing, I remembered liking how it sounded when I told people I was a private detective. It wouldn't hurt to talk to someone for a few minutes, right? At least it would distract me from the brewing hellscape in my mind.

Sure, I texted back, and the phone rang.

A husky voice said, "Hey."

"So you were in the audience that night?" I asked. "What'd you think of my set?"

A pause. "It was okay."

I laughed. "Your tone makes it seem like a proctology exam would be preferable."

"Hey, those exams can be funny if you're in the right mood. If you can't get in that headspace, that's your problem, not the doctor's."

My caller was a woman, and young, or at least energetic from caffeine or nerves or both: she rattled out her words like machine-gun fire, barely pausing for breath. "How'd you get this number?"

"I asked Bridget at the club. She might be good at booking acts, but mister, she's not great at data security. She gave me your number for a six-pack of beer."

"I hope it was good beer."

"It was decent. I told her I was on a budget, no fancy hipster beers that cost ten bucks a can and taste like a chocolate bar."

"I'm glad she sold me out for middling quality. What's your name?"

"We'll get to that. This investigation, it's sensitive. I want to see if you're amenable, first."

"What makes you think I can help?"

"Okay, c'mon, don't treat me like I'm stupid, okay?" Brassy laughter, so loud I had to tip the phone away from my ear. "I might be dumb, but I'm not stupid. You stand up there, offering cash if anyone can tell you anything, and later that night they find Karl? You can't tell me that's a coincidence. How'd you do it?"

"I'm not a licensed detective, if that's what you're thinking."

"I don't care if you have a detective license. I need someone who can find things out."

"What do you need found out?"

"It's better if I tell you in person. You like burritos?" She laughed again. "Even if you don't, you're going to love this food truck downtown, its chorizo burrito will change your life. Just agree we'll meet at noon today, okay? Okay. Let me give you the exact address. I'm the chick wearing the big coat. You can't miss me."

After the cavern-like dimness of my apartment, it was a shock to creep into the larger world again. It was still boiling hot, but the air had that razor freshness when the wind sweeps away the smoke and exhaust. If you're an optimist, you can smell a hint of the ocean in the hazy distance. The freeway downtown was blessedly empty, and instead of the air conditioning I cracked the windows so the warm slipstream could play with my hair. Combined with the four glasses of water and two aspirin I downed before leaving home, I felt like I was operating at almost full capacity.

The engine rattled and coughed but held its speed, and I gave the dashboard a reassuring pat after I found a parking space near MOCA. The food truck in question was named *Los Lobos,* and its side featured a spraypainted mural of a gray wolf tearing into a giant neon burrito. It was parked in the shadow of The Broad, the oddly textured cube of a museum on the corner of Grand and 2nd, across the street from the Walt Disney Concert Hall, which always reminded me of a giant, wadded-up ball of aluminum foil. When you're rich enough, who'll dare accuse you of having bad taste in architects?

Except I was too hungry and hot to focus on poor design. The sun slurped moisture from my skin. The temperature's too high for a big coat, I thought as I shuffled across the street toward the food truck and the small crowd gathered before it. What kind of lunatic would wear something like that in weather like this?

I spotted a flash of velvety black at the edge of that cluster of noontime workers. The next thing I noticed was the hair, red as a forest fire and shoulder-length. It spilled down the quilted shoulders of a Navy greatcoat with two rows of brass buttons down the front. The coat was open enough to reveal a black t-shirt with 'NAH' written across the front in jagged type.

She brushed away the hair curtaining her face. She had the kind of eyes a casting director would kill for, crackling with electricity, above freckled cheeks, thin lips, a strong chin.

When she saw me staring at her, she waved. Between the coat and the black jeans and the combat boots, she looked ready to walk the icy deck of a battlecruiser in the North Atlantic in December, and yet she wasn't sweating. How weird was that?

"Either you're the guy I called," she said as I stopped a few feet away, "or you're my next random stalker."

"I'm the guy. My name's Dash."

We shook hands. Her palm was dry, her grip strong. "Madeline," she said, nodding toward the food truck. "I hope you brought your appetite. How're you on spice?"

"The hotter the better." I'm trying to hasten the retreat of a nasty hangover, I didn't add.

"You look like a masochist, so ask them for the Nuke Sauce. It'll torch your tongue clean off. Myself, I always go for the weak stuff, because I get this mild IBS and it's really a wonder to behold if I've eaten too much hotness, it's–"

I winced. "Too much information, is what that is. Let's order? Then you can tell me why I'm here."

I read the chalkboard menu beside the food truck's order window. I wasn't a connoisseur of L.A. food trucks, but I hated the ones that took a great cuisine – Mexican, Korean, BBQ, what-have-you – and tried to "fuse" it with something else. The last thing I wanted on my chicken burrito was kimchi or pickled ginger. *Los Lobos* specialized in no-frills Mexican, deliciously loaded with all the calories my body craved after living off whiskey and noodles for too long. I went for the chorizo Big Dog burrito and a Coke while Madeline opted for three fried-fish tacos and a bottle of water.

After ordering and receiving our food, we perched midway up the massive concrete steps outside the concert hall, above the unending tide of office workers and homeless folks, where we could enjoy our calories in relative peace. My hangover was in full retreat. Maybe it was the combination of a blazing sun and hot sauce forcing me to sweat out the toxins from the past few days. Maybe it was the chance to talk to another interesting, weird human being.

"Hot enough for you?" she asked after a minute.

I gave her a thumbs-up. "You know what? This is hardcore."

"Glad to help. If you're not a licensed detective, what are you?"

The great existential question. "I used to be an investigator for a company," I said. Again, only a few clicks away from the truth. "I didn't like how they ran things, so I left. I guess I'm exploring what it'd mean to be an independent."

"What happened with Karl?"

I shook my head. "Couldn't tell you."

"You keep secrets, good. You pass my rigorous vetting." She crunched down more food. "Can I tell you about my issue?"

"Sure. I don't sign NDAs, by the way." Was she a journalist or a blogger? Did she have a recording device tucked into that greatcoat? My instincts told me she was after something other than a few quotes about a star's death. Besides, reporters always have a desperate gaze, like a Pomeranian that hasn't eaten real meat in a month.

"I wouldn't know the first thing about writing an NDA," she said. "My full name's Madeline Ironwood. My father was Ken Ironwood. You ever hear of him?"

"No."

She pointed across the street at the giant banner hanging from the side of a building. The top of the banner featured a black-and-white image of a thin, severe man in a pale suit, a cigarette between his lips and an antique pistol in his left hand. Bullets, sprays of white powder, and reels of film were scattered across the image and the title beneath: 'SLINGER: A TRUE CRIME SERIES'. And below that, the red logo of the world's largest streaming company.

"That's him," she said. "Reduced to eight hour-long episodes, I'm sure it'll be a big hit, but I won't see it. I think there's a podcast, too, but I won't listen to it. Insult to injury, they're not paying me a dime, either."

"I'm sorry." I pointed at the pistol in the man's hand. "Was he an assassin or something?"

She laughed. "No, he was obsessed with old cowboy movies, the ones where two guys have a showdown at high noon? He even bought one of the prop pistols from 'The

Good, The Bad, and the Ugly'. My father was a big smuggler, mostly drugs. When I was a kid, they told me if it came through a port on the West Coast, he touched it at some point along the line. I'm not sure I believe that – criminals love to exaggerate – but he was big. He used to hang out with movie stars, singers, all kinds of famous people. I have a photo of him at a party, standing next to Bruce Willis and Ah-nold."

"That end up in the series?" I was already thinking of ways to verify her story. Trust but verify, Manny always told me. I think he stole that from Ronald Reagan.

"No, but other photos did. He disappeared when I was two, so I don't remember much of him except for some flashes. My mother got remarried within, like, six months."

"They never found him?"

"The cops did their best, but after a couple years of not finding a body, they gave up the search. They had lots of theories. So did the FBI. There were roughly a thousand suspects. The Columbians, the Mexicans, the Triads, a pissed-off movie star, hell, even LAPD."

"That's not the whole story."

She took her time wiping her fingers with a paper napkin. "You're psychic. That's indeed not the whole story. You ever hear of San Douglas?"

"Sure, it's north of Santa Barbara, near Santa Ynez. They have a bunch of wineries. Some good restaurants, too." I had driven through it once. I recalled a main street lined with a cute post office, a few touristy wine stores, and an upscale steakhouse. The kind of place that existed for the pleasure of the millionaires and billionaires who owned expansive compounds in the surrounding hills. At least it wasn't one of those desert hellscapes filled with redneck outlaws and trailer parks.

"They also have a big lake, which is drying up. Where the water's receding, they're finding things." Opening her greatcoat, she reached into an interior pocket and drew a folded stack of paper. "Take a look."

I folded the papers open. It was a terrible copy of a digital photo, high-contrast and pixelated, and I had to flip the image a few times before I recognized the dark blur as a rusted barrel poking from wet mud. The next page was a beginning of a medical examiner's report, breaking down in clinical detail the skeletonized remains found inside that barrel. In the tattered remains of the skeleton's suit, the cops had discovered a wallet with Ken Ironwood's driver's license in it, along with four hundred dollars in cash and a plastic poker chip.

The condition of the remains made it difficult to determine the cause of death. Several blows to the jaw and lower skull had removed nearly all the teeth, and two ribs were broken, although it was impossible to tell if those injuries had happened pre- or post-mortem.

Madeline sighed. "It's been almost two months since they told me. I want to grieve for him. I keep trying to make myself cry. Nothing comes."

"I'm sorry." I flipped to the last pages. The condition of the skeleton made any toxicology report impossible, of course. There was also a topographical map of a lake and the surrounding roads, with a tiny X at the leftmost edge. "You got this fast."

"What?"

"The medical examiner's report. Usually they have a backlog, it takes them forever to put one out."

"Yeah, that's what they told me. The San Douglas Sheriff's Department doesn't care about this. Even if they did, they don't have the resources to tackle it, because the whole department is four people, I think. LAPD says it's out of their jurisdiction. I've tried calling the FBI, and they keep blowing me off."

"Which is why you called me, a guy you saw in a comedy club."

She laughed. "If it makes you feel better, you weren't my first choice. I tried hiring three private detectives. The first two stopped returning my calls, the third one was a creep."

"I have another suggestion you might absolutely hate."

"Getting the documentary guys involved?"

"Yep. They have the resources, right?"

"I tried that, too. You know what they said? The episodes were locked, but if enough people watched it, they'd be happy to consider doing another season. I won't sit on my ass and wait for a studio exec to greenlight the answer to my life's biggest question."

"Sounds wise."

"Besides, these documentary guys? They're daredevil types. They're probably paragliding in the Andes. Which sounds like a darn good way to lower your life expectancy, but I'm known for my lack of fun."

"I like keeping my feet on the ground. If we were meant to soar through the air, we would've grown wings." I waved my hands beside my ears.

She stared at me. Her pupils were large and dark in a way that reminded me of Amber Rodney – galactic in the right light. "So that all leads me to you," she said. "I got no idea who you are, but if you could find Karl Quaid, maybe you can help me find out what happened to my father. And I'll pay, of course, if it's reasonable."

"What's your goal here?"

"I'm the vengeful type," she said. "Whoever killed him, if they're alive, I want them in jail. Or if they're dead, I'd want you to find out whether they were cremated or buried, because if it's the latter, I fully intend to take a piss on their grave while humming 'The Star-Spangled Banner'. I bet they're dead."

"Why?"

"Because he was likely killed by another criminal, and being a criminal has a way of lowering your life expectancy."

"True. Most criminals are absolute morons. I once knew a guy who tried to rob a gun show."

"They shot him?"

"Saying they shot him is kind of an understatement. They mopped up what was left of him with a sponge."

She gave me that speculative look again. "It's hard to tell when you're joking. Can I trust you with this? Like you said, it's not like you have a license."

"Give me time to think about it, but not too long," I said. I closed my eyes and saw Karl bleeding on his kitchen floor. "When it comes to vengeance, I'm not going to kill anyone, okay? I used to be violent, but I've sworn off it."

She smirked. "That's a deal, scary man."

"Great." I stood. "Thanks for the food."

I drove home again, windows down in case I caught a fresh scent of the ocean. The clear sunlight sparked off the looming glass towers. I was intensely aware of myself as a microscopic speck within an infinite sprawl of concrete and metal that would exist long after I was dust. Taking this job might be good for me. When I had nothing to do, I lived too much in my own head. But could I really trust this woman? And could she trust me to do the job?

Traffic was light on the way home. Entering my apartment, I dropped my keys on the table in my entranceway – and paused.

Something was wrong.

A shivery bolt of fear sizzled down my spine. I braced a hand against the wall, my pulse speeding.

What the hell? Where was this coming from?

The apartment looked normal, although I could only see part of the living room from the entranceway. The sunlight streamed through the windows. Had I opened the blinds before leaving? I must have. The door was locked. Nobody had a key, not even the super.

I stepped forward, the floorboards creaking under my weight. My heartbeat was a heavy metal drum solo. Did this count as a panic attack? I was used to my body's meltdowns, especially in the months after I quit working for Manny, except this felt more intense, like I was about to melt into a puddle. I opened my mouth, tempted to shout a greeting, or maybe a warning – but what if someone answered back?

I wished I hadn't sold my gun.

I reached the living room, and from here I could see the empty bedroom and its open closet, the bathroom with its clear shower door, the tiny nook I once called an office that currently served as the storage space for stacks of books and plastic crates. Nobody here. I almost wheezed my relief. You paranoid dork, I told myself. Why would anyone break into your…

I stopped.

The cat statue was on the floor. Or pieces of it, rather.

Despite my hangover, I would have remembered shattering it into a half-dozen chunks before I left.

I pictured Mister Skull floating across my street, through the shadowy lobby of my building, up the stairwell to my apartment. Not a phantom or a hallucination – absolutely real.

What did he want with me?

Even if I wasn't sure I could do this job for Madeline, getting out of town suddenly sounded like a great idea.

9.

Shifting crates in my home office revealed the small safe bolted to the bottom shelf of the bookcase. I entered the code into the keypad on the lid and opened it. Manny's cash, my passport, will, lockpicks, and a few other items sat inside, untouched.

After being almost broke for so long, I took perverse pleasure in withdrawing a thousand bucks and slipping it in my wallet. It made me feel like a big-time hustler who'd won the game. Only the giddiness didn't last. As I locked the safe again, my throat tightened, like an aftershock of fear. I squatted, willing my body to relax, wondering if I was losing my mind.

What if I'd broken the cat sculpture by accident, and just not noticed?

What if Mister Skull was a figment of my drunken imagination?

I wanted a drink, but there was nothing in the apartment. That was a good thing, since I would need my wits for the next few hours. Remembering a tactic from an old James Bond movie, I exited the apartment, locked the door, and plucked a hair from my scalp. Taking a knee, I used a bit of spit to glue the hair across the gap between door and jamb. If anyone tried to enter while I was gone, the hair would snap.

Unless a slight breeze broke the hair, of course. Then I could have all the joys of standing in the hallway, sweaty and paranoid, wondering whether a masked killer was really waiting for me on the other side of the door. Call it Schrodinger's stalker.

I took the stairs to the roof, where the landlord had built a sad tiki lounge with a plastic palm tree and a trio of dented lawn chairs. It offered a panoramic view of the streets below. The light was clear, the sun high, but the wind was dying, and the distant hills were dissolving in a gray haze.

I debated what to do next. Option A was sitting in my apartment with a bottle until I ran out of money or they found my rotting corpse in front of the television, whichever came first. Option B was doing the job for Madeline. The idea of using my skills for something other than a movie studio's reputation intrigued me. I needed to know more, though.

I opened the web browser on my phone and searched the digital world for Ken Ironwood until I found a couple of fluff pieces about the upcoming miniseries, but they contained precious little detail beyond "smuggler" and "friend of Hollywood stars" and "mysterious disappearance". The L.A. Times had a handful of articles from the 80s and 90s, with only a few more tidbits: an indictment for stolen property tossed out of court, an "alleged" murder or two, a rumored connection to the robbery of a shipping container loaded with artifacts bound for a museum.

That last part sounded interesting, so I clicked deeper. On a true-crime website, I found an alleged manifest for the shipping container: twenty statues from the Romans and Etruscans, along with a set of gold funeral masks from ancient Greece, all of it bound for the Getty Villa before someone climbed aboard the ship while it idled off the Port of Los Angeles, popped open the container's doors, and loaded the loot onto a smaller boat. If the thieves had found an unscrupulous art collector, they might have made millions off the masks alone.

The website suggested Ken was involved, but nobody could prove anything.

If Ken had been a big player, he'd also been a good one, leaving few ripples as he swam in L.A.'s darker waters. None of the articles mentioned whether he had a family. Next, I searched for Madeline Ironwood and found a few social-media profiles protected from strangers, plus a horror-film database listing credits for bit parts and voiceover work. She'd appeared as 'Redheaded Victim' in a "Scream" sequel and 'Angry Driver' in a direct-to-streaming movie starring Nicolas Cage.

She was like a million other people in the city.

I needed real information.

I steeled myself and called Manny.

"I knew you'd see the light," he yelped. "I knew it."

"Sorry to ruin your day," I said, "but the answer's still 'no'. I got a question, and I need a favor."

"You got some balls," he said, flipping from cheerful to angry.

"I could make any number of jokes in poor taste, but I'll get to the point. When you were up at Karl's house, did you notice a guy wearing a skull mask?"

"What? No, everyone scattered by the time we got there, except a couple kids drunk by the pool. Skull mask?"

"Yeah, a guy in a skull mask. I saw him up there. I think I might have seen him afterwards, too."

"What kind of psycho walks around wearing a skull mask, even in this town?"

"That's exactly what concerns me."

"No, I haven't seen any guy like that. I'd probably rip off his stupid mask if I did, on general principles." Anger cooled into concern. "You hitting the bottle too hard?"

"No," I lied. "Here's the favor: I need to speak to Angie."

"Oh, hell no. Why?"

"She might have known a guy, back in the day."

"What guy?"

"Ken Ironwood."

"They're making that documentary on him. I saw the trailer the other night. Don't tell me you're starting up a true crime podcast. I'll shoot you myself."

"Nothing like that. I can explain the situation to her, but I need the meeting set up. Today, preferably. A phone call will do if she doesn't want to see anyone."

"She hates phones. Always thinks they're bugged." He sighed. "Okay, champ. Keep your line open."

I checked my email, then the news. Nothing new on Karl beyond all the "tributes" to a "brave soul" who "brought joy to the lives of millions". The studio's regular PR firm was working overtime via its bloggers and flaks and other online weirdos to bury Karl's sins beneath a metric ton of postings, social-media waves, photo slideshows via the bigger content mills, and every other pixel they could find. By this time Friday, they were going to transform Karl into the patron saint of hipsters.

Manny called back. "Can you get out to Santa Monica within an hour?"

"If the traffic's not too bad."

"Do it. I'll text you her address. I'll be there, too."

"You don't have to..."

"I'm in the neighborhood. I've been remiss in seeing her. Don't argue."

Angie – born Angela Stoddert – had taken the bus from her hometown of Omaha to Los Angeles the week after the Rodney King riots. Unlike so many of those before and after her who arrived in the City of Angels with big dreams of becoming a movie star, or at least guest star in a half-decent sitcom, she wanted one thing: power. She started out as an assistant flack in a major studio's PR arm, a job known for crushing the weak. Her boss demanded all women in the office wear ultra-short skirts and offer him bumps of cocaine whenever he asked. That kind of life taught her very quickly that sheer ruthlessness was the key to unlocking her desires.

Her golden opportunity arrived in the last hours of the 20th century. A scumbag photographer had snuck into a star-studded party in Beverly Hills, where he took a few snaps through a bathroom window of a young pop star doing heroin on the john. His camera's flash alerted the party's security to the infiltration, but by the time they activated, it was too late – the scumbag was already over the gate and in his car, barreling downhill for the basin. Angie, standing in the driveway while berating one of the host's underlings about an unrelated issue, realized what was happening and "borrowed" a famous rapper's Hummer from the valet. The big vehicle's engine was more than enough to catch up to the photographer's Honda, and what happened next made Angie one of the most famous figures in L.A.'s secret history: she slammed on the gas, driving the Humvee over the Honda, which imploded beneath those massive wheels like a soda can beneath a giant's foot, the photographer pancaked.

Before the cops arrived, Angie pried the photographer's

camera from the wreckage and took the memory card. LAPD let her walk, writing it off as an unfortunate accident.

After that, anyone with serious money and equally serious problems, from the studio heads and politicians to the billionaires, gave Angie a call. She was the Great White Shark who would swallow your issues whole.

She was also Manny's mentor, teaching him everything about Hollywood's evil arts, and relentlessly criticizing his fashion sense until he was unable to walk out the door in the morning without looking like a refugee from a high-end catalog spread. Which made her my mentor by proxy, although I'd only met her a handful of times.

Like J. Edgar Hoover, Angie had several safes full of secrets, and when the time came, she had arranged for the studios to give her a clean-money payout, via a producer credit on a trilogy of blockbuster fantasy movies that won an armful of Oscars and nerd awards. That credit entitled her to four percent of the overall gross, which was more than enough to buy a large house in Santa Monica, three blocks from the beach and tucked behind a pristine white wall.

Traffic to Santa Monica was better than I expected. When I arrived at the address, I found Manny waiting beside his car, puffing on his vape. "You owe me," he said.

"I'll buy you an ice cream. I'll even spring for two scoops."

"Ha." Slipping the vape into his pocket, he squinted at the red door in the wall. "Okay, I have enough nicotine in my blood to handle this. Let's go."

We buzzed the intercom, and the door opened onto a sandy garden sprinkled with desert plants, blue and pink blossoms scenting the air like candy. The house beyond was a concrete box painted the same blazing white as the wall, its expanse broken by a wide glass door, which slid open to frame Angie in a black pantsuit with a white shirt beneath, her graying hair knotted in a tight bun atop her head, her skin deeply wrinkled and tanned.

"Welcome to my bunker," she called out, before turning and disappearing into the interior.

We entered, and the door whispered shut behind us. The interior of Angie's house was all sharp angles of marble and glass, its geometry broken in places by plush chairs, vases filled with orchids, antique furniture. The air was frigid and clean. We followed her retreating form into a sunken living room, where a pale glow from a skylight seeped over four couches arranged around a glass table.

"Thanks for seeing us," I said. "I know you're busy." There was no art on the walls, no books on shelves, nothing you could use to glean Angie's taste or hopes or interests.

"Dash, you've always been one of the real ones," she said, all surface cheer and whitened teeth as she bustled to the marble sideboard loaded with glasses and bottles, where she poured three short glasses of lemonade from a tall pitcher. "Manny told me you're reluctant to take your old job back."

"That's right."

"A healthy choice, maybe," she said, lifting a bottle of vodka from a silver tray beside the lemonade pitcher. "Want a little boost?"

I hesitated before shaking my head. "No, thanks."

"How about you, Manny?"

"Nah, I got to drive all the way back," Manny said. "Not in the mood to trade paint with other drivers today."

"Surprised at you, Dash," she said, handing us our lemonades. "You getting religious on us? Found the Lord?"

"Nah," I said, clinking glasses with them. "If I can hold

off drinking before nightfall, I can convince myself I'm not a functioning alcoholic."

"That's dark," she said, her face twitching, and I realized too late she might have taken the comment as an insult. "Fortunately, I have no such compunctions. I buried this town's miserable secrets for decades, and I fully intend to pickle my liver in the highest-quality spirits."

"Whatever works," I said. My experiences at Hell House had scarred my soul. Angie had a life full of Hell Houses. If she wanted a slow, high-proof suicide, that was her prerogative.

"Sit," she said, pointing at the couches. "Let's chat."

The couches were upholstered in the buttery hide of an exotic animal and cost more than a new Tesla. I sank into the nearest one like quicksand. Manny did his best to surf the cushion to my left while Angie sat across from us, smirking at our predicament. "I feel like I'm about to drown," I said, "in rich Corinthian leather."

"Yeah, I had the couches overstuffed," she said. "It's a power move. You feel low to the floor, even a little trapped? The whole house is like this. In the dining room, all the chairs except mine have a half-inch shaved off their legs, just enough to make everyone feel short."

"You're a master of the game," Manny said.

"You always were a great bootlicker, Manny," she said, "but these days, I only leave my fortress of solitude when it's my ass on the line." Her attention shifted to me: "Dash, what did you need?"

"Back in the day, you ever run across a guy named Ken Ironwood? He was a thug, a smuggler, but he was also friends with a lot of talent."

She traded a look with Manny. "Why do you ask?"

"They found his body up the coast," I said. "In a barrel. Someone threw him in a lake, meaning to disappear him forever, but the lake dried up. Someone wants to pay me to care about it."

"Who?"

"Ken Ironwood's daughter, and my gut says she's legit, but I couldn't find much online about her. Or him."

"There's that new series coming out," Manny said. "Those documentary guys."

"Those dumb pricks." She snorted. "You know the biggest problem with all these true crime documentaries, Dash? The people who make them. They start calling around, asking who's responsible for someone's overdose back in the day, or whether some car crash was murder."

"They ever find your number?" That surprised me. Angie was very good at staying hidden.

"No, but they end up harassing some wine-o-clock bitch from regular PR who doesn't know squat. Imagine if they actually managed to reach me." She mimed holding a phone to her ear. "Sure, I'll tell you about that time I drowned a 'Saturday Night Live' cast member in a tub. Drive on over."

Manny's lips twitched, like he was unsure whether to laugh.

"Yeah, I knew Ken." Angie paused to sip her drink. "I had to. A guy like that, partying with the stars, he's like a lit stick of dynamite in a daycare. The last thing I needed was an Oscar winner funding a half-assed smuggling operation because he thought it was 'fun', or getting shot because Ken liked to duel."

"Duel?" I asked.

"Duel." Angie mimed firing a pistol. "Ken was obsessed with Westerns. Maybe a year before he disappeared, he even tried to finance a movie with Clint Eastwood, probably with cocaine money. I helped deep-six that one, not that Clint bothered thanking me. Anyway, Ken had a set of six-shooters he liked to fire off whenever he was drunk. I always felt it was a matter of time before he tried challenging someone to a Spaghetti Western standoff."

"But he disappeared," Manny said.

"But he disappeared." Her eyebrows shot up. "Did you realize that smuggling drugs is dangerous? The more you know."

"I heard he stole artwork, too," I said.

She nodded slowly. "Lots of artwork gets redistributed onto the private market. Some of my old clients, whenever they threw a house party, I had to check their invite list for art historians. Last thing you want is someone screaming the Picasso on the wall was taken from a museum. Really ruins the mood."

"I bet. You hear any rumors about who killed him?"

"Sure. He backstabbed the wrong partners. No idea which partners, but you can take your pick – the cartels don't regard that kind of thing kindly. They dumped the body, and I guess it would have stayed hidden until the end of time if it wasn't for climate change."

"You think I can find out who did it?"

She drained her glass. "No. And that's not a reflection on your skills. You don't have access to the same resources as the cops or the FBI. My advice? Take the money, do as little as possible, and forget about it. How's the daughter?"

"Good, I think? She didn't seem all that traumatized."

She waggled her empty glass in irritation. "I mean, what's she like? Hip? A bit eccentric? If so, she's a chip off the old block."

"Yeah, she's a tad weird. Wears a big Navy coat in this heat."

"That's a real cry for help. What's she drive?"

"No idea."

"Please, Dash, for the love of everything holy, come work for me," Manny interrupted. "You're better than this nickel crap. The way you handled that Karl situation was masterful."

"No." Angie raised a finger. "The Karl situation was the best Dash could do under the circumstances. Manny, you let that situation get out of control. If I was in charge, I would have taken Karl long before this, shoved him on ice somewhere, not let him loose until the premiere."

Manny shrugged, but I could tell he was hurt. "He was crazy, unpredictable. We just couldn't get in front of him."

"That's the very definition of your job," she said. "Anticipate and bury. Now you have the mother of all cleanups, and I don't envy you a bit."

"You'll get everyone past it," I told Manny, seized by the absurd urge to defend him. "Well, everyone except Karl. But between all of us in this room, Karl had it coming."

"We all have it coming," Angie said.

"I always loved your cheerful outlook on life," I said, standing. "Angie, anything you can tell me that'll help? Anything to start off?"

She examined her empty glass like it held an answer. "I have no idea why they found Ken's body in the sticks. Maybe he was up there to party. Don't be too disappointed if you don't find anything."

"Thank you both," I said, disappointed by her lack of information. But should I have expected any different? Even Angie couldn't keep track of every miscreant who ever crawled along Hollywood's underbelly. "I don't want to waste any more of your time."

"It was good to see you," she said. "Be careful. I've always been a big fan of letting the past lie."

10.

Outside Angie's place, Manny slammed a mammoth paw on my spine hard enough to jostle my fillings. "That help?" he asked.

"Not as much as I'd hoped," I said. "But thanks for setting it up."

"Racking up my chits with you." He drew the vape from his pocket, sucked, blasted vapor from his nostrils. "Angie's right. This assignment of yours, it's a waste. I mean, if you want to take someone's cash, feel free, but don't burn too much time on it."

"Manny…"

"Shut up, you happy idiot." He smiled when he said it, at least. "Come back, and we'll fix whatever went wrong the last time around, okay?"

Unless Manny could raise people from the dead, he was wrong on that front. "You're worse than a jilted ex," I said, opening my car door. "I need time to think."

"I understand regret. But it's a useless emotion, okay? Move on."

"You don't want forgiveness?" I said, climbing into the driver's seat and shutting the door.

"Only in the morning," he called out. He might have said something else, too, but I already had the engine running.

I boomed from Santa Monica, the traffic gods smiling upon me once again as I cruised a relatively empty PCH into the belly of the beast. After clipping my phone to the dash, I called Madeline. "I'll take the job," I told her.

She whooped. "Excellent."

"I'll drive up to San Douglas, see what I can see. Give me two, three days for five hundred bucks total, plus expenses. I'll itemize whatever I spend."

"Eight hundred."

"You're paying me more?"

"A real detective would cost a hundred bucks an hour, easy. I'm getting a deal. And one other thing: I'm coming with you."

"What?"

"They shipped my father's ashes to me, but the cops up there held onto a bunch of his things. They want me to pick them up. Whatever's there might be useful for you, too."

"You sure about this? Investigative work, it's a lot more boring than what you see in movies." I had no idea about that, but it sounded right. Name me a job that isn't a grinding bore once you've done it enough.

"I need to get out of town anyway, and we can take my car. It's a sweet lime-green Mustang, old school, needs some time on the open road. C'mon, it'll be fun. You don't have a wife, girlfriend?"

"No, why?"

"Because I don't want some random lady getting jealous."

"Maybe I'm gay."

"Or a boyfriend wondering if you're suddenly bi."

"I'm single, thanks for asking."

"Fantastic. So am I, but we're keeping professional boundaries. That clear?"

"Yep." I wasn't a creep, and besides, I was nurturing a little crush on Ellie James, who was cute and could talk about murder, what else did you need? "One addendum to all that."

"Shoot."

"I'll take my car, too. Just in case we need to split up." I didn't like the idea of depending on someone else's wheels. I hoped my own aging vehicle had the stamina for a three-hour trip north. "And I'll find an Airbnb to book. Someplace with separate rooms. Unless you want something different, like a hotel or sleeping in the woods."

"I don't do well in tents. And from what I can see online, all the hotels up there are bougie bed-and-breakfast, say that five times fast. So, yeah, find us a house. Lemme give you my address. Figure we can caravan it out of the city at ten tomorrow, dodge rush hour?"

"Rush hour never ends."

"True. Still, show up at ten. I like to sleep in."

She gave me the address and I ended the call. I slowed for thickening traffic around my exit and tried to assemble a mental list of whatever a detective might need to investigate a decades-old murder. A change of pants was essential. Lockpicks might come in useful, although my skills were rusty. Aside from that and some cash, what else did I need?

A gun, whispered an older part of me. Because Angie was right: when you poke the past, it has a nasty way of poking back. And even if I got through San Douglas without any trouble, Mister Skull was lurking around, wasn't he?

I'd sold my old piece, a snub-nosed Raging Bull manufactured by Taurus, after quitting my job with Manny. It was chambered for .454 Casull – good for large game, Manny told me, as if I would someday encounter a grizzly bear wandering down Hollywood Boulevard. I never had a concealed carry permit and so packing it had always made me nervous, even with the LAPD on speed dial.

A reputable gun dealer in Burbank had bought the pistol for eight hundred bucks, and I promptly spent the money on car repairs, expensive sushi, and an ounce of premium weed. Now I had the cash for a new weapon, but the state enforced a ten-day waiting period on new firearms purchases.

Traffic slowed, brake lights flashing like red blood cells in a clogged artery. I called Ellie James.

"You ever heard of texting?" she asked. Wind snapped in the background, punctuated by a faint horn, like she was driving with the windows down.

"This is too sensitive," I said. "Can you get me a gun? And a holster?"

"I might. Why do you need one?"

"Protection."

"You needing protection definitely worries me."

"I can take care of myself. I got to get this done."

"And by 'holster', you mean like something for your hip?"

"One that goes inside the waistband if they have it. Which I'm betting your friendly neighborhood arms dealer will."

Another long pause. "Let me call some people? Then I'll text?"

"Call me instead."

"Okay, neanderthal. Sorry, I didn't mean that. You're acting old-fashioned."

"Not the worst thing to be." I ended the call. I was thinking about the restaurant across the street and the window where Mister Skull appeared.

As I bumped onto the exit ramp, Ellie called back and said she could meet me in an hour with a suitable firearm. I gave her the address of a burrito place a few blocks away from my house. It would be my second burrito of the day, another thousand calories of premium meats and hot sauce, but my body had flipped the switch from nauseous to ravenous.

I parked a few blocks away and walked over to the restaurant, my head on a swivel for anything suspicious. Did I really expect my skull-masked friend to lurk in broad daylight? I didn't know. This town had more than its fair share of psychos.

After Ellie arrived and we ordered our burritos (fake meat for her, chicken for me), we retired to a picnic bench on the cracked concrete that separated the parking lot from the street. She opened her shoulder bag and tilted it so I could see the black grip and shiny silver body of a pistol, a six-shot .38 Special revolver that would fit easily in my waistband. It lay atop a leather holster.

"Perfect," I said.

"It's loaded," she added. "I am a full-service gun runner like that."

"You do this kind of thing often?"

She winced. "No, because guns give me the creeps. Pistol plus extra bullets plus holster will cost you seven hundred. Full disclosure, I got it all for five hundred from a dude who called himself the Drone Warrior, and he spent the whole transaction staring at my ass, so the extra two hundred bucks is for my trouble, okay? Don't haggle with me."

"Zero intention of doing so." I pulled my wallet and retrieved seven of Manny's crisp bills, rolling them into a tight tube I tucked into my palm. So much for conserving my cash.

Her lips pressed into a bloodless line. "This have anything to do with Karl's death? The other night, you were in front of his place."

"It's related to that, yeah. Or it might be. I'm not sure."

"Did you see Karl before he died?"

"I'd like to tell you, but it's probably not wise. You don't want to be wrapped up in anything."

"You just don't want me to sell it to a tabloid site."

"Couldn't care less about that. You make that dough." I shoved the roll of bills at her. "Trust me, I'm sparing you from something bad."

"Okay." Pocketing the money, she reached out and rubbed my bicep. "When was the last time you slept? You look like you could use a few hours."

"I could use a lot of things," I said, scanning the street. No pedestrians on the sidewalk, nobody ordering food from the burrito place's takeout window, all cars stopped at the red light a block up. I snatched the .38 and holster from her shoulder satchel and stuffed them in the greasy paper bag that had once held our burritos.

"You don't ever need to be a tough guy with me," she said. "It's sexy to admit fragility."

"If I admit fragility I'm going to collapse," I said. "Into a puddle."

She rolled her eyes and stood up. "Be safe, okay? Believe it or not, I'd like to see you again, and not just from running into you randomly."

I want to see you, too, I almost said, except she had already pushed away from the bench. She sped down the sidewalk, glancing briefly over her shoulder before turning the corner. I tried to figure out the last time I'd been on a date, which made me think about my ex, which made me think about the cat statue shattered in my apartment.

Greasy bag of gun in hand, I walked toward my place. When I was a block away, I took a right, heading down a smaller street, then another right into the alley paralleling La Cienega. The dead restaurant's rear was a white wall with a steel door, bracketed by dumpsters overflowing with crushed drywall and flattened cardboard boxes.

I paused to pull the .38 Special from the bag. I knew someone like Manny, who prided himself as a connoisseur of death-dealing firearms, would pooh-pooh such a weapon as weak on stopping power, not to mention a mere six rounds before you needed to reload. I didn't intend to get into any gunfights, though. If you're in a gunfight requiring a reload, you've already messed up badly.

I popped open the pistol's cylinder and examined a bullet. Its flat head suggested a fracturing round, but I wasn't enough of a gun nut to know for sure. I returned the bullet to its chamber and snapped the cylinder shut again. Like so much else in my life, it would have to do.

Taking the holster from my bag, I clipped it to the inside of my waistband. The stiff leather would keep the holster open, affording me a quick draw. If I wore a loose shirt over it, people might mistake it for a love handle.

After tossing the bag in a dumpster, I tried the door, pistol in my right hand. The handle turned. I debated whether to walk away. Maybe my alcohol-saturated brain cells had conjured Mister Skull and maybe the cat statue had fallen off the couch on its own and shattered, and all I would find in this restaurant were empty floors and dusty tables. I deserved a little good luck, didn't I?

I opened the door and slipped into the darkness beyond, clutching the .38 in a two-handed grip, the hammer pulled back and the barrel aimed at the floor. My reflexes were good, I could acquire a target and aim and fire with outlaw speed, or at least that's what I told myself as I navigated the dim confines of what had once been a kitchen. Dented metal racks formed a narrow aisle leading beyond the dark stoves and counters, toward a pair of swinging doors.

The tiled floor was torn up in places and creaked beneath my weight. I was quiet as a herd of elephants, so I traded stealth for speed, throwing open one of the swinging doors and darting through, moving to the left against the wall. In my old job, they had paid for me to take classes at a gunnery range in Simi Valley, the kind of place they train SWAT cops and action stars to clear rooms, and I knew how to reduce my chances of a bullet in the head while moving through unfamiliar space.

I slammed into the room's far corner and swept my pistol's sights over a cluster of overturned tables, their legs poking into the air like dead insects. Amber light filtered through the dirty windows, playing over an empty bar, a wall stripped down to the studs, and a pile of crushed furniture. My hands were shaking. *Get a grip.*

I leaned against the bar and guzzled air.

Well, damn. Maybe I was too paranoid for my own good. Sometimes cat statues fall and shatter on their own.

"Cut back on the booze," I ordered myself, lowering the pistol.

As I turned to leave, I scanned the place a final time. The sun filtering through the smeared windows drifted across a dusty patch of floor, spotlighting a faint pair of footprints. And yeah, they could have been left by some long-ago construction worker – but what kind of worker walked around barefoot?

I stepped closer, drawing my phone from my pocket. The left footprint was missing its ring and middle toes. As I snapped two photos for posterity, I estimated the feet were maybe size 9. A smaller guy, not that it meant anything. Even a small guy is deadly with a weapon.

I exited the restaurant, knowing I wouldn't sleep much tonight.

11.

That lone hair remained in the gap between my front door and jamb. I kept my gun drawn as I entered my apartment and swept each room carefully. Yet again, my place was empty, and I jammed a chair beneath the front doorknob before packing my duffel bag with whatever I might need for the trip north.

I opened my closet to select the right shoes. My old suits hung in bags on the rear rod. Despite my financial troubles, I'd never considered selling them online. They were cut from fine wool and stitched together by ancient men who'd learned their art in Italy. The craftsmanship gave the suits a peculiar power: when you wore one, you could freeze time in whatever room you entered.

I debated whether to take one with me. Bespoke tailoring was a little too slick for wine country. This weekend called for invisibility, and besides, I wasn't that guy anymore. I selected my hiking sneakers along with khakis, jeans, a few button-down shirts and t-shirts, and my lockpicks.

Bag packed, I booted up my laptop and searched for a suitable abode in the vicinity of San Douglas that wasn't too expensive and also didn't look like it belonged to a psycho cannibal cult. I settled on a small house ten miles outside the city limits, which the website assured me had two bedrooms, running water, and presumably zero mutants lurking on the premises.

I texted the link to Madeline: *Is this OK?*

What? No four-star hotel? NO! she texted back, then followed up with: *Hahaha, no it's fine.*

After booking the house, I cleared my web browser and used my laptop to watch five episodes of a forgettable action series. I kept the volume low, tensing at every creak and pop in the apartment, but after two episodes I had relaxed a little, and by the end of the fifth I was drifting off. In the dream that followed I was standing on a two-lane highway slicing through the desert, its asphalt shiny as black ice in the light of the full moon. A wolf crouched on the center line, gnawing apart the bloody mess of a heart. I knelt and ran my fingers through the slick hair between its ears. Its golden eyes met mine. It growled companionably.

I woke up an hour before dawn, feeling so energized I barely recognized my own body as I rolled out of bed and sprang onto my toes. Advocate all you want for massages or cocaine or kale smoothies as the ultimate cures for hurt and fatigue, but I'm here to tell you nothing refills your batteries like a few hours of deep sleep.

I wrote 'SCREW YOU MISTER SKULL' on a notecard, punctuated by a smiley face, and left it on the kitchen counter, just in case my new friend visited in my absence. I found two energy bars in the back of the snack cabinet and added them to my bag.

Before I drove to Madeline's, I tossed my bag in my trunk and slipped my new gun and holster into the glove compartment, burying it beneath a geologic layer of Chinese takeout menus and yellowing owner's manuals. The morning was blessedly cool and clear as I drove into

Koreatown, where Madeline lived in an older apartment building. I found an empty parking space behind a car I guessed was hers, a green Mustang that looked like it belonged in an automobile museum, all tight lines and chrome highlights. I wondered if it handled as beautifully as in the movies.

I was also surprised Madeline risked parking it on the street, because a ride like that was worth a hundred grand, easy. Maybe she splurged on a slot in a garage.

I phoned Madeline. "Coming down," she said.

She exited the building wearing her signature Navy greatcoat and gray jeans and combat boots, having subbed out the 'NAH' t-shirt for one with Taylor Swift's pixelated face on it. She had a small leather bag looped over her left shoulder.

"He arrives in our darkest hour, here to save us from ourselves," she said, lowering her voice to the ominous growl of a movie-trailer narrator. "Don't let his clothing choices fool you, he's heroic to the core."

I plucked at my khakis and button-down shirt. "I'm blending in," I said. "Innocuous."

"Innocuous." She smirked. "You look ready to sell me a plan for whole life insurance."

"Nice car," I said, jutting my chin at the Mustang.

"Thanks. Inherited it from my mom. She once shot a guy who tried to steal it."

"Sounds like a good story for later. That's all you're packing?" I said, pointing at her bag.

"What, should I be carrying three massive suitcases for a three-day trip? A hundred pounds of dresses, something for every occasion?" Her voice rose. "You think all women pack heavy? What kind of sexism is that?"

I raised my hands in surrender. "Kidding."

"So am I," she said. "My other bags are in there. It's not a hundred pounds of clothing, but it's close. Dress so they can't ignore you, that's my motto. Can we get on the road? I don't like to stop except for gas, by the way. Think you can keep up?"

"Of course," I said, hoping my words held some dark magic capable of helping my car keep up with a Steve McQueen sexmobile.

We started off. My phone told me it would take two and a half hours to drive to San Douglas, US-101 N to exit 101B beyond Santa Barbara, then CA-154 over the mountains and inland. According to the interactive map, the route was blessedly free of traffic except for some snarls around Studio City and Sherman Oaks. I had a full tank of gas and the dashboard's warning lights were dark.

Madeline drove it like she stole it. She took every turn at speed, the Mustang's ass swinging wide, her shock of red hair swirling with the g-forces. When we reached the onramp for the 101, she stomped the gas, the Mustang's tailpipe briefly farting gray smoke as it growled up the incline.

Only by flattening the gas pedal to the floor could I hope to keep up with her car's glorious cylinders. I'm as environmentally friendly as the next mammal trapped on a burning planet, but the sight of that sleek steel shimmering in the California sunlight, the traffic parting before it as if blessed, made me a little sad for the extinction of those great, gas-powered beasts that had once roamed this endless country. In a decade or two – if humanity survived – everyone would be driving a battery-powered lozenge.

The traffic around Studio City and Sherman Oaks wasn't

nearly as bad as the map predicted, and soon we were booming north out of L.A. I was tempted to flick on the radio for any breaking updates on the latest mess in Hell House, before thinking better of it. If a cop wanted to drag me into a windowless room for a friendly chat, they would let me know soon enough. Instead, I sorted through my music on my phone, past the ambient playlist from the other night, before settling on a set of old-school metal songs. Lemmy bellowed out the start of "Ace of Spades" and the notes sliced through me, cutting away the weights on my mind.

I thought about all the long road trips I'd taken as a kid, my dad at the wheel of our old stick-shift, laughing and smoking and monologuing about all the mysteries of the world, everything I ever wanted to know about war and girls and whether Bigfoot existed. We always drove at night, the two of us in our metal cocoon, the world outside reduced to white and red lights skittering against the black.

That was a long time ago.

Maybe that was the last time I'd felt truly safe.

My mind drifted to Madeline. Imagine spending your life wondering what happened to your father, only for a bored cop to call and tell you that your old man's moldering remains were found in a barrel in a dried-up lake. It would have shaken my soul to its foundations. No wonder she wanted answers.

We made record time up the coast, the glittering Mustang weaving past slower cars. At this rate we would reach San Douglas at the two-hour mark.

On the way out of L.A., I kept checking the rearview mirror. The first thing you realize when watching for a tail on a highway is how many cars come in the same color and model. As we approached Santa Barbara, the traffic thinned out enough for me to keep an eye on specific vehicles, and no cars or trucks followed when we took the exit to CA-154.

My playlist ended. In the silence, I remembered how my dad and I would sometimes spend the long car rides with the radio set to seek, giggling at the weirdo snippets drifting in from the stratosphere. Short clips of men talking about alligator wrestling and blowing up state capitols, interspersed with snatches of music. I imagined I was calling in to one of those radio stations (did people even do that anymore?) to vent about my issues during a long drive, and I was also the bored radio host fielding calls from nowhere, maybe with an ashtray full of cigarette butts by my left elbow:

"Dash from L.A., you're on the air.

"Thanks for taking my call, DJ Bobby. Longtime listener, first-time caller. I have a bit of a weird situation: I was at a movie star's house the other night and I saw a guy wearing a skull mask. I think that guy's following me around, maybe with bad intentions.

"Sounds like a heck of a night. Which movie star?

"Doesn't matter. They're dead.

"Well, I guess that rules him out as your mystery man. This guy in the mask, you think he was also famous? Maybe you should ask him for an autograph, see if that scares him off.

"Nah, I'm betting he's just a persistent bugger. But what does he want with me?

"Dash, that sounds like one heck of a conundrum. Maybe it's someone you knew from a previous life who happened to be at that party, chilling out in a skull mask? And maybe when they saw you, they said to themselves, 'Hey, it's the perfect time to reconnect with an old buddy.'

"Nobody wants to connect with me that badly.

"All I'm saying is, keep it in mind. You've heard that phrase, that L.A. is a small town? We run into people all the time. You know anyone who hates you enough to lurk outside your apartment late at night, maybe break in?

"People who hate me? That's a really long list, DJ Bobby. It'd fill a book.

"Sounds like you're good at making friends!

"I blame my old job."

A faint roar from behind, followed by a flash of red in my peripheral vision. A Dodge Challenger swooped into the oncoming lane to pass me. I glimpsed the driver: a purple-haired woman shouting something I couldn't hear. The Challenger skewed into my lane, so close my front bumper almost tapped her 'Honk If You Love Darwin' bumper sticker, before accelerating at a healthy fraction of light speed. I resisted the urge to flash her a middle finger.

A hundred yards ahead, the Challenger tried the same trick with the Mustang. Madeline swung the wheel, jerking toward the Challenger's flank, and the other driver overcorrected, skidding across the lane and onto the gravel shoulder, brake lights flaring through a rising cloud of dust. I imagined Madeline chuckling behind the wheel, maybe waggling her eyebrows like Groucho Marx in an old movie.

Madeline was nuts.

The punky lady in the Challenger bumped to a halt onto the shoulder. A quarter-mile later I lost sight of her around a bend, and that was fine, because I had to shift my attention to the steepening grade as we climbed the San Marcos Pass. The Mustang had no trouble with the hill, zipping with ease around a rattling pickup truck loaded with chickens, but I had my gas pedal to the floor and the engine was whining in pain.

"C'mon," I begged. "Don't fail me."

A warning light flickered on the dashboard, the RPM needle edging into seizure territory. I eased up on the gas, slowing my ascent, which invited an irritated honking from the cars stacking behind me. I yelped with joy when I topped the rise and the road descended into yellowing valleys. We were on top of the fault line, and I felt the Earth's pent-up energy as a tingling deep in my brain. Yesterday, cruising through downtown L.A., I'd pictured myself as the tiniest of specks amidst the enormities of concrete and steel, a sense of nothingness that now returned, magnified, as I inched along this jagged rock plunging for thousands of miles to the planet's core, ready to crush us all with a shudder.

The Mustang veered off the highway onto a narrower two-lane. I followed it into a valley scorched by fire, toward a distant town like a white scar against the black. In the oncoming lane, a cloud of dust solidified into a fire truck, its sides smeared brown, its driver a pale blur behind a sooty windshield. It boomed past, siren wailing.

I lowered my window and sniffed at the breeze. It smelled like a million trees burning. In this part of the state, it was fire season for most of the year. My car had survived the trip here. I had zero desire to test whether it could escape an inferno.

A small sign snapped past, pocked with shotgun pellets, announcing 'San Douglas'. A half-mile later, another sign said the speed limit was 25 mph within town. The blasted terrain ended at a dry arroyo spanned by a metal bridge, and beyond it stretched the town's main street: a strip of cute buildings covered with a thin layer of soot and dirt, lined with windows filmy like dead eyes. I flicked my brights and Madeline heaved the Mustang to the curb. I stopped behind her and climbed out, wincing as my knees cracked after the long drive.

"Damn," Madeline called out as she exited her car, a half-smoked cigarette between her lips. "Guess it was a hot time in the ol' town last night."

"I didn't see anything about it on the news," I said.

"I don't read the news. You're welcome, by the way."

"For what?"

"For how I dealt with that bitch in the Challenger. She almost took you off the road, remember?"

"Be careful with road rage," I said. "People have guns."

She snorted. "I have a gun."

"Do you?"

"Nah," she said, flashing teeth. "I'm kidding. I just can't stand assholes on the road, okay?"

"Okay." I chose to believe her about the gun.

"I bet you're hungry," she said, "and we'll get food, but we need to take a stop first."

"Where?"

"We got to pick up my father's things. From the Sheriff. If the Sheriff's office didn't burn down, that is." She sighed and tossed her cigarette between her feet and crushed it under her heel. "I'm warning you, this won't be pretty."

12.

Last night, after booking our home away from home, and before binging several episodes of a show I'd already forgotten, I searched for some facts about San Douglas. The Wikipedia page told me the town's population was a tad under five thousand people as of the last census, and that it had a warm-summer Mediterranean climate, perfect for the wineries dotting the nearby hills. The town sat in the 19th Senate District, represented by Democrat Ron Bennett.

There was precious little on the town's history, though. A website run by San Douglas Chamber of Commerce described how the land was owned by the Mexican government in the early 19th century, then the Catholic Church, which established the original settlement. In the 1880s, the railroad cut through the valley, sparking a boom of hotels and businesses. During the Silent Era, the studios used the area as a backdrop for cowboy films. In recent years, it was an up-and-comer on the winery scene, thanks in large part to the rise of Vonn Wines, producers of ultra-popular (and ultra-cheap) merlot that came in oversized bottles.

I bet it had some nasty secrets. You don't survive as a town for more than two centuries without burying a lot of bodies.

Beneath the grime from recent fires, the town's

establishments were tailor-made for an Instagrammer's lens, no doubt paired with a winning hashtag like #ultimatevacation or #bestlife. We drove past wine stores and gift boutiques and a place that sold artisanal cupcakes, all of them empty of customers. I guessed the fire had forced everyone to evacuate. After a few blocks, San Douglas felt as abandoned as an outpost in a post-apocalyptic movie. It gave me the creeps.

At the edge of town, we found the Sheriff's office, a white adobe building with a red roof and three official SUVs parked along the side. The air conditioners crammed into the smoked-glass windows drooled water onto the pavement.

As Madeline and I parked our cars at the curb and climbed out, the station's front door opened, framing a bearish man in a tan uniform. His thick muttonchops made him look like a Victorian era refugee. He had a clipboard in his right hand and a clear plastic bag in his left. The bag was stuffed with brown and black objects. He waved the clipboard as he descended the steps to us.

Madeline waved back at him before pulling a crumpled pack of cigarettes and a lighter from her greatcoat pocket. "Howdy," she called out.

"Hello. I'm Jim Reid. Deputy Sheriff around these parts." His gray-steel eyes flicked between us before settling on Madeline. "Saw you stop in town. You're Madeline, right? You look like your photo."

"That's correct."

"Nice to meet you," Reid said. "That's quite a coat. You cool enough? It'll be a scorcher all week."

Madeline pinched her coat's lapels. "It's got an air conditioning unit built in."

"Okay," he said. Like most cops, he lacked a tolerance

for weirdness. Turning to me, he asked, "Who are you, sir? Family?"

"My name's Dash Fuller," I said. "I'm a friend of Madeline's."

Reid blinked. "You're from L.A., too?"

"That's right. You said you saw us stop in town?"

Reid shifted, adjusting his belt. He struck me as the kind of cop who would smash you upside the head, given half an excuse and a broken bodycam. "We got cameras all over," he said. "Feed back to the station here. Lot of folks left before the fire came through, and we've had some looters."

"That's too bad," I said.

"They're not local, those looters," he added. "They're from out of town. I'm guessing more than a few from L.A. You said you were a friend. What kind of friend?"

Madeline opened her mouth, surely ready to deploy a joke, but I beat her to the punch. "I'm a private detective," I said, my heart hammering, because there was every chance this guy would search a database for my name, followed by a few calls to folks in the Big City. Depending on who he called, things could get interesting.

"Huh," he said. "Okay."

"Listen, Sheriff?" Madeline torched a cigarette and blasted out a plume of smoke. "You have something for me?"

"Oh, yes," Reid said, offering the bag, which had an official-looking form taped to the front. "Here are your father's personal effects. I'm very sorry for your loss. I hope you can get some closure from this."

His attempt at condolences had the warmth and energy of a robocall selling loan forgiveness. Madeline's gaze shifted from his face to the bag and back again, and her jaw tightened.

I took the bag and tilted it for a better angle on the contents, which included a rusty key with an oversized plastic fob, a wallet softened by age, and a smaller plastic bag filled with a driver's license, credit cards, and other scraps.

"She's gotta sign," Reid said, presenting the clipboard.

Madeline freed the pen from behind the clipboard's clasp and slashed it across the form's signature line. Reid jabbed his thumb at the station and said, "I apologize for meeting you out here like this. Under ordinary circumstances, we'd do this inside, in my office, like civilized people. But we had an incident this morning and we're cleaning up."

"What kind of incident?" I asked.

"One that needs a lot of cleaning up. Don't worry your pretty little head about it."

Madeline thrust the clipboard back, almost hitting Reid in the chest. "What about the investigation?" she asked. "Can you give us an update?"

"We found a .38 revolver in the barrel with the body. Sent it for ballistics analysis. Maybe it'll connect to another cold case." Reid's tone suggested that scenario had a snowball's chance in hell, but he needed to say the words anyway.

Madeline took the bag from me. "This is everything you have?" she asked the cop, her voice hitching slightly.

"There's nothing else for you," he said. "We'll let you know if we have any updates. Do you have any other questions at this time?"

Madeline squinted as she pulled on the cigarette, then blew an atomic cloud of smoke in Reid's face. The cop stepped back, his fists clenching. I touched Madeline's elbow, trying to guide her back to the Mustang before the situation spun out of control.

Instead of exploding, Reid coughed and shook his head.

"Take care," he said, turning away. As he strode up the steps to the station, Madeline sneered at his enormous back before hocking a loogie between her feet, and I struggled to suppress a smile. Once he disappeared inside, Madeline stuffed the plastic bag in her greatcoat pocket.

"We should get out of here," I said. "Grab some food, get to the house. Maybe swing by the lake if you're up for it?"

"None of that sounds as satisfying as going in there and beating up that prick," she growled.

She didn't know the power of a cop like Reid in a small town like this. If he wanted to kill us, they'd never find our bodies. Or he could frame us for something terrible, make sure we spent the rest of our lives only talking to family through the scarred glass of a prison visiting booth. A cop like that could do anything to you.

13.

Every establishment in town was closed, including the liquor store, which was for the best. Madeline was my client, and despite the devil on my shoulder muttering that I deserved a drink or two after that stressful drive and the encounter with Reid – hell, maybe three – I didn't want to make a bad impression. Didn't want to appear *unprofessional*, which was a welcome change from the past year or so, when sometimes I didn't bother to change clothes for a week.

The map on my phone alerted us to a restaurant with good reviews a few miles down the road. The exterior was a concrete pillbox with a rusted rocket on the roof and a neon sign announcing 'BURGERS', a relic from an era before the big chain restaurants took over fast food. We parked our cars in the narrow band of shade presented by the stand's far wall, and I climbed out to examine the menu bolted to the side of the order window. The place didn't sell any carnivorous fare. Instead, my options included a "Sloppy Rick" (a roll stuffed with seaweed and frizzled onion), a tofu burger dubbed "The Magnificent Silken", fried rice and beans, burnt broccoli salad, homemade soda, and vegan cornbread.

The lady taking our orders had skin so sun-darkened it was almost purple, her gray hair knotted in a tight bun against her tiny skull. She reminded me of a burned-out match.

"No meat?" I asked.

She shook her head. "Jim – he's the owner – said we'd become part of the problem. Cows putting too much bad stuff in the atmosphere. So, we switched. You want a meat-like experience, the Sloppy Rick is your best bet."

"I knew a Sloppy Rick," said Madeline beside me. "He lived in a cardboard box in my alley."

"Not nice," I said, shooting her a sideways glance.

The order lady laughed. "We got a secret menu, too. Just like In-N-Out. It's a beet burger we call 'Big Red'. Comes with yucca fries."

"I'll take a Sloppy Rick," I said. L.A. is stuffed with restaurants that will serve you a sliver of marinated tofu on a bed of astringent greens, often for the cost of a wagyu steak, and I'd always prided myself on avoiding all of them in favor of joints dedicated to clogging your arteries. I could afford to eat a little healthier.

Madeline ordered a Big Red. While her cook fried and flipped our food, the order lady leaned out the window and told us about her trailer burning to the foundations. Lot of folks up in the hills lost their homes, she said. Whole lives turned to smoke. They'd kept this restaurant open to support the firefighters, who paid in kind by cutting firebreaks around the parking lot.

If our rental home was a pile of blackened sticks, it would complicate our weekend plans. I regretted not sending a check-in email to the owner before we left.

The lone picnic bench in front of the stand lacked an umbrella, and the sun had baked its coated metal hot enough to burn through cloth, scorch skin. We sat on the hood of my car, spreading our plastic baskets of food between us. Between sips of soda, I tore into my Sloppy Rick. The order lady was right: it was a curiously meat-like experience, especially the texture. The sweet and savory unleashed a sparkling wave of dopamine in my brain.

"Back there, the cop said they had an incident," Madeline said. "What'd you think they were doing?"

"Hiding a body," I said.

"Really?"

"No, but I also don't put anything past a cop in a small town. They think they're gods."

"You deal with them a lot? In your other life?"

"A couple times. Nothing I'll talk about."

She sighed. "Fine, be that way."

"It was interesting how quickly he wanted us out of there." I mimed shoving a bag into our hands. "In my experience, cops ask a lot of questions, especially if there's an open case. They can't help themselves."

"I told you, these cops don't care about it. That's why I hired you."

"Except this guy said he'd seen your photo. Which suggests they've been poking around. And you're a difficult person to research. You don't leave a lot out there."

"Yeah, I'm kind of itinerant." She studied my face. "You researched me?"

"Part of the gig. I saw you did some movie stuff."

"Yeah, an ex of mine produced horror movies. Mostly low-budget stuff, total crap, but it paid enough to get me through some lean times. Can you guess the worst part of it?"

"Getting covered in fake blood?"

"No, that was cool. The worst part are the creeps who

have *boob databases* out there. They watch movies, take screenshots of every time a girl's shirtless, post it to the site, index it. Like Wikipedia, but for tits. Surprised you didn't see any of that, since they take great pains to get those sites at the very top of search results." She winked. "Unless you did, and you're just being a gentleman."

"I must have not typed in the right search terms."

"Thanks for not being a creep. In the meantime, shall we confront the inevitable?" She finished her burger in two bites, wiped her hands on a wad of napkin, and drew the bag of her father's items from her pocket. Placing it on the hood, she tapped the stubby key through the plastic. I noted a symbol etched into the plastic fob: a circle studded along its circumference with sharp angles and tiny points, like an angry star. Below it, a cluster of lines that might have been a letter or number.

"It's too small for a door key," I said. "Maybe for a locker or a big padlock, something like that?"

"I'm leaving my mind open," she said. "Whatever it goes with, I bet it's long gone."

"I have an idea," I said as I took my phone from my pocket, opened the camera app, and snapped three closeup images of the key and fob. "I'll send these to a friend. He's good at symbol stuff."

"Okay, but don't tell him what we're doing up here? Please?"

I set my phone on the hood and locked eyes with her. "You're my boss. Whatever you say, I do."

She waggled her eyebrows. "Anything?"

"No killing."

"Okay, but anything short of killing? Like, say, I asked you to jump into a sewer?"

"I'd definitely need a good reason for that. Not to mention a bonus. Let's keep going." I drew out the wallet. Decades in a barrel had reduced the leather to a flaky mess. I peeled it open slowly. The cop who'd extracted the wallet's contents had shredded the pockets and billfold. I set it on my crumpled sandwich wrapper before reaching into the bag again for the mangled cards.

"I told you they sent me his ashes?" Madeline said, turning away so her face was in profile. She grabbed a yucca fry from the bag and devoured it, then wiped her eyes. "I haven't done anything respectful with them. They're just sitting in a cardboard box on my desk at home. I keep thinking if someone breaks in, they're gonna tear open the box, see a bag with white power in it, and think it's coke."

"Wouldn't be the first time that's happened," I said.

"Getting snorted up a random criminal's nose would be a fitting end for my dad's biological remains," she said. "He'd have appreciated it. But I still feel bad, like I should buy him a nice urn or something."

"You're up here trying to figure out what happened to him. I'd say that was respectful enough. Take a look at this," I said, spreading out a faded driver's license, two credit cards, a tattered hundred-dollar bill, and a shred of photograph. With the tip of my thumb, I edged the driver's license toward her. Time and water had rendered the letters and numbers almost too faint to read, but the ghost of her father's face was visible in relief, the curve of the jaw so much like his daughter's.

She examined the license first. "He took a decent DMV photo. That's a skill."

I passed her the photograph. She lifted it by the softened edges, careful to avoid tearing it. Its colors had waned into pale swirls of yellow and brown, but the image was clear: Ken sitting on a set of concrete steps leading to a brown door, a little girl on his knee. The girl's face was reduced to a whitish blotch, but the shock of red hair was instantly recognizable.

Madeline hissed air between her teeth, loud and whistling. Her eyes watered. I wanted to tell her to let it come, that the energy behind those tears had to go somewhere, but I also knew you can't give advice about grief to someone in its throes. It's their storm to survive.

I placed a hand on her shoulder. She brushed it off before snatching the plastic bag off the hood and dumping the driver's license, wallet, and cards into it. She sealed it with a vicious swipe before returning it to her greatcoat. Taking out her own wallet, a pink-nylon number with a cute cat stitched on the front, she slipped the photograph into its see-through pocket, behind her driver's license.

"Well, damn," she said. "I guess this makes me cry after all."

"There's no shame in it. You see these things, and it makes what happened to him real."

"Tell me a joke."

"What?"

"You're trying to be a standup comedian, right? Tell me a joke."

"What's the difference between an Afghan preschool and an ISIS training camp?"

"Oh God, I regret this already." But she was smiling.

"I don't know, I just fly the drone."

"Drone jokes go over my head."

I squinted at her. "You never get to make fun of any puns again."

"Small price to pay. Let's go to the house." Her smile died, something shifting behind her eyes. It was like watching a curtain descend over a window, shutting off the world from view. Whatever pain she was feeling, she didn't want me to see.

14.

I searched the address for our rental house using the Maps app on my phone. While a colored wheel spun on the screen and I waited for the directions to load, the sun needled my forehead. The heat was like a living thing out here, crisping the grass yellow, baking the horizon's elms into brown spears piercing the cloudless sky, slurping up the last mud from drainage ditches, frying lizards scrambling across the road. And this was the future: it would never get cooler or greener on this ball of rock hurtling through space.

The map snapped to life, distracting me from the slow-motion apocalypse. A red pin skewered the target address eight miles away.

"I'll lead off," I told Madeline.

Behind the wheel, I twisted the air conditioning to maximum and sent a text to Vincent, my friend in L.A. who worked for one of the big special-effects contractors:

Can you clean up an image for me? Old piece of plastic, there's a symbol on it. I want to know what it is.

I included my photos of the key and fob. Chances were good that Vincent was locked in a deathmatch with his keyboard, trying to finish an effects shot for a big superhero movie, so I didn't wait for an immediate response. Clipping my phone to the dashboard, I started off, leading Madeline from the burger stand's parking lot onto the open road. In this new direction, the fire damage was patchier, blackened hills alternating with pastures and the occasional house that had survived the inferno untouched.

My phone beeped with a text from Vincent:

Sure, yeah, I got some apps I can run this thru. YOU PAYING?

I tapped the text app's microphone button and said, "A good bottle of whiskey is yours." Wonder of wonders, the phone's software transcribed my words without error, and I hit the send button.

Another Vincent text:

Deal. Computer, ENHANCE!

I always appreciated a good Blade Runner reference. I shifted back to the map as we crested a rise and dipped into a shallow valley. The road straightened and it was a pleasure to press the gas pedal down and push my car's engine to the shuddering edge. We shot past rows of wilting grapevines, broken at intervals by driveways guarded by elaborate metal gates, leading to estates tucked out of sight. The fire had spared this area. I kept returning to the rearview mirror, watchful for any cars shadowing us, but we were alone in the big nowhere.

Well, almost alone. Despite the dust and heat and blistering sunlight, a bicyclist in bright yellow spandex sped along the road's narrow shoulder. He was pedaling at an impressive clip, and his ride was an expensive one, with a one-piece frame crafted from carbon fiber, his spokes shielded by black plastic discs. I veered into the oncoming lane as we passed to give him more space. He was old, with lined cheeks and a white goatee, but the popping veins in his neck and arms suggested he had cardio superior to someone half his age.

A mile after the bicyclist, my phone beeped, directing me

to take the next right turn onto another two-lane. From there, it was another mile until a left onto a gravel drive lined by fields. Nothing had burned in this part of the country, the grass thick and tangled as grizzly fur. We crested a small rise and the house shot into view like a switchblade made of oak and glass and shingle: an A-frame that looked like it belonged in the pages of a glossy architectural magazine.

We parked on the gravel beside the house. Before climbing out of the car, I checked for Madeline, who stood with her back to me, examining the facade. I opened the glove compartment, retrieved the holster, snapped it onto the inside of my waistband, and slipped the pistol into it. Better safe than sorry. As I'd hoped, my shirt draped over the handle without leaving too much of a bulge.

"It's like Tim Burton and the world's bougiest architect got together over a bottle of whiskey and decided to design something," Madeline said as we stood in front of the place. "What do you think they were trying to go for? Whimsy with a big dose of pretention? It doesn't look anything like the photos."

She was right. The owner had snapped the exterior photos from a tight angle that blocked out the house's razor lines. It was a minor thing, easily ignored, except after the run-in with Reid, I was in no mood for more weirdness.

"Hopefully there isn't a torture chamber," I told her, returning to the Nissan for my duffel bag before mounting the porch steps. Beside the front door was a lockbox with a keypad. I inputted the code the owner had emailed after I made the reservation, and the lockbox popped open, displaying a pair of keys.

"So far, so good," I said, and unlocked the door, entering an open space that encompassed the kitchen and living room, split by a marble-top island. A purple couch like an alien blob dominated the living room, bracketed on either side by yellow chairs with whimsically curved backs. An enormous flat-screen television dominated the long wall, alongside a giant sign that invited any visitors to 'LIVE LOVE LAUGH'.

"Hey, it's not filled with creepy dolls," Madeline said, rubbing a finger along the back of the chairs. "The biggest sin here is cheap IKEA crap."

"As long as it's got air conditioning and a half-decent mattress, I don't care," I said. Dumping my bag beside the door, I walked deeper into the house, past a bathroom and two bedrooms, where a glass sliding door opened onto a small patio with sweeping views of the hills. A narrow set of floating stairs beside the bathroom led to a loft area upstairs, with another bedroom and a closet-sized bathroom. On every wall, colorful signs advised me to 'CHILL OUT' and 'HANG IN THERE' and '#INSPIRE'. I would have taken creepy dolls instead.

I checked the corners and light fixtures for hidden cameras and microphones, because I'd read too many articles about the owners of rental properties who videoed their guests for unsettling ends. The last thing I wanted was footage of me snoring to end up on a sleep fetish site.

I didn't find any cameras, but the floor-to-ceiling windows made me feel like I was in an aquarium. I opened the closets (empty) and the drawers in the bedrooms (also empty) before returning to the kitchen area, where Madeline was tapping at the small touchscreen that regulated the house's temperature.

"Seventy," she said as the vents above us clicked and blasted coolness.

"It'll do," I said, stepping beyond her and out the front door. From the porch, I scanned the gravel drive and the hills beyond. The sightlines blew. Someone could crouch on a nearby ridge and watch us for hours. At least the rising land blocked any view of us from the road.

"The lack of chainsaw-swinging psychos is a win," Madeline said, following me outside. She sat on the railing, her legs kicking in space. "I'm taking the upstairs bedroom, by the way. If someone breaks in, I'm betting he'll get you first."

I imagined Mister Skull slipping through a window, looming over my sleeping form, and I tried not to shudder. "Your concern is touching."

"All I'm asking is that you scream as the knife goes in. It'll give me time to crawl out a window."

I wanted to tell her to stop, but I was afraid it'd sound like whining. "The windows don't open," I said. "It's all floor-to-ceiling glass."

"Damn, there goes my escape."

"I guess you'll just have to shoot them."

"I didn't bring a gun. I said that to freak you out."

"Really?"

"Really."

"Because I did," I said, pulling up my shirt to reveal the holstered pistol. "Are you okay with that?"

Some people behave oddly around guns. No matter what your intentions with the weapon – even if you're there for protection – they treat you like a mass murderer waiting for any excuse to snap off. Madeline gave me an exaggerated shrug, like she wanted to show how little it bothered her. "Why that kind of gun?" she asked. "Why not a—what you call it—automatic?"

"It was all my arms dealer could get me on short notice," I said.

"In America? Your arms dealer needs to go into another line of work." She pulled out her cigarettes. "I don't see a 'no smoking' sign."

"Just toss it into all that dry scrub over there when you're done."

She snorted. "You see that bicyclist?"

"He was doing about forty miles an hour, I think. Pretty impressive for an old dude, especially when it's a billion degrees out."

"You ever watch the second 'Top Gun' movie where Tom Cruise is on that final bomb run, and the g-forces are pulling him back in his seat, so he's puffing heroically, trying to stay conscious, all that? Older men on bikes remind me of that. They think they're Tom Cruise on a top-secret mission, but they're really an aging dude sweating it out while dressed like a sausage."

"On that note," I said, "shall we look at the lake?"

"Yeah." She tucked a cigarette behind her ear, unlit. "That's a good idea. Let's see where they planted my old man."

15.

We took the Mustang. It was exceptionally well-preserved for a vehicle that had rolled off the assembly line during the Johnson administration, the seats upholstered in buttery soft leather, the chrome dials gleaming on the dashboard. It had the original stick shift and a suicide knob on the steering wheel, the better to pilot the beast one-handed through the worst of L.A. traffic.

"You know what I love about a stick shift?" Madeline said as she twisted the key in the ignition, the Mustang's engine starting up with a deep rumble I felt in my nether regions.

"What's that?"

"It's a Millennial anti-theft device. Nobody knows how to drive these things anymore," she said, shifting into first and steering us away from the house.

"I guess that's one way to prevent it from getting stolen."

She eased us onto the road and slammed on the gas, double shifting into third. "Yeah, but that doesn't stop miscreants from trying to mess with it. After the third or fourth time my windows got busted, I started paying to put it in a garage, and someone *still* tried to break in. I shift garages every couple of months, if you can believe it. Almost more trouble than it's worth." She patted the dashboard. "Sorry, baby."

"Back in my old job, my boss assigned me to watch this movie star for a weekend." I settled back in my seat, the pistol digging softly into my hip. "He was a junkie, and I had to stop him from meeting his dealer, getting high, doing anything to screw up his life before this big press junket. He wanted to grab a taco from this place in East L.A., and he wanted to drive there in his beautiful purple Rolls Royce."

"New Rolls, or one of those vintage ones?"

"The new ones, they manufacture them for Saudi princes, Moscow oil barons, people like that. Totally gaudy. When it was dark, it even had pinprick lights in the ceiling supposed to look like a constellation. Anyway, we drive down there and there are no garages where we can park this thing, no options but the curb."

She took the cigarette from behind her ear and lit it one-handed. "That sounds like a bad idea."

"Oh, it was. I didn't have a dog in this fight. I was supposed to keep him clean until Monday morning. We circle the block seven, eight times and finally find a spot right in front of this restaurant. Problem solved? Yeah, right. We're standing there in line at this place, and he's totally freaking out, trying to look out the windows in case someone's messing with his car, and I couldn't help but think if someone so much as scratches the Rolls, that's probably twenty grand in damage right there."

"You're probably right. Did that happen? You walk outside and find it stripped for parts?"

"No, nobody touched it. But that was when I first realized that owning ultra-luxury goods isn't what it's cracked up to be. That stuff ends up owning you." I pulled out my phone and double-checked the map. "You'll want to take a right at the next intersection. You got this car from your mom?"

"Yeah, she's gone now," she said. "By the way, you need to relax more, you sexist pig."

"Excuse me?"

"You're a little tense," she said. "Which makes me nervous. What, you're not used to women driving?"

"I'm not nervous."

"Good." She jutted her chin at the windshield. "Because if you are, you're really gonna crap yourself at what I'm about to do."

Fifty yards ahead of us, a tan sedan was cruising at maybe ten miles below the speed limit, its rear window coated with a fine layer of dust. A quarter mile beyond, in the oncoming lane, the sunlight reflected off the windshield of a bright yellow big rig.

"You can always wait for the road to cleeeaaa…" I began, but Madeline shifted from third to fourth gear and stood on the gas, her lips peeling back in a vicious grin, and above the engine's rising roar I heard her growl like an animal making its last stand in a cave. The Mustang leapt forward. She wrapped a finger around the suicide knob, deftly notching us into the oncoming lane, the semitruck's horn blaring as it rumbled toward us like a steel wall, like death itself –

I glimpsed the driver of the sedan through the dusty windows, a man soft and pink as a scoop of strawberry ice cream left in the sun. In the dimness, his face was a mask of surprise, the mouth a black oval, and I could almost hear him screaming –

We passed the sedan and Madeline swooped the suicide knob again, tucking us into our lane as the semitruck blasted past with no more than an inch or two to spare, its brakes screeching, the stench of burning rubber stinging my nose. She shifted from fourth to fifth, powering beyond the wavering sedan and braking truck, and I heard my dad in my head: *The one thing that will save you is speed.*

"I'm sorry," Madeline said, but she didn't sound sorry at all. "I'm so sorry. I don't why I do it. Maybe I should see a shrink."

"You almost killed us," I said, proud of how steady I sounded despite the gallons of adrenaline frying my nerves.

"Except I didn't. I'm very good," she said. "And this Mustang is a tank. Even in a high-speed crash, I bet we have, like, a fifty percent chance of survival."

"Slow down, please."

She downshifted elegantly from fifth to fourth, then to third, dropping us below the speed limit. "I'm sorry," she said, meaning it more. "I like driving like a maniac. But I'm very safe."

"Don't do that again," I said. "That's all I'm asking."

We fell into an awkward silence for the rest of the fifteen-minute drive to the lake. A sign directed us from the two-lane onto a gravel road, and the surrounding grassland dipped into a brown wasteland. We bumped down a narrow causeway, dust spewing in our wake, and she downshifted to first. The 'lake' was cracked dirt for two hundred yards on either side of the causeway, transitioning beyond that to muddy flats shimmering in the sun.

"Again, I'm sorry," she said. "Are we cool?"

"Yeah, we're cool. Tell me the next time you're about to do a Mario Andretti impersonation."

"Who's that?"

"Oh my God, you're so young."

"Relax, you're not that much older than me. Shall we get down to business?" She waved the smoking stub of her cigarette at the landscape. "According to the map in that medical examiner's packet, the spot was at the end of this elevated road thingy." She took a contemplative drag as she studied the scorched landscape. "Must have been beautiful once."

"Probably." If I squinted, the brown flats and fire-hazard hills blurred away, and I saw this area as it existed forty years ago: lush with rain, the lake waters deep and blue and cool. Small white boats would have sliced the waves, the beaches a spray of colorful umbrellas and beach chairs and screaming families.

"There," she said, her hand jabbing past my face, the cigarette tip almost burning my eye. To our right, I spotted a tangle of yellow crime-scene tape out in the flats, fluttering in the dry breeze.

She braked and shut off the Mustang. I climbed out, my skin already roasting in the afternoon breeze. It smelled like a brick kiln out here. The causeway's flanks had crumbled into loose rock, and I had some trouble picking my way down to the lakebed, but Madeline in her combat boots took the incline like a goat, leaping onto the bigger boulders. The lakebed crackled and split beneath my soles.

"This is the part where I narrate what the cops originally told me over the phone," she said, striding toward the crime-scene tape. "There's a winery over that ridge there, and they give horseback tours. Under normal circumstances, they stay on their property, but one morning they decided to shake things up, ride in this direction. One of the guests noticed a reflection on the flats. At first, they thought it was part of a boat. I guess when this area dried up, it revealed a lot of sunken boats."

"The barrel was gleaming? It wasn't rusted out?"

"Almost all of it was buried in the mud except for one bit

poking up. It was rusted, yeah, but the rim had some blue paint on it and that caught the light? I don't know. What I do know is that they rode out here, saw the barrel, called the cops."

"When did they call you?"

"About a week later, once they made the identification." She stopped at the edge of the tape. I expected a deep hole beyond it, instead of a narrow depression filled with loose dirt.

I turned on my heel, trying to examine the scene from all angles. That's what private detectives did, right? The causeway and the Mustang looked like scale models from here, the shoreline a wavering blur.

"When did this part dry up?" I studied the ground around us, as if the cops had missed a vital clue. Sweat bloomed between my shoulders, cooling as it trickled down my spine toward my waistband.

"They told me it was really shallow out here for a couple years, but it didn't actually drain out until maybe six months ago." She sighed. "What a wasteland. Like friggin' 'Mad Max'."

"You want my opinion?"

"I'm paying for it, right?"

"Whatever happened, they didn't dump the barrel from the causeway. Something that heavy wouldn't have floated all the way over here. They wouldn't have dumped it from shore for the same reason."

"Which means they dumped it from a boat."

"Yeah." I pulled out my phone and tapped the map, then pinched my screen until I had a view of the lake in its entirety. "We need to find docks, ports that have been around for a couple decades. Ask around, see if anyone remembers something from back in the day. It's probably a snowball's chance in hell, but I don't have any better ideas."

"You don't think the cops did that, whatchamacallit, 'canvasing the area'?"

"Maybe. But if they did, they didn't share it with you, did they?"

"Look," Madeline said, pointing behind me.

I turned. Atop the causeway, another car slowed to a stop behind the Mustang. Was it trying to pass? There was nothing beyond the causeway: when it reached the far shore, it transformed into a gravel path that petered out within a hundred yards, at the base of the nearest hills. The car was neon green and comically tiny, barely large enough to fit two adults.

"Huh," I said.

If they stole the Mustang, it was a long walk back to the house in the killing heat. No, I told myself, don't get too paranoid quite yet. Maybe they're ordinary folks driving around, like you. Maybe they're producers from a streaming network, here to scout the scene for their next series based off a true crime.

Or maybe they're here to kill you.

Shut up, I told my traitorous brain. Not every situation is DEFCON-1.

But my right hand drifted toward my pistol.

"Maybe we should see what they want?" Madeline said, walking toward the causeway. The wind had picked up again, scraping the flats, flapping her hair like a red flag.

I followed. The bright sun reflected off the mini-car's windows, hiding its occupants from view. It was one of those newer models, maybe electric, with a body designed to make it look cute and friendly. Except it didn't feel friendly. Not one bit.

The mini-car's doors opened, dispensing two men onto the causeway. It was difficult to see their faces at this distance, except one was stocky, his shoulders thick with muscle beneath a nylon jacket, his face shadowed by a baseball cap. The other guy was lean, his head like a raised cleaver in silhouette, and dressed in a similar jacket.

Madeline raised a hand and waggled her fingers.

I didn't like this. No, that was an understatement. I was *fearful.* If one of those guys had a gun with any range, we had zero cover out here. I figured I'd draw and fire and keep firing while moving Madeline toward the shoreline, blocking her with my body. We'd have roughly the same chances of survival as a cockroach at ground zero of an atomic blast.

The Lean Man stepped in front of his car, reaching into his jacket. He turned, the light playing across his head from a different angle – his skin was blue. No, he was wearing a blue mask over the lower part of his face.

From his jacket, the Lean Man took a squarish object and placed it on the Mustang's trunk. Raising his hands, palms out, he retreated to his mini-car and climbed behind the wheel again, the Stocky Dude tucking into the passenger side almost in sync. We were fifty yards away when their vehicle shifted into reverse and backed down the causeway at high speed.

"Who the hell was that?" Madeline said.

"No idea," I replied.

It took a bit of billy-goating to climb to the top of the causeway, with both of us pausing to set our feet on stable stones while looking for the next step. I approached the

Mustang with caution, waving for Madeline to stay back. The lean man had left a flat package wrapped in brown paper.

"What is it?" Madeline asked.

"The good news is, it's too small to be a head in a box," I said. "Beyond that, I'm not sure." Manny had trained me for many things, but not detecting bombs and booby traps. Unless it had wires poking out or a burning fuse, I had no way of telling whether a package was stuffed full of explosives.

Ah, screw it. Why blow us up? I slipped a thumb beneath the package and lifted an inch. It was lighter than I expected, too. I was holding my breath. I exhaled and popped the tape holding the folds, then peeled the paper away, revealing a purple box with no logos or writing on it. I eased the lid open. Inside were four rows of tiny chocolates, and not the cheap kind, either. This high-end assortment was designed for husbands who need a gift to bring home to the spouse after they catastrophically screw up.

There was a pink envelope taped to the underside of the lid. "We have a secret admirer," I said, opening it and drawing out a folded slip of paper.

"God, I hope it's not cheesy poetry," she said, snatching the paper from my hand. "It says, 'Enjoy the chocolates. Get out of town'. Doesn't even rhyme, you goobers. I thought all poetry was supposed to rhyme."

I checked the horizon for the car, spotting it at the point where the road sliced over the distant hills. The driver had stopped. They might have been studying us through binoculars, wondering what we'd do.

Madeline plucked a bonbon from the top row.

"Careful," I muttered. "You know what they say about strangers and candy…"

"Yeah, but I'm hungry," she said, popping a dark chocolate sphere into her mouth. She chewed – and stopped. Her eyes widened, frantic, as she gagged deep in her throat.

I grabbed her elbow, ready to hustle her into the car. Had our new friends poisoned the box? Where was the nearest hospital?

She spat the chocolate at her feet. "I really hate cherry filling."

"Oh." I loosened my grip, relieved.

She winked. "I should have faked a seizure. Screamed 'cyanide'. Really freaked you out."

"I'm so glad you didn't. We should keep the box, though. Might give us some insights."

"Into what? Catching diabetes?" She squinted at the greenish dot of the car in the distance, then extended both arms straight up, middle fingers raised. "What do those creeps want?"

"For us to leave, like it said on the note."

"I know, but why?"

"I bet it has to do with your father. What else could it be?" The car disappeared behind the hills. I bet we would see them again if we stuck around.

We climbed into the Mustang. I was ready to suggest we drive around the lake, scope out the nearest docks, when my phone beeped with a new message from Vincent:

Found yer SYMBOL! It's WEIRD!

16.

Inside the Mustang, I angled the phone so Madeline could see Vincent's follow-up texts and images. "A winery?" she asked, squinting at the screen. "It's a winery logo?"

"And not just any winery," I said, swiping away from the text app and opening a web browser. "Vonn Wines. They're the biggest producers around. Merlot, mainly, but I think some other vintages, too."

I searched for Vonn Wines, bringing up their logo: the outline of a sun with wavy rays. I flicked to the text app and Vincent's enhanced, color-corrected images, the same logo standing out against the key fob's corroded plastic in sharp relief. Because he thought virtually everyone on the planet was a drooling idiot, including me, Vincent had helpfully traced out the logo with thin red lines.

"It's too small to be a door key," I said. "But I'll bet this goes to a wine locker."

"My dad wasn't a wine guy," she said. "Based on what people told me, beer was more his speed. Whiskey, sometimes."

"I'll tell you a fun fact," I said, summoning the browser again and searching for the Vonn Wines website. "A lot of people, they're not wine people, but they want everyone to think they're wine people, because wine has that air of sophistication. Your dad was big into appearances, no?"

"Sure," she said.

The Vonn Wines website popped to life: flowery text against a background of emerald-green vineyards. I tapped on the 'Memberships' tab and scrolled through the wine-subscription options until I reached the 'Vault' option. For a few hundred dollars per year, I could have my own climate-controlled locker in the depths of the winery's "special cave", provided I always stored a dozen bottles or more. I bet the winery had a deal like that since its founding.

"Even if my dad had a locker there, which is no guarantee, it's long gone," she said.

"Sure, but there might be a record." I tapped on the website's 'History' tab, summoning a page of dense text. Three generations of the Vonn family had overseen the winery, focusing their energy and passion on creating some of the greatest wines that California's fertile soil could yield. A lot of love was poured into those ten-dollar bottles that most people bought because they were late for a party and the label had a cool jester on the front.

"Your buddy, the guy who figured this logo out, what's he do?" she asked.

"Special effects for movies. Creating digital creatures, stuff like that. But he started out as a history major, and he likes using his computer skills on actual problems."

"A useful guy to know."

"He's helped me out before. You need an image enhanced or cleaned up, he's your guy. What's wrong?"

"It was so long ago," she said, staring out the windshield at the dry pit that had once been a lake. "We're not going to find anything, are we?"

I felt the heat pressing against the windows. It would be

so easy to tell her yes, this quest was pointless, and drive back to L.A. On more than one occasion in my ignoble career, I'd used someone's momentary loss of faith like a chain around their neck, dragging them someplace they never wanted to go.

"A day ago, I would have agreed with you, a hundred percent," I said. "But we've found more than I expected, and we've been here, what, three hours?"

"I don't know."

"If there was nothing here, creepy guys wouldn't be leaving chocolates on your car."

She smiled. "True."

I checked the time on my screen. "This winery's close. I think we should drive up there, see what's what."

"Okay," she said, gunning the Mustang. "But then we find some food, head back to the ranch, and crash out early, okay? Because I'm wiped out."

"Deal. I'll navigate." I set the winery's address into my phone, activated the directions, and placed the device on my thigh so she could see the screen. The Vonn Wines Estate lay along a ridgeline fifteen minutes north of here. "Step one: go backwards. Try not to plop us in the lake."

"If this is gonna work out, you'll need to develop more faith in my kickass driving skills," she said as she leadfooted in reverse, the speedometer creeping toward twenty miles an hour. When we jolted off the causeway, she spun the suicide knob with two fingers, pirouetting the car with the grace of a ballerina.

"Between this and the truck, I'm convinced," I squeaked as she shifted into first and slammed down the accelerator, leaving the lake and its ghosts behind. Once we hit the paved road and our dust lessened, I zipped down the window and tilted the passenger-side mirror so I could watch the road behind us. A long time ago, I spent a few days every year at a racetrack in Victorville, learning evasion techniques from a grizzled dude who claimed he'd served in the IDF but spoke with a Kansas accent. Manny wanted me capable of driving like a Secret Service agent if I ever had to zoom a pop star from a stalker or a paparazzi frenzy.

Despite that top-shelf instruction, I never learned how to drift a car at high speed around a corner, or any other physics-defying tricks. That aside, the grizzled dude had taught me some of the finer points of picking up a tail. You could run a red light and see if anyone tries to follow you through it, or drive onto the highway and immediately exit again. Out in the countryside, it was much easier to detect a pursuer, which did jack-squat to ease my paranoia.

Who knew we were out here?

Who wanted us gone?

What was the deal with the chocolates?

One hand on the wheel, Madeline pried open the box and levered out another melting bonbon, popping it into her open mouth without looking. "Ugh, zero for two," she said. "It's nougat."

"Are there any flavors you actually like?"

"Polonium. Has that nice tang." She winked at me. "You know, if they poisoned these things. You're such a paranoid android. Here's another and equally scary idea: what if they put a tracker in one of these candies? We swallow it, they know where we are at all times."

"Until we go to the bathroom."

"I guess that's the downside. I'll check my poo for metal gizmos later, just in case."

"You tell anyone we drove up here?"

"Hell no. My friends probably think I'm back in my apartment, chain-smoking and binging television, like the exciting scamp I am."

"I'm wondering how they found us." Maybe there was a tracker in the Mustang? Except the car hadn't been out of our sight since we arrived in town.

"Maybe the cop told them we were here. Then they just drove around until they found us."

"Maybe."

We drove in silence for another few miles before she asked, "How did you get into it?"

"Get into what?"

"Your previous line of work. Cleaning up famous folks' messes, or however you want to phrase it."

"I met this guy named Manny. He's one of those people you never hear about, who's never on the news, but they get all the dirty work done. Everyone in Hollywood wants him solving their problems, so he basically lives in his car, always on his phone, driving from crisis to crisis."

"Sounds horrible."

"Not if you're a workaholic. He lives for the action. If you're a child star who got busted for an underage DUI? He's your phone call. Dead body in your pool? Give him fifteen minutes, he's pulling up in a van with a bunch of sketchy dudes, ready to disappear that corpse."

"Like that guy in 'Pulp Fiction', the one who Harvey Keitel played."

"The Wolf, yeah. Sort of like that, except he's not working with gangsters. A guy like Manny will only do jobs for the rich and powerful, and only the ones who are ostensibly legit. People who pay well, and won't ever talk, because they have too much to lose."

"So, how'd you end up working for him? You give him a resume? Apply online?"

"Nah, none of the above. I got in a fender-bender with him. We start talking and end up on the topic of the DMV, and I mention I have a friend who works there. Manny offers me a thousand bucks if I can persuade my friend to get a big singer's license renewed without the guy having to come in, line up, cause a scene."

"And you did it."

"I gave half the cash to my friend to do it, but yeah. Then Manny asked me to do it again, and again. My buddy renewed the licenses for a bunch of Oscar and Golden Globe winners, plus maybe half the folks on the Billboard charts. That was the start of it." I paused, wondering how much I wanted to tell her. "Then Manny started giving me different work."

"Dead bodies in pools?"

"Not at first. In the beginning, it was making sure clients left jail without the paparazzi seeing them, stuff like that. A couple of times I had to persuade the cops not to break up parties at clients' mansions. Sometimes that's harder than you think – when you live in a ten-million-dollar house, your neighbor is probably a rich prick with connections, and they don't appreciate it when DJ Solomun or whoever is spinning in your yard for three days straight."

"How do you do it?"

"Get the cops to not break up a huge party in the Hollywood Hills?"

"Yeah. For when I buy my big mansion."

"You get friendly with as many high-ranking cops as you can find. Captains, commanders, guys like that." Like Brian Pinto, the deputy chief out of West Bureau, who once ordered his men to drag a poisoned girl into Hell House's garage so she could die out of sight, then lied to the girl's family about what happened. "You find out what they like, and how to give it to them."

"Please tell me you didn't give a cop a handie. Please."

I grinned. "No, thankfully. They want tickets to premieres, maybe a walk-on as an extra, stuff like that. It wasn't difficult once you knew what they wanted."

"But it got difficult."

The poisoned girl's name had been Eugenia. When her family visited the station, Pinto allowed me to sit in the room while they begged the detectives to do their jobs. Nobody told them who I was or what I was doing there; they must have assumed I was another cop. Eugenia's sister Natalia could have been her twin, and the sight of her made me want to turn to stone.

I swallowed, trying to work some spit into my mouth. "Yeah, real difficult," I said, "and do you mind if we don't talk about it? I can't talk about it. I signed a bunch of NDAs."

"You're worried about NDAs?"

"Oh yeah, they'll bleed you dry in a week. Totally ruin your life. I've seen it. Let me turn the tables on you. You were an actress–"

"For a hot minute," she said. "I tried the musician's life, too, because I enjoy being a cliché."

"How'd that pan out? Take a left here, by the way."

"Thanks. It worked out about as well as the acting career."

"What do you do now?"

"This and that."

"In my world, that's code for drug dealer. Or screenwriter."

"I've delivered packages. Never asked what was in

them. It paid well, though." She snorted. "Like father, like daughter."

"A living's a living."

"Yeah, it beats screenwriting." She chortled. "You'll like this. I had a friend who was asked to take a stab at a remake of 'The Wild Bunch'? Only updated to contemporary Mexico. He was super-excited, because Peckinpah was one of his heroes, but, get this, the executives said they wanted him to rewrite it so the gang survives at the end. Spoiler alert if you haven't seen the original."

"I've only seen it roughly a thousand times."

"He couldn't do it, not even for rent money. He took a job at a box store instead. Said it was better for his soul. Anyway, back to the situation at hand. If your phone's correct, we should be almost to the winery, right?"

"Yeah, we're here." To our right, a pair of stone pillars bracketed the driveway to the estate. Embedded in the left pillar was a brass plaque with 'VONN' stamped on it. Given the cheapness of Vonn's plonk and the gaudy ads it splashed across social media, I half-expected a neon sign, along with a fleet of exhaust-farting tour buses in the driveway, perhaps accompanied by a few bridesmaids puking their lunches on the lawn.

Madeline deftly maneuvered between the gates and onto a gravel lane sweeping past an imposing, Spanish-style mansion screened by browning pines. The lane curved again, slithering through gentle hills studded with neat rows of rough stumps: the grapevines, their future progress marked by long strings stretched between tall sticks. I'd taken a few wine tours in my time, and knew these operations consumed enormous amounts of water. Given climate change, how long could these valleys continue to produce wine?

I spotted a camera bolted to the mansion's tile roof, plus another one on a pole alongside the lane. If this place had any security, they knew we were coming.

The lane carried the Mustang up the hillside, where the gravel lane transitioned to pavement before widening into a parking lot, which was empty except for a vintage silver Porsche at the opposite end. Beyond the Porsche, a short walkway led to an enormous concrete structure embedded into the side of the hill, defined by neo-modernist angles and narrow windows. It looked like a giant robot bursting from the earth.

"How do you make a small fortune in the wine business?" I asked as Madeline braked the Mustang in a slot at the furthest corner of the lot.

"Tell me."

"You start with a large one."

"You didn't use that joke during your standup set, did you?"

"No, I spared the masses that particular brilliance." I nodded at the structure. "I'd say these people are making a large fortune, though. This isn't some quaint winery."

"The welcome party's here," she said, shutting off the engine.

The glass doors at the end of the walkway had opened, and a man in a pale linen suit and blue shirt strode into the light. I recognized his goatee and sharp cheekbones, the athletic shoulders pressing against the tailored fabric. "You remember that bicyclist from the road?"

"The old guy?" She grunted. "Damn, you're right. It's him."

"Small world," I said, debating whether to unclip my pistol and leave it in the Mustang's glove compartment. A winery wasn't dangerous to anything except your wallet and blood-alcohol level. Except I was in a paranoid mood after our lake sojourn.

I stayed strapped as I exited the car, double-checking that my shirt cloaked the lump above my waistband. A blessedly cool breeze caressed my face. Beyond a low stone wall edging the parking lot, the land dropped steeply, presenting a scenic angle on the rolling vineyards, the black lines of gnarled vines stretching to infinity. I had a better view of the mansion tucked within a cluster of shady trees, and another cluster of older, smaller buildings along the dry riverbed that marked the vineyards' border.

The goateed man raised a hand as he approached. "Greetings," he said.

"Howdy," I replied. The guy's two-piece was off-the-rack, baggy in the pants and tight in the jacket. I should have worn a suit. People who lack style are intimidated, and sometimes awed, by good tailoring.

"I'm sorry, but we usually do our tours in the morning, so I can't offer one," he said, hooking back his left sleeve to check the time. Despite the cheaper suit, he wore a Panerai Luminor that cost more than I made in my best six months, which I knew because Manny had once bragged about buying one after we stopped a famous director's affair from blowing into the open.

"We're not here for a tour," Madeline said, locking the Mustang.

"Well, if you're here to visit the shop, you're in luck, because it's open for another ho–" The man looked up from his watch, caught sight of Madeline, and paused.

"Are you okay?" I asked him, feeling a faint surge of pleasure. In my old life, I'd always enjoyed when all the pieces of a puzzle began to click together. The way the man looked at Madeline told me we'd stumbled upon a big piece.

"Was your father Ken Ironwood?" the man asked.

"Yes," Madeline said.

The man flashed shiny teeth. "Well, I'll be damned. I saw a photo of you once. You were very small, but you already had that amazing hair."

"I'm Madeline," she said, extending her hand. "And you are?"

"I'm Mike Vonn," he said as they shook. "I'm the owner. And I'm very sorry for your loss. I lost my parents a few years ago, and it's unbelievably difficult."

"Thank you," she said. "I didn't know him well, but..."

"We'd love to talk to you about Ken," I said.

He pivoted to me. "You're the boyfriend? Husband?"

"Neither. I'm a friend helping her out."

He hesitated, his weight shifting onto his back foot. I wondered if he'd entertained the idea of seducing her, a task my presence made far more difficult. These aging executives, they always thought of themselves as alpha males who effortlessly took whatever they wanted, as if they weren't popping Viagra like candy and injecting themselves with enough testosterone for an NFL team. Or maybe I was being unkind.

Like a machine clicking back into gear, Vonn's hosting instincts took over, and he stepped to me, his hand enclosing mine in a crushing grip that reminded me of Manny's. "Mike Vonn," he said, his smile hardening into a slight snarl.

"I caught it before," I said. "I'm Dash."

Turning to Madeline again, he said, "I wasn't friends with your father, exactly, but he was a good customer. We had many a happy interaction."

"He came here often?" I asked.

Vonn's head flicked toward me. A flash of irritation. "Not so often," he said. "But he stored some bottles of wine on the property. Kept a regular account. Would you like to come in? I can give you a special tour. I always love showing off the place."

"Sure," Madeline said, sneaking a look at me for confirmation. I nodded.

He spun, flicking a finger for us to follow him through the doors to the underworld.

17.

The winery's entranceway reminded me of a subway tunnel: a pale concrete tube stretching into infinity, with carveouts and nooks punched into its curve every few feet. A strip of fluorescent lights glimmered off the red tile floor. "It's a little industrial," Vonn called over his shoulder. "But that's because it's a working winery. Trucks bring the grapes up to the parking lot, and the workers carry them through here."

We passed the entranceway to the winery's store, its wooden shelves lined with bottles and coffee-table books, the table beside the register bright with colorful knick-knacks and souvenir bottle openers and boxes of snacks. Beyond it, doorways led to offices filled with desks, filing cabinets, workers hunched over screens.

"Hollowing out this mountain was a genius move on my part, if I do say so myself," Vonn shrugged with false modesty, as if a phantom audience had burst into applause. "Ultimate in natural climate control. Good for the wine."

"And when the apocalypse hits, you got a doomsday bunker," Madeline said.

"I suppose I do. Madeline, what brings you here?"

"We were going through my dad's effects. Found a key with your logo on it."

A hitch in his step. "Ah, yes. That would have gone to his wine locker."

A few yards past the offices, a stone archway opened onto a sunken living room with leather couches and a wall-mounted screen big enough for a movie theater. Two teenagers sat on the central couch, their attention on the phones in their hands. On the big screen, Karl Quaid flashed the camera a steely glare as he opened his mouth, long fangs sliding from his gums. I expected to feel something, considering how I watched him die a few days ago.

Instead, I felt nothing.

Maybe that was progress.

Vonn noticed me hesitating in the doorway. "You see that superhero movie, vampire movie, whatever it is?" he said. "My grandkids made me watch it twice. I don't usually go for that sort of thing, but it wasn't bad."

Madeline edged into my view, trying to read my face. "The guy just died," she said. "I read somewhere he was a real jerk."

"Yeah, I read he got shot or something," Vonn said. "The kids were pretty broken up about it."

The kids continued to swipe at their phone screens, ignoring the colorful pyrotechnics onscreen. Karl Quaid's costume crackled with digital lightning as he flew through an explosion, his slipstream unleashing a hurricane of debris on a collapsing city. Here was his afterlife, trapped in the same crowd-pleasing loop until the last server farm with his films shut down for good.

"Let's keep moving," Vonn said. "I want to show you the winery's beating heart."

The tunnel ended at another archway. We stepped onto a catwalk suspended three stories over the floor of an enormous cavern. Below us, ten stainless-steel fermentation vats ringed the space, each large enough to hold thousands of liters. A pair of steel machines dominated the center of the floor. I expected an overpowering smell of wine, but the only thing I sniffed was cleaning fluid.

"Vats and presses. This is where the magic happens. We've got the whole thing monitored by sensors. Temperature in the vats gets out of whack, we're alerted to it in seconds." Vonn led us along the catwalk's arc to a set of elevator doors. "Cost lots of money, took years to earn any kind of profit."

"How long did it take you to build all this?" I asked.

"This part of the property? Five years." The elevator doors binged open. The car was large enough to accommodate fifty people. "When we were hollowing out the caverns, the military asked us if they could use the space on weekends for Special Forces training. This was after 9/11. I like to think we helped those boys get a better handle on Afghanistan."

"Quick," Madeline said to me. "Tell him your drone joke."

"Not the right time," I said.

Vonn grunted.

"Sorry," she added. "Reflexive cynicism. I didn't mean any offense."

"You remind me very much of your father," Vonn said. We descended so gently I barely felt it. The elevator doors whispered open, and the fermentation vats towered above us, silent despite the liters of wine burbling in their vast bellies. We slipped between the presses on our way toward yet another doorway, this one large enough to accommodate a truck. Beyond it, rows of oak barrels stretched into the distant void.

It felt too empty down here. Where were the workers?

You'd expect to see at least one person scrubbing the floors or moving a barrel.

Maybe Vonn doesn't want any witnesses.

I slipped a hand to my side, tapping the pistol grip beneath my shirt.

"Where are we going?" I asked, my voice echoing off the cavern's curving walls. I was almost yelling, I realized. My forehead sweaty, my heartbeat accelerating like a runner off the blocks.

Vonn turned to me with a quizzical smile. "I have a place where we can talk more."

His suit jacket was loose, he could have anything under there, a knife or a gun or –

"No," I blurted. "We can talk here."

My heart slammed against my ribs to get out, out, out. A panic attack, like in Hell House. Maybe it was seeing Karl in that movie clip or maybe it was this rich prick in his weird kingdom reminding me of the rich pricks whose messes I'd spent years sweeping up but whatever the trigger, everything was out of control, and I couldn't –

"Hey."

Madeline's gaze held mine.

"Hey," she said again, gifting me a slight smile. Her eyes flicked down, guiding my attention to her hand hovering over her coat pocket. Her thumb and forefinger pinched a pebbled-leather handle with a silver button at one end. A switchblade. She had her body angled to hide the weapon from Vonn's sight.

"It's okay," she said, and opened her fingers so the blade dropped back into her pocket. "Still don't like underground spaces, huh?"

My heart slowed.

I blinked and shook my head, my eyes clearing.

"Yeah," I said. "Yeah, sorry. Subways are hell for me."

Vonn laughed. "Sure, I've had some problems down here, too. Lack of sunlight. But like I said, it's good for temperature control. Shall we?"

When he disappeared through the archway, I gripped Madeline's shoulder and squeezed. She tilted her head toward mine.

"I'm a woman," she whispered. "You think I'd let a strange man lead me somewhere without backup?"

"You coming?" Vonn called from somewhere beyond the barrels. "I want to show you something cool."

"I hope it's not a gun," I said, but I felt better as we entered the new tunnel. Whatever happened, she had my back. And I had hers.

18.

It was a maze down here. The far end of the tunnel split into a four-way intersection, the other three tunnels likewise lined with hundreds of barrels. Still no workers in sight. I was a little calmer, resisting the urge to tap my pistol yet again.

I wondered if someone had told Vonn about our presence in town. Like a deputy sheriff, perhaps. Or two men in a mini-car loaded with chocolates and menace.

In the center of the intersection stood an oak table topped with two fat candles in bronze holders, three wine bottles, and a row of glasses. Vonn examined the label of the leftmost bottle. "Our Cabernet Sauvignon from two years ago," he said. "Nice, ripe tannins, so it's got some solid depth, nice flavors. I always taste blackberries, leather, and earth. Would you like a glass?"

"Sure," Madeline said.

"Just a splash," I seconded, figuring it would quiet my jangled nerves.

"Fantastic. Nothing's better than wine with new friends." Pulling a winery-branded corkscrew from his jacket pocket, he popped the cork and poured two glasses. "Let it air a moment."

"You always have a couple bottles down here for guests?" Madeline asked.

Vonn laughed. "No, we have some high rollers coming around this evening for dinner. We have a full kitchen operating upstairs, too. Hosting events is a lucrative part of the business. Whenever we have guests down here in the cellar, I usually give them the same spiel, starting with how my family first came to this valley in 1870. They said my great granddaddy was a criminal, maybe a murderer, who escaped jail in San Francisco and made his way down to these parts. He ended up buying a hundred acres right along the ridgeline, which was a good start, but a fraction of what we currently possess. I don't know where he found the money – they said bank robbery, but who knows? You saw the house by the gate?"

I nodded. "How could you miss it?"

"He built that, too. It had a bowling alley, a distillery, stables for horses, and something called a milk house, if you can believe it. It's my main residence."

"You keep the bowling alley?" I asked.

"No, but the indoor pool is something to see. It has gray slate imported from Florence, and at considerable expense, I might add." He splashed wine into two of the glasses and handed them to us. "Cheers."

I stuck my nose in the glass and smelled a slight smokiness. Did the fires seep into the taste of the grapes? I took a sip, imagining I was drinking liquid ash, the planet's pain.

"He and his sons – my grandfather and my grand-uncle – started this wine business." Vonn helped himself to a full glass. "It did well until Prohibition. Those idiot Feds, they forced every winery in California to shut its doors, but they didn't know who the hell they were dealing with. My family, they started selling bootleg hooch instead, throwing huge parties here. Movie stars drove up all the way from

L.A. to sample the goods – there's a photograph upstairs of Clark Gable in the garden, magnificently drunk."

"When'd you start selling wine again?" Madeline asked. "And by 'you', I mean your father or whoever."

"Oh, my father had zero interest in the business. The revival, it was all me." Vonn puffed his chest like a proud pigeon. "This place had fallen apart by the time I inherited it. My father was living in two rooms upstairs, the rest of it was a ruin. I'd made a fortune up in Silicon Valley – if you use social media, you're welcome – and I decided to bring the family heritage back."

"I don't use social media," I said. "I think it's poison."

"Oh, I don't disagree," Vonn said. "I don't use it myself. But I came up with some of the solutions for the backend cloud infrastructure that allowed it to scale, back in the day. I like to tell the kids I'm the one responsible for a billion cat videos."

"You ever think, 'Oh God, what horrors have I unleashed on the world?'" Madeline asked. "You know, like Oppenheimer when they set off the atomic bomb?"

"You're funny," Vonn told her, before turning to me. "She's funny."

"When did you meet her father?" I asked.

"Get to the point, huh?" He nodded. "I suppose I've been rambling on a bit. What can I say? I'm proud of this place. Truth is, I don't remember exactly when I first met Ken, but it wasn't long after we opened. It was Bill Clinton's second term in office, because the Lewinsky affair was all over the news."

"He liked the wines?" I asked.

"We're not Napa. We're not Sonoma." He swirled his glass before the candles, fire flickering in the wine's crimson depths. "But the terroir here is fantastic. We grow grapes in the basin, but also up on the hillside. I think your dad appreciated what we were trying to do."

"You said you weren't friends?" Madeline asked.

"We were friendly. He was a good customer. Stopped by a few times a year, but I don't think we were the sole reason for his trips. I'd heard rumors about his line of work, and, well, given my family's history, you can imagine I was sympathetic. Criminals are just another kind of entrepreneur." He cocked an eyebrow. "You're both wondering if he confided in me."

"It crossed my mind," I said.

"The answer is 'no'. I wouldn't think to ask, and he was too much of a professional." The eyebrow stayed cocked, but his tone sharpened. "You strike me as a former cop, son."

"I'm not," I said. "I used to do PR."

"Oh really? Maybe you could give my PR person a few tips. All he does is write shoddy press releases and dumb posts."

"You should fire him," Madeline said.

"Sure, except he's also my son, and otherwise he'd sit around stoned all day." Vonn sighed. "We've all got our crosses to bear. The truth is, I haven't the faintest clue what happened to Ken. He just never showed up again, and one day we cleared out his locker and transferred it to another customer. I'm sure we sold off his wines, although I'd be more than happy to have the accountant go back through the books, find how much he's owed."

"That's okay," Madeline said.

"Are you sure? I can throw in some interest. It might be a sizable sum." Vonn lifted the bottle, offering us a fresh pour. I raised my hand, palm out, proud of myself for declining.

"Thanks, but I'm done," Madeline said. "And thank you for telling us all of that. We don't want to take up too much more of your time."

"It's no trouble," Vonn said, placing our glasses on the table. "Come back anytime. I'm serious. We can throw in a discount on a wine subscription."

"Sure." Madeline had already turned away, striding for the circle of white light that marked the entrance to the winemaking cavern. I could tell she was frustrated.

Vonn presented me with one of the unopened bottles, a five-year old Merlot. "Spicy oak and chocolate," he said. "A full-bodied finish. For the ride back."

I accepted the gift with a slight nod. "Do you sell chocolates in the store up there? We could go for some chocolates, too."

"Yes," he said, and hesitated, scrutinizing my face in the candlelight. "I've told you all I know about Ken. If she doesn't want the money, that's fine. But she won't gain anything by digging further. You understand?"

"Yeah," I said.

He pointed at my waistband. "And next time, please leave the firearm in your car. We usually don't allow them on winery grounds, but I let it slide this time."

I looked down. My sweat had traced a faint outline of the holster onto the fabric of my shirt. "You can't be too careful," I said.

"Nope." He tugged at his left inseam, raising it enough for me to see why he wore his trousers baggy: he had a black holster clipped to his ankle, heavy with a small revolver. "You certainly can't. I'll show you to our lovely store, but after that, I want you off the property. Understood?"

I nodded. From deeper in the caverns echoed a faint boom, maybe a door slamming, and I wondered who else was down here. A burst of cooler air swept over us, and I shivered. The space felt like a tomb.

19.

The winery's chocolates came in a white, rectangular box with the Vonn logo on the lid. As Madeline eased the Mustang through the winery's front gate, I opened it and found fifteen chocolates in three rows. A small card taped to the underside of the lid broke down the flavors: the chocolates were "infused" with port, Merlot, and Zinfandel, whatever that meant.

Setting aside the Vonn chocolates, I retrieved the box left for us at the lake and examined the remaining bonbons, which looked different from the ones I bought. Madeline had eaten three more while I was distracted. "Did any of these taste like wine?" I asked.

"What?"

"The chocolates from the lake. Did they taste like wine, port, anything like that?"

She stuck out her tongue. "Gross. No."

I stacked the two chocolate boxes at my feet, beside Vonn's gifted bottle of wine. "So those guys at the lake didn't get these chocolates from the winery."

The road was empty, so she accelerated to highway speeds, the Mustang straining to go airborne on the harder bumps. "You thought Vonn might have sent those guys?"

"It did cross my mind."

"Why would he do that?"

"He knew your father. He lives in the area. Maybe he was lying about them not being friends."

"Maybe." She cocked her head. "Maybe my dad was laundering cash through the winery. It would make sense, wouldn't it? I'm not a winery expert, but I bet they burn through a lot of cash, it's hard to keep track of expenses."

"Sure. It's as good a theory as any."

"We don't have any other theories."

"I want to drive around the lake, see what we can find."

"We can do that tomorrow. It's been the longest of long days, I need some friggin' food before I pass out." She mimed falling asleep, her forehead tapping the wheel, and the Mustang jerked toward the shoulder before she corrected.

I clutched my door handle. "Please don't. I don't want them to ship what's left of me back to L.A. in a tiny baggie."

"Oh, relax. This car hits anything else on the road, it'll plow right through it."

"Let's not test that theory. I like my organs in their current places."

She pouted. "You're no fun. Where are we eating?"

"We could hit that roadside place with the curiously vegetarian menu."

"I'm all for that. Then, sleep. Unless you want to try to find a bar."

"Given how things are going so far, I'd probably get into a brawl with some redneck within five minutes."

"Don't worry, I'd bet on you. Unless the guy was particularly large and mean-looking."

At the roadside place, we both opted for Sloppy Ricks and yucca fries. The sun looked like an egg yolk losing its shape on a broiling pan as it descended toward the hills, and it was cool enough in the stand's shade. As we waited for our food, Madeline retrieved the box of Vonn chocolates, examining them with the skepticism of a scientist peering at a mutant bug. She finally selected a square morsel and popped it in her mouth, chewing with her gaze fixed into the distance beyond the stand.

"Verdict?" I asked.

She swallowed with a grimace. "Like a wad of tissue soaked in prison plonk. Whoever made these wasn't the same person who made those other chocolates. Those were total quality."

"I guess that's settled, then."

"When our food comes out, I might give this box to them as a tip. Unless you want them for your own snacking pleasure?"

"Nah, give them away."

"Good." She turned from the horizon, locking on me. "I've been avoiding asking you this, but I feel like I need to. And when you answer me, I need a real answer from you, okay? No manly growling like 'nothing' or 'I feel fine', okay?"

"Okay?"

"Okay. Down in the winery, you looked like you were having a serious panic attack. You were sweating, all that stuff. I was worried. Something trigger you?"

I debated whether to share anything about Hell House or my past with Manny or any of the other thousand things that had melted my brain into a sparking lump of neuroses over the years. I could have told her how I tried to make amends, how the week after Hell House I had my cop contacts give me Natalia's phone number and address. How I called Natalia late at night on a burner phone, meaning to confess, only for my jaw to snap shut. How I tried visiting her after the incident with Karl Quaid and still couldn't find the right words. Would she have any sympathy?

Probably not. Nor should she.

"It reminded me a bit too much of something I'd been through before," I said. "Another rich guy in an isolated place."

"What happened?"

"The rich guy in question did something bad. I had to clean it up."

"Someone die?"

"Yes," I said. "Someone with a family. Parents. A sister. They never learned the truth. That's what chews at me – they're out there, wondering what happened, and they'll never really know."

"I'm sorry."

"I am, too." I remembered Natalia cursing me in the street. "I can't fix it, can I? But it's my thing to deal with. And it's not going to impact what I do, how I perform."

The corner of her mouth twisted upward. "'How you perform'. What are you, a car?"

"You're paying me to deliver a result."

"That's true, I am. But you're not a piece of machinery. Something bothers you, I want you to call it out, okay? For your sake and mine."

"I liked your switchblade, by the way."

"It's vintage, like the coat." She pinched her lapels. "The difference is, I found the coat in a thrift shop in Long Beach, but the knife was my father's."

"Do you know how–"

"To use it? Yes. It's even had a taste of blood. I had a friend who was really into Japanese culture – actually, that's a lie, he was really into cyberpunk and yakuza movies. Like most white boys, he wasn't even aware that culture fetishization is cringe. Moving on: one night, he got high on questionable mushrooms and wanted me to chop off his pinkie finger. It's a yakuza ritual."

"Yubitsume."

She looked surprised.

I raised my hands, palms out. "Hey, I watch a lot of yakuza movies, too."

"That's the word for it, yeah. We were in a club, tons of people around, but I was drunk. And angry, I guess, because I'd been sitting there for hours listening to him rant about honor and respect and some cyberpunk video game. So, I pull out the knife and tell him, 'You really want this? Let's do it.' And he gives me this big smile and puts his hand on the bar."

"And you did it."

"I was angry and hungry and all the other things that make you impulsively chop up a friend. I didn't expect it to bleed nearly as much as it did. Plus, he started screaming and waving his arm around, which really didn't help keep the blood contained. The bartender gets a bunch in his eyes so he's also running around screaming, the finger goes flying onto the dance floor..."

"Most of this story is an outright lie, isn't it?"

She struggled not to laugh. "No, it's all true, I swear. I guess at that point I was thinking they could still attach the finger. It's a sharp switchblade, and I'd made a nice, clean cut. But this girl with tiny five-inch heels, I swear to God, she steps wrong and spears the thing like a cocktail weenie, and that was it for my friend's finger. Looks like our food's ready."

A sunburned hand extended from the stand's order window, clutching an oily bag bulging with carbohydrates and fried seaweed and onion. I brought it back to the car. "Let's eat at the house," Madeline said, unlocking the doors. "I could use the air conditioning. Also, a shower."

"Me too," I said, distracted by a flash on the horizon: the low sun reflecting off the windshield of a car rocketing toward the shack. What if Mister Skull had tracked me all the way out here? No, that idea was ridiculous.

Or was it?

The car resolved into a smudge of browns and whites: a sheriff's SUV breaking the speed limit by a healthy margin. I froze. If the local cops wanted our scalps, we wouldn't stand a chance.

"Maybe he really needs some yucca fries," Madeline said, sounding worried.

"Maybe." There were three workers inside the shack, which meant three witnesses if something went weird. Why was I thinking this? Was I too paranoid?

Spewing a gritty cloud behind it, the SUV veered into the shack's parking lot and slammed on the brakes, stopping a car's length from the Mustang's bumper. The driver's door opened and out strode Deputy Sheriff Reid, grinning like a werewolf. His campaign hat cast his face in shadow.

"Sorry," he called to the workers in the shack, who greeted him with tired waves. "Sorry," he said to us, pushing his hat brim higher up his forehead. "I like to go fast sometimes. Livens up the miles."

"How's it going?" I said, shifting so my body blocked his view of the bulge on my waist.

"Nothing's on fire today, so I'm counting that as a good thing." He pointed at the bag in my hand. "Got yourself a little veggie burger? They used to serve real food here. Never understood all the pussies scared about eating meat. Eating meat's what we're meant to do. Eating meat's how we live forever." He crooked his left arm into a bodybuilder's pose. "Look at these guns, you don't believe me."

Madeline traded looks with me, confused. I understood how she felt. The Reid we'd met a few hours ago had been the stereotype of a taciturn cop. Now he was manic, cheerful, less like a law officer and more like your best buddy who'd drive a flaming car the wrong way down a highway after a few drinks. Had he forgotten to take his meds this afternoon?

"We were about to leave," I said, placing a hand on the Mustang's door handle. "Is there something we could help you with?"

Reid snorted, rose on the balls of his feet, and said, "Heard you took a trip out to Vonn's winery." Even his voice sounded different: higher pitched, almost strangled.

"Correct," Madeline said. "We heard their vintages are second to none. Truly a once-in-a-lifetime journey. Napa better be shaking in their custom footwear." Her voice was deadpan, but I caught the tension humming beneath it.

"Vonn is an upstanding member of this community," Reid said, settling back down on his heels.

"Yeah?" I said, hoping to draw his attention away from Madeline.

He cracked that wolfish smile again. "And if you believe that, I have a bridge to sell you. In a nice place called Brooklyn."

"We're being stalked," I told him. "Two guys in a tiny car, like one of those electric models. One's big, the other's small. You see anyone like that?"

He tilted his head. "Where'd you see them?"

"By the lake," I said.

"What were you doing out there?"

"Visiting where they found my father," Madeline said. "Paying our respects, I guess."

"I don't recall seeing anyone like that," Reid said. "Like I told you before, we're getting a lot of Martians up here. Crazy critters who maybe want to take advantage of these wildfires, rob some empty houses."

"They weren't those kinds of crazy critters," I said.

"How do you know that?"

"Weren't any houses around. Who told you we visited the winery? And why would you care?"

"It wasn't Vonn, if that's what concerns you," he said. "I like keeping track of all the local flora and fauna. You're a pair of crazy critters yourselves, just a different species. You see what you needed to see?"

"What?" Madeline said.

"Out at the lake," Reid barked. "You saw where they found your dad, you have his effects, what else do you need?"

"We'll leave as soon as we're able," I said. "Don't worry about it. You finally clean up that situation at the station?"

He hitched his belt, thrusting his crotch at us, all mirrored shades and dark energy and sun-bleached muttonchops. "You enjoy the rest of the time in our fair county, understand?" he said. "And then you get the heck out. Crazy critters, they get eaten. It's the cycle of life. Some friendly advice from your local lawman."

20.

Madeline waited until the shack had disappeared around the bend before slamming the gas and shifting into third gear, then fourth. She shuddered, a fresh cigarette jittering between her lips. "He shot us finger guns," she said, "as we pulled out."

"What?" I said, checking the side mirror.

"*Finger guns,*" she said. "And I don't think in a buddy-buddy sort of way."

"Crazy," I said. Had Reid guessed where we were staying? There were only so many rental places in the area, and he likely knew all of them.

"Here's an even crazier idea," she said. "What if our Deputy Sheriff Reid was actually a pair of twins? A normal one and a crazy one? It'd be right out of a Cronenberg movie."

"Write that screenplay. Like Jim Thompson's 'The Killer Inside Me', updated for the #MeToo era. Or something."

"This might stun you, but I'm the only person in L.A. without a screenplay stuffed in a desk drawer."

"I knew there was a reason I liked you."

She checked the rearview. "Seriously, what should we do?"

"Nothing we can do, except try and stay out of his way.

He's a cop, and if a cop wants to do something to you, they'll do it."

"On that comforting note, what's our next step?"

"Like I said before, we drive around the lake. See if there's anyone that remembers your old man. It's a needle in a stack of needles, but it's all I can think of."

She lit her cigarette and rolled down the window, blasting smoke out her nostrils. "We could head back to the winery, talk to Vonn again. That dude is shady as hell."

Yet again, I mulled whether Vonn was involved in Ken Ironwood's death. It was as good a theory as any, but we would need proof. And if Vonn was responsible in some way, he would have destroyed any evidence a long time ago. Someone capable of building a winery that doubled as a supervillain lair was likely good at long-term planning.

"We talk to him again, we better bring something to use as leverage," I said. "It's not like we can interrogate him. I left my brass knuckles at home."

"Oh, we'll resort to the switchblade. I'll ram it under his kneecap. Pop it like an oyster shell."

"You scare me."

"Good, that keeps things interesting. Here's our home away from home." She turned onto the gravel lane that led to the rental. The sun was descending beyond the high ridge to our west, casting long shadows across the grass, and the house's windows blazed with orange light, making it impossible to see inside. She parked beside my car and shut the engine down.

As we sat in the ticking silence, I felt a deep exhaustion sinking into my flesh like lead. Had we only just left L.A. this morning? It felt like a thousand years ago. I wanted so badly to stuff my stomach and pass out on the nearest mattress until morning. Yet there were too many lurkers out there, thinking our names, and I knew I would awaken in the small hours and sit in a chair with a good view of the hills, the lights off, my gun within easy reach.

21.

My eyes snapped open. Something was in the house with us. I had fallen asleep on the couch, my pistol and phone on the cushion beside me. The tiny green numbers of the stove clock glowed like cats' eyes in the dark. It was quarter to two, one of those times when the planet's blood slows and the spirits drift into view.

I retrieved the pistol and stood, listening. From upstairs came Madeline's faint snores. I walked to the front door and peered into the deeper shadows of the yard, the faint moonlight glinting off the car windshields. Unlocking the door, I opened it slowly to keep the hinges from creaking and stepped onto the porch, the wood surprisingly warm against my bare soles.

Insects buzzed and clicked in the tall grass. I opened my mouth slightly because a soldier told me once it would incrementally improve your hearing, allow soundwaves a clearer channel through your mouth to your ears. Whether or not that long-dead dude was messing with me, I heard nothing other than nature at work.

I stepped back inside and locked the door.

When I turned, Mister Skull was sitting on the couch. The white mask glowed in the dark. He wore a black jumpsuit and black boots and black gloves. He reached onto the cushion beside him and lifted a thick scrapbook with brown covers, the kind your grandmother might have owned back in the day. He set it on his lap and opened it to the first page, displaying faded photographs of Madeline as a small child, Ken Ironwood dressed in a purple suit with big lapels.

Stop, I tried to say, but my throat was paralyzed.

Mister Skull flipped pages, revealing more photographs: Ken Ironwood behind the wheel of the Mustang, standing in a vineyard, crouching on the concrete beneath a massive loading crane. And images of Madeline as she grew, her red hair sprouting over her shoulders, her lanky body enclosed in that Navy greatcoat like a wool cocoon…

I wanted to point my pistol at his face, but my arm muscles felt like concrete, the nerves severed. I tried stepping forward – *I'll knock the mask off* – and my feet refused to move.

Mister Skull's eyeholes burned into me. It was infinity in there, a void of no return. He slapped the scrapbook onto the couch and rose on cracking knees and strode toward me, unhurried, methodical, ready to end me here–

My eyes snapped open to white light and heat.

I was sprawled on the couch. The angle of the sun spearing through the windows told me it was early morning, and I could feel the day's heat already pressing against the glass, seeking a way in. I gasped for oxygen like a beached fish and when I no longer felt like I was suffocating I stood, the world tilting slightly on its axis.

Madeline was in the kitchen, her back to me, tapping a wooden spoon against the side of the coffee maker in a loose rhythm that sounded vaguely familiar. A Guns N' Roses song, maybe. She was clearly into vintage stuff.

"The creature, it lives," she called over her shoulder.

"You're up early."

"I'm always up early. Seize the day, and all that Insta influencer crap." She turned. "You were thrashing. I almost woke you up."

"Bad dreams," I said.

"I get those, too. I keep having this one where I'm trapped at a Taylor Swift concert, and someone says they're gonna do at least fifty encores, and I start screaming until I wake up. How do you take your coffee?"

"Black. Like my mood."

"Excellent." She opened one of the cabinets over the sink and pulled down two oversized travel mugs. "I'm figuring it'll be a long day, so we want to get on the road, like, ASAP?"

"Yep." I dropped to all fours, then tented my body into a downward-facing dog. My knees shook slightly, and my core muscles quivered like gelatin, but the pose held. My head felt okay, all things considered. No hangover. No fuzziness.

The coffee machine hummed and spat caffeine into the first mug. She leaned against the counter, watching me. She had a loose t-shirt with the poster from John Carpenter's "Big Trouble in Little China" on the front, along with a pair of tight jeans. It was odd seeing her without the coat. "Bend your legs a little more," she said. "You don't need to have them stiff like that. And loosen your elbows just a tad."

I followed her suggestion. "You do yoga?"

"I used to teach it, buddy. For about six months, part time."

"You're full of surprises." I felt energetic enough to shift into a plank, my biceps trembling after a few seconds. I needed to get into shape again.

"Not really. Half the people in L.A. teach yoga or Pilates

or whatever. It's a good way to pay rent, especially when you're broke."

I settled onto my stomach, then rolled over and stood. I smelled of sweat and smoke and dust. "You never considered selling the Mustang? Even when you were low on cash?"

She shook her head. "Never. Not even when my bank account was down to a buck fifty. The thought of some rich prick getting yet another new toy was more than I could bear."

"I like your principles," I said. "Let me grab a shower, then I'm at your service."

Once I cleaned up and changed into fresh clothes, I sipped my coffee on the porch while sweeping through a local map on my phone. Five marinas dotted the perimeter of the lake, only one of which had a webpage. I estimated it would take us a few hours to hit them all. I planned on taking the pistol. Even in the harsh light of day, Mister Skull refused to leave my mind.

Madeline stepped onto the porch and locked the door behind her. Her greatcoat swallowed her small frame. It reminded me of a kid playing with their grandfather's old military gear. "Let's throw this snowball into Hell," she said.

I debated whether to rig the house to detect intruders, as I'd done in L.A. with the strand of hair across my apartment door. The hair trick wouldn't work outside because the breeze was too strong. Besides, unless we were dealing with the purest breed of idiot, a sticker or piece of tape would be too obvious. No, we'd have to hope nobody visited while we were gone. Not much of a plan.

Armed with our coffee in travel mugs, a gun, and a fresh pack of cigarettes for Madeline, we motored into the county. "I must admit," she said, pressing her mug between her thighs as she shifted gears and popped the day's first coffin-nail from its pack, "the cop still worries me."

"Me, too."

"I felt like I was up half the night, worrying about it. What if we run into him again?"

"Smile and wave," I said, trying for the joke, but my smile crashed and burned on liftoff.

"Or run for our lives." We had reached the two-lane road tracing the shoreline. After three miles, the dry flats turned muddy before disappearing beneath greenish water. On our left, the first marina on our list swung into view: a white shack with a sun-bleached sign announcing 'BOATS', and beyond it a pair of wooden piers extending into the lake like arthritic fingers. A few small sailboats and motorboats bobbed in the shallows. Madeline swung into the gravel lot and parked along the side of the shack. The sun stabbed through the windshield and prickled the backs of my hands.

The shack's door opened, and an old man walked out. He had a rail-thin body and a tiny head topped with wisps of cotton-tuft hair, but his oily hands were huge, blocky, veined. He looked like he could crush a sparkplug to slag with his thumbs.

Madeline strummed an imaginary banjo. "'Deliverance', here we come."

"Hush," I said, opening my door. "I got this."

The old man drew a stained rag from the back pocket of his jeans and wiped his sweaty forehead, leaving a faint streak of black over his eyes. "Morning," he said.

"Howdy," I said. "You the owner?"

"That's right," he said, tilting his head for a better view of Madeline. "You want a boat, I ain't got any to rent, sorry to say."

"No, I'm not in the rental market. You familiar with that guy they found in the barrel? It was all over the news."

"Oh damn, you another reporter?"

"No. I'm a detective," I said.

"A what now?"

"A detective, like in the movies." I sensed things trembling at the edge of control. A true detective would have dreamed up a better plan than driving circuits around a lake, hoping against hope for a clue.

I pointed over my shoulder toward the Mustang. "The young lady in there, she's the daughter of that guy they found in the barrel," I said. "She's paying me to find out what happened to him."

"Oh yeah?" The man made a noise like an engine throwing a rod. "I'm sorry for her, but from everything I heard, the guy had it coming."

"That's not my place to decide. I'm just doing a job." I stuck out a hand. "My name's Dash."

"Howard." His handshake was crushing. I was in the kingdom of men with iron grips.

"How long you own this place, Howard?" I asked, prying my hand loose with most of the bones intact.

"Forty-three years next January," he said. "We had two reporters come through the other day – I told them to screw off. That was after the cop who came around, and I'll tell you what I told 'em: I never forget a face, and I never saw that guy in my marina in all my years here. Nobody gets in my marina without me knowing it."

"Maybe they rolled him here in the barrel." I stepped to the left, trying to see beyond Howard into the shack. He mirrored my movement, blocking my view.

"Buddy," he said. "It was a long time ago, and I want to be left to my business. Clear?"

"Clear. Those reporters, what were their names?"

"I didn't care to write them down." In that moment he sounded almost imperial, like an old British lord plopped into rural California. "All I know is they were filming a television show or something."

"A documentary?"

"If you say so. They kept waving phones around, filming stuff."

"Reporters, they're sure annoying." I nodded at the piers. "You mind if I take a quick look around, with your permission? I won't take any photos."

"Knock yourself out."

I turned to the Mustang and lifted a finger in a just-one-minute gesture. Madeline saluted me back. I circled the shack, noting the rusty cage of propane tanks leaning against the rear wall, along with plastic gallon jugs leaking an oily liquid. One lit match would turn this place into a rocket. I continued onto the nearest pier, trying to ignore Harold glaring at me from the parking lot, his enormous fists wringing the life from that stained rag. He was nervous about something, or maybe he didn't like visitors asking about decades-old murder cases.

Water lapped against the pier like a cat's tongue. When I reached the fuel pump at the end, I shaded my eyes and spotted what I thought was the thin brown line of the causeway against the trembling horizon. If the boat ferrying Ken's body to its final resting place had departed from here, it wouldn't have needed to travel very far. How many more years would it take before this part of the lake dried up, turning the marina into another relic of a gone world?

I turned to check Howard's position. To my utter lack of surprise, he stood where I left him, doing his best to kill me with a look. I decided to irritate him by taking my sweet time examining the three boats tied to the pier. The first two were motorized skiffs, but the larger sailboat to my left was a real beauty, a single-masted antique with a gently curving hull and a pristine deck. I noted the name emblazoned on the stern – *DJANGO* – and the golden icon painted beneath.

I blinked.

That was interesting.

As I passed the shack, I gave Howard a slight nod. "Thanks," I said. "I really like that sailboat."

Howard grunted and spat between his feet. I climbed into the Mustang and gestured for Madeline to start the engine. "Let's get out of here," I said, pulling out my phone and checking the map again. "Take a right, drive down a half-mile, then take a left onto a lane."

"What's there?" she asked, throwing the car into reverse.

"If this is correct," I said, pinching and zooming, "that dirt road goes up along these hills. We're gonna find a place where we can watch our new friend."

"Why?"

We bumped onto the road, and I checked my side mirror for Howard, who had disappeared into the shack. "Because he knows way more than he's letting on," I said.

22.

The road looping across the ridge above the lake might have been private, and I hoped we wouldn't encounter a gate, but the turnoff was clearly marked. Madeline popped a chocolate from her greatcoat as we hit the turn, chewing while she spun the wheel one-handed, the Mustang's tires rumbling onto loose gravel.

"I thought you hated those chocolates," I said.

"I chopped off a guy's finger when I was hungry, remember?"

"Touché."

A weather-faded 'No Trespassing' sign flickered past on our right, bolted to a bleached pole. I bet we could disregard it: if someone stopped us, we would pretend to be airhead tourists out for a drive.

The path circuited a dead tree before ascending the hill, the Mustang's tires clawing at the steepening grade. Madeline pushed to the shuddering edge of first gear, the engine's pitch rising. "Slow down," I said. "Like, way down."

"Don't you trust my driving?"

"I do. But we're casting up a lot of dust."

She eased to a walking pace as we crested the rise. I had my phone in my lap, tracking the blue dot of our progress until we were roughly level with the marina below. The road was behind the ridge enough to block our view of the shoreline. On either side of us, the grass rose to nearly the level of our windows: perfect for concealment, but it also made me paranoid about snakes, coyotes, and other creatures with teeth.

"Stop the car," I told her.

She hit the brakes. I sat, willing to let the silence become increasingly uncomfortable, as I puzzled out strategy. In an ideal world, I would have a small, battery-powered camera I could attach to a convenient rock, a gee-whiz spy device that would send me footage as I sat in air-conditioned splendor somewhere, sipping a beer. I had done enough surveillance in my life to recognize what I was in for: too many hours of fighting sleep and numb legs, staring at the same distant point while my mind spun illusions to break the boredom. And that effort might still yield nothing.

"You going to fill me in?" she said.

"What were the names of the guys who did the documentary on your father?"

"Brian Golden and Tommy Dove. Why?"

"I think they were here. They really irritated Howard there."

"Huh," she said. "One of them tried calling me the other day, but he didn't leave a message."

"Which day?"

"Same day I met you?"

"I wonder if they're lurking."

"The cop didn't say anything about them."

I shifted topics: "Your Dad ever own a boat?"

She shook her head. "He robbed boats, but I don't think he owned any. Not that I know of. My mom never mentioned one."

"Okay, here's my plan: you're going to drive back down to the road, find us some food. Mexican, whatever – I'm not picky, just as long as it's not friggin' vegetarian." I grinned. "Meanwhile, I'm going to find a halfway comfortable place, sit, and stare at that marina. We spooked that guy. He might do something stupid."

"And I'm supposed to drive off and let you play detective."

"We'll need the food. You don't understand, surveillance is boring as hell. I'm sparing you a few minutes of it." I opened my door. "Be careful driving out. Map said there's a loop up ahead, it'll take you back down."

"Okay. Don't do anything dumb while I'm gone."

"I guarantee nothing. And get bottled water. A lot of it," I said, climbing out. After she motored off, I moved toward the ridge, crouching so my head was below the level of the grass. The land fell away in a gentle slope, and I snuck five yards below the ridgeline before settling on a flat rock behind a low screen of bushes. From here I had an amphitheater view of the marina and a half-mile of road in either direction.

The rock rubbed against the bottom of my holster. I unclipped it from my waistband and set it on the warm ground beside me. A gun would make it an even fight against any rattlers.

The marina was still. I assumed Howard was in the shack. The antique sailboat bobbed in the gentle current, its mast swaying, its brass fixtures glittering in the sun. *Django*. Like the character played by Franco Nero in the old Spaghetti Westerns, or Jamie Foxx in the Tarantino flick. The kind of movies Ken Ironwood had loved.

I pulled out my phone and typed in "Django sailboat northern California" and received a basket of random search results: sailing manuals, sailing magazines, boat sales pages, even a website devoted to the adventures of a border collie named Django that lived with its owner on a sailboat crossing the Atlantic. I clicked on the first link offering boats for sale – and hit gold: the images at the top of the page were unmistakably the craft from the marina. It was an archived webpage from five years ago, when a company named 'New Marine' had sold it for a cool half-million to an unknown buyer. According to the 'Boat Details' tab, *Django* had been built in the late 1990s and technically counted as a sloop, with a four-blade propeller powered by a diesel engine.

From there, I searched for 'New Marine', receiving roughly a million hits in return. A boat-sales company in San Francisco looked promising. I dialed the number on their website. A bored-sounding woman picked up on the fourth ring.

"Hello," I said. "I'm calling about a sailboat named *Django* that you sold a couple years back. A sloop with a wooden hull. I'm interested in buying it, and I was wondering if you could put me in contact with the owner?"

A long pause. "Sorry, who're you?"

"I represent a foreign client," I said, trying to slip an added note of prissiness into my voice. "Cost no object, but we really would like to get this done as soon as possible."

"Unfortunately, we don't reveal the names of clients. But we have many sailboats we can sell you."

"My client's really hung up on this one."

"We have many wooden sloops, including some new ones with premium amenities I'm sure your client will love." She had shifted into sales mode, robotically seductive. "I'm impressed with these models myself. In fact, you won't find a better..."

"No, like I said, my client's locked on this specific one," I said, prepping my final Hail Mary toss. "Tell you what: you don't have to tell me who bought that boat. But if you reach out to them, tell them about this offer, and if they make a deal with us? We'll pay you a hefty finder's fee. Sound good?"

"Please hold," she said, and the line clicked to muzak. Whatever your feelings about Jimi Hendrix, he didn't deserve his guitarwork reduced to an easy listening melody. The wind was picking up, whitecapping the lake's shallow waters, drying the sweat on my forehead to a salty crust.

A click. "Hello?" the woman said.

"Hello."

"We'll forward the request to the buyer," she said. "Can you give me a phone number to reach you?"

I rattled it off and ended the call. Anyone searching for my phone number online wouldn't find anything useful: I lacked much of a digital trail. The boat had been built a few years before Ken disappeared, and something about it itched my brain. If this thread led nowhere useful, I would try to track down those documentarians next. I was sure they were the 'reporters' Howard had mentioned.

On the road to my left, a flashing dot resolved into the Mustang. It turned onto the gravel road and disappeared from my sightline, but I heard it rumbling up the hill. Madeline stopped a few yards north of me. When she opened her door, I clucked my tongue, and she clucked buck. I kept clucking until she crunched through the grass on my right, her body bent over an oversized paper bag.

"Success?" I asked.

"Yeah." She settled onto the rock beside me. "Mexican

up the road. Not a chain. I got us chicken quesadillas, plus waters. Sound good?"

"Oh yeah."

"Any movement?"

"None." I opened the bag and eased out the scorching foil packets with our food. "I got a lead on the boat's owner."

"Who is it?"

"Not sure. I'm hoping someone will call me back."

"Who do you think owns it?"

"Vonn, maybe. But I think your dad owned it before that."

She pursed her lips. "Why would my dad have a boat all the way up here?"

"Because I'm betting he had a whole different life up here. The winery was a part of it. I'm on thin ice with this, but the boat is named *Django*, which is an old cowboy movie name, and your dad dug those movies."

"You're right, that's thinner than a supermodel. And if the owner's Vonn?"

"It gives us some leverage when we talk to him again."

She unwrapped the foil and nibbled the edge of her quesadilla. "Vonn takes him out on the boat. Kills him. Dumps him out there."

"Or killed him somewhere else, used the boat to dump the body."

"It's a theory."

"It's a theory."

"Apropos of nothing, I got us a present." From her coat pocket, she drew two new baseball caps, the price stickers attached. "The Mexican place was selling them. I figured they'd save us from heatstroke."

The front of the blue cap stated, 'Women Want Me/Fish

Fear Me', while the red cap announced, 'I Pee in Pools'. I snatched the fishing-themed one and slid it on, positioning the bill so it covered my neck. Madeline stuffed the red cap over her thick crimson hair.

I had eaten half of my quesadilla when she pointed at the road and said, "Isn't that our buddies?"

A pastel-green smear approached from the south, resolving into the mini-car from yesterday.

"It must be," I said.

"Maybe they're out to buy more chocolates."

"I don't think so."

The mini-car turned into the marina's lot, and the shack door slammed open. Howard stumbled into the sun, swiping the air with both hands, the rag clenched in his right hand. The Lean Man and the Stocky Dude squeezed from their car, waving like they wanted Howard to calm down. Howard pointed at the pier and shouted something we could almost hear from the ridge. Even with my new baseball cap shading my eyes, the sun was too bright to see the pair's faces clearly.

The Stocky Dude placed a hand on Howard's shoulder. I drew my phone and opened the camera app and snapped a few shots of them together. The Lean Man disappeared around the side of the shack. Howard pointed at the pier again, his head dipping in what could have been disappointment, and the Stocky Dude said something to him.

The Lean Man walked onto the second pier as the Stocky Dude and Howard entered the shack. I shifted my aim and snapped a few more photos of the Lean Man walking past the antique sailboat – never sparing it a glance – and stopping in front of the fuel pump.

Madeline tensed.

I shifted the camera app from photo to video mode and started filming. The Lean Man unhooked the fuel nozzle and dropped it on the dock. He fiddled with the pump, his back blocking his hands from our sight. When he turned and trotted back to shore, I didn't notice anything different with the machinery, no sparks or leaking fuel or anything preceding a big boom.

The Lean Man opened the driver's door of the mini-car and climbed in. Its engine whined above the rising hum of the wind as he gunned it. The Stocky Dude stepped into the sunlight, wiping his hands on his pants, and over the engine's snarl I caught a snatch of high-pitched yelling that must have come from the Lean Man inside the car. He sounded angry. The Stocky Dude sprinted for the passenger door and leapt inside as the Lean Man threw the car into reverse and skidded onto the main road, heading north.

Madeline exhaled loudly and said, "You think they hurt him?"

"Howard?"

"Yeah."

"Maybe." He's probably dead, I didn't add. I flicked through the new photos on my phone, zooming in tight on the ones of the Stocky Dude and Howard, but the distance reduced any details to pixelated blurs. Slipping the device into my pocket, I exhaled loudly, frustrated.

"They hurt him because you asked some questions?" she asked.

"I don't know." I tried to suppress a fresh pang of guilt. I had panicked Howard into calling two people to help clean up a problem, only Howard didn't realize he had become part of the problem. If Stocky Dude had killed him, I hoped it was quick.

"Maybe we should go down," Madeline said, speaking faster. "If he's hurt, we need to help him–"

A flash of white and a wave of heat. Madeline yelped. My ears popped. A cloud of black smoke boiled from what was left of the pier. Flaming bits of fiberglass marked where the two skiffs had sunk. The antique sailboat listed at a sharp angle, taking on water, its port side reduced to smoking wood and burning ropes.

"Oh fuck," Madeline shouted, jumping to her feet, scattering our food. "Oh fuck, oh fuck."

The roof of the shack was alight. Clouds of orange and red embers swirled in the breeze, drifting across the road into the brush. I stuffed my phone in my pocket, the pistol in my left hand as I sprinted up the ridge to the car, Madeline on my heels. If those embers sparked a grass fire it would sweep over us before we could take more than a few steps.

Below, the sailboat's fuel tank cooked off with an echoing thump. The mast flared, sparkling within a cloud of foul steam.

"Damn it," Madeline yelled, the car key slipping from her hand. She knelt for it, but I was faster. I unlocked the driver's door and pushed her through to the passenger side before ducking behind the wheel. Even if a firestorm wasn't about to cook us alive, we needed to leave here before the cops and the fire department arrived.

I shifted into first gear, the Mustang bucking as I almost fumbled the clutch. The gravel path swooped to the right, away from the ridge, before descending toward the lower fields and the main road. Madeline stared out the window, murmuring "fuck" under her breath like a benediction.

I was going to follow the mini-car. It was a stupid idea. Also my only idea.

I slowed at the turnoff. I didn't want to turn onto the main road only for a fire engine to blindside us. The lanes were clear in either direction and I spun the wheel north and floored it. In the rearview mirror, the shack exploded into a mushroom of greasy flame, followed by a shock wave thumping our rear window like a fist. I thought I caught a whiff of burning fuel and wood.

"Oh man," Madeline said. "Oh man, oh man. We are in so much trouble."

"Not us," I said. "We just asked some questions."

"Everything's on fire."

"Look," I said. "We're following these guys. It's dangerous. I need your head in the game, okay?" The speedometer edged toward eighty miles an hour. The mini-car didn't have much of a lead over us. How long would it take old-fashioned American horsepower to catch up with a granola-crunching, eco-friendly engine?

"Okay." She fumbled her smokes from her coat and lit one, flaring through half of it on the first long puff. "Nicotine to the rescue. Oh man. Oh fuck. What now?"

"We follow," I said, thankful again for having a gun. Things were moving too fast, piling down, crashing into death. We needed to stay ahead of the wave.

23.

Too late, I realized a major flaw in my plan: I was driving a museum piece, the opposite of inconspicuous, especially to two guys who'd left a creepy box of chocolates on its trunk. Making the situation more interesting, the two-lane along the lake was curvy but largely free of trees or buildings that might provide cover.

Even our stupid baseball caps wouldn't help us.

The panic snarled in my chest, but I refused to let it sink its claws into me.

At least I had the pleasure of driving the Mustang. It growled agreeably as I pushed it faster, until I spotted the mini-car swooping through the next curve. I eased off the gas and let our speed drop to fifty while I debated what to do. A yellow Lamborghini overtook us in the opposite lane, its engine growling like a buzzsaw, before dipping in front of us. I was grateful for its bright bulk hiding us from our prey.

Madeline exhaled loudly and shook her head clear. "I'm okay," she said. "I'm okay."

"Good."

"You think those guys work for Vonn?"

"Who else?"

I took the curb at speed, almost riding the Lamborghini's bumper, and she white-knuckled her door handle. "For a guy who's a real ninny about my driving," she said, "you're really doing a Steve McQueen here."

"Hey, you know the name of one actual film star."

"It was a real caveman move how you grabbed my keys back there," she said, and smirked. "Way to really take charge."

"Sorry," I said. "We needed to move." I didn't feel sorry at all. I understood why she liked to daredevil in this beast. Sure, it got ten miles to the gallon and ejected enough carbon to melt an ice cap, but the power made my lizard brain screech for joy.

She tried slotting a cigarette between her lips, but it slipped free and landed in her lap. She retrieved it only for her trembling fingers to drop it a second time. "Damn," she said. "I'm so sorry about that guy."

"Don't be."

"We caused it." She pinned the cigarette's filter between her front teeth and patted her pockets for her lighter, hard, like she was hitting herself.

"Stop." I touched her wrist. "We're not responsible. These guys are."

I avoided telling her the truth: if we'd done things a little smarter, Howard would still be upright and sucking oxygen. He wasn't the first person I'd killed indirectly. Manny and I had probably triggered more overdoses and car crashes and suicides than we would ever admit in polite company. You take away a D-lister's career, and a year later you read about how they drove off a bridge overpass; maybe you remember their name, maybe you don't.

The universe could put Howard on my tab.

But I didn't want Madeline to wrestle with that sort of weight.

She didn't deserve to feel like me.

We followed the lakeside road through a small settlement. A gas station with a row of electric chargers shared a gravel lot with a diner and a windowless concrete building. A few sun-bleached double-wides were tucked in the grove of yellow pines beyond. The mini-car banged a left turn at the lone intersection with a traffic light, following another two-lane into the hills. The light flicked to yellow as the Lamborghini knifed through, following the lake road toward whatever rich-prick adventures lay beyond.

I resisted the urge to run the red, hoping the buildings would provide some cover if the mini-car's driver was scanning his rearview for any signs of pursuit. Without the Lamborghini, I would need to drop back even further to prevent being seen. I just had to hope the road didn't branch after a few hundred yards.

Our luck held on that front. The road rose into the hills, looping after the first few miles into a series of fearsome curves and switchbacks that demanded I lower my speed to forty, then thirty. We passed a peloton of bikers in bright spandex chugging up the incline. "God," Madeline said, flicking her lighter. "Why do drivers hate bicyclists? Like, really hate them?"

"I have a sense you'll tell me."

"It's not because they try to take up too much of the road, which they do." She rolled down her window, her hair snapping in the burst of dry air. "It's because they're being so damn healthy. It makes everyone jealous."

"I'm exhausted looking at them," I said, accelerating once the bicyclists fell behind us. We took another curve in time to spot the mini-car disappearing behind a ridge. No signs of civilization in sight. Where were they going?

I slowed as we approached the top of the ridge – if they wanted to ambush and riddle us with bullets like Bonnie and Clyde, it was the perfect location. Flexing my hands on the wheel, I tried to remember everything I was taught about spinning a car around at speed – you put the clutch in, then spun the wheel, or was it wheel-then-clutch? But no sooner had I started worrying about it than we were over the ridge. The road beyond was clear and straight through more flammable grassland. In the middle distance, the mini-car turned into a tree-lined driveway blocked by an iron gate between two stucco pillars. I slowed until the gate opened and the mini-car disappeared onto the private lane beyond.

"Looking it up," Madeline said, flicking through her phone. "My signal is surprisingly strong up here."

As I cruised past the gate, I noted the empty security booth on the pebbled median between entrance and exit lanes. If you wanted to open the gate, you needed to tap a code into the keypad bolted to a metal stalk. No signs announced whatever lay beyond the iron barrier.

I accelerated again. A deep ditch and white wooden fence traced the compound's perimeter, and I assumed there were cameras. Above the fence jutted the edges of tiled roofs and the tips of browning trees.

"Private community. Golden Lake, it's called. Sounds like a euphemism for piss," she said, slipping her phone back into her pocket. "It's new, too. Units on sale. Starting from the low three millions."

"Easily affordable," I said. "We can dig some change out of the couch cushions."

"Well, we're not getting in without a code," she said. "What now?"

I drove another hundred yards before pulling onto the

shoulder. "It doesn't make sense," I said. "These guys are driving around, leaving chocolates on strangers' cars, blowing up a whole marina, then heading back to their really expensive house in a gated community?"

"You're suddenly expecting this weekend to make sense?"

"Maybe Vonn has a house here. They're meeting him here to share details. Beats talking on the phone."

We fell silent.

It'll only get rougher from here, murmured the devil on my shoulder. This path only gets heavier. If you turn back, you can call the state police from L.A., explain whatever you've found, let them take care of it. They'll have to care now, right? You've discovered so much.

You know the state cops will never listen, countered my better angel. They might even think you were a part of it, throw you in a room, start asking questions. What happens if they really dig? How much of your past will end up in the light? You'll be left with nothing. Worse than nothing.

I have to do this, I yelled at my dueling selves, and imagined them blowing up in respective clouds of brimstone and cotton candy.

The first of the sweaty bicyclists shot past us, a colorful blur in their skintight outfits. The slower ones followed, their faces twisted into nearly identical rictuses of pain as they struggled against the stiffening wind and their exhaustion, their legs churning the pedals of their titanium-frame bikes. Madeline winked at me before unbuckling her seatbelt, tucking her knees under her, and extending her upper body through her open window, all the better for her to shout at those exhausted athletes: *"I'm being corrupted!"*

"Subtle," I said, once she slid back inside.

She punched me lightly on the shoulder. "Oh, come on. They loved it. Besides, you're way too uptight."

"Back in my old job," I said, "I once had to deal with this guy named Eryk Johnson. He looked almost exactly like Keanu Reeves, and he would show up at premieres, parties, whatever was happening that night. Tell the door guy he was Keanu, sign some autographs, and walk right in."

"Okay, Mister Random. Why are you telling me this?"

"Because I have an idea." Pulling out my phone, I found the Golden Lake's website. It would boast one hundred and fifty houses when it was completed, and twenty of those were already finished and on sale. You could arrange a tour by dialing the number at the top of the web page or filling out an online form.

I dialed the number. A perky realtor named Tiffany answered, and I proceeded to spin a tapestry of lies tailored to make someone in the luxury real estate business salivate like Pavlov's dog. In my snottiest tone, I explained how I was a stockbroker based in San Francisco, specializing in crypto. I said my name was Bernie Debs, and I was itching to buy a substantial chunk of real estate in picturesque San Douglas as soon as possible. I hoped the prospect of a big sale excited them enough to forget researching my background.

"I'm in the area," I said. "I was wondering if you had any availability today for a tour?"

"You could come over right now," Tiffany burbled, rattling off the address. "If you use code two-one-three when you get to the gate, it'll let you in. Then it's a quick left and a right at the next intersection."

"Wonderful. We're twenty minutes away." I thanked her and ended the call.

Madeline giggled. "That was an impressive show. There's one problem, though."

"What's that?"

"You don't look like a billionaire trader or whatever. And I don't look like some billionaire trader's hoochie mama."

I smiled. "You don't have any idea of how this works, do you? That Eryk Johnson guy, any halfway-smart person knew he wasn't actually Keanu. But they wanted to believe."

24.

My years working for Hollywood's grimiest taught me about the nature of power. If you need something from other people – a loan, a favor, a hundred million dollars to shoot your big space epic – you arrive at the meeting looking your best. You suit up in that clothing you spent a fortune on. You splurge on an ultra-hip haircut. You want to project how you're at the top of your game.

Instead, it makes you look weak.

Dressing up for an important meeting, it's like you're begging for approval.

The tech CEOs, the movie stars (however many of them still exist), the rock gods with a gazillion song streams a week, they show up to meetings in a t-shirt and jeans. They drift through the doors of ultra-expensive restaurants in a stained leather jacket. What are you going to do, kick them out? Tell them you won't fund their next project, especially after their last one bought the building you're sitting in?

When you dress down for a big-money moment, you're saying this isn't a big deal to you. That you have infinite power.

If you can throw in a few eccentricities, even better. I once heard of a tech CEO who hosted a dinner for reporters while wearing a tall purple hat right out of Willy Wonka's closet. None dared mention his sartorial choices in print, but they praised the hell out of his latest electronic doodad.

That's why I rolled up to a mansion in my street clothes, accompanied by a woman dressed like she was ready to stand guard at Buckingham Palace. We looked like people who made untold millions of dollars off a couple lines of computer code. As much as I loved my suits, I appreciated how well this tactic worked.

I entered the right combination into the keypad and the gate wheezed open. The road beyond wove between gravel medians studded with prickly desert plants, which opened onto a grid of beige mansions of numbingly similar design. They'd spent so much money and effort to flatten the land, pipe water through a near-desert, truck tons of lumber and stone to this spot – and then built the same McMansions you'd find in suburban Cleveland. Maybe humanity deserved everything coming to it.

Madeline pulled out her phone and opened the map for our location, which displayed only a gray square in place of streets or buildings. Whoever was building this place refused to allow the big tech companies to scan it.

The sameness of the roads and houses made it difficult to find the right address, but I knew we'd arrived when I spotted the blonde in the white pantsuit standing in the driveway, a leather binder in her hand. Her skin was so pale I was surprised she didn't explode upon contact with sunlight.

"Mister Debs," she said, approaching us with hand outstretched. "I'm Tiffany."

"Thanks for showing us around," I said, making sure to apply extra crush to my handshake, like a crypto bro always trying to dominate whoever he met. When her smile flickered, I released my grip and turned to Madeline. "This is my lovely wife, Amber."

"How goes it?" Madeline said, jutting her chin at the house behind us. "This it? Looks bland."

I shot her a look: be cool. If we wanted to hunt for our friends in the mini-car without attracting much attention, we needed to take this tour first. Sure, a real detective might have come up with a better plan, but if she had a problem with that, she shouldn't have hired a burnout.

"The outside is designed explicitly to blend seamlessly into the beauty of the surrounding environment," Tiffany purred, her smile stretching again to maximum length. A shimmering drop of sweat threatened to escape her hairline and run down her temple. "And the interior will really blow your socks off. Shall we go in?"

"Will it blow off my shoes, too?" Madeline said, trailing me as Tiffany led us through the double doors into a marble foyer that could have fit an 18-wheeler with room to spare. The foyer opened onto a cavernous space with two ornate staircases curving toward the second floor, lit by three-story windows on either side of us. We marched through an enormous set of doors into a living room that was more like a greenhouse, with glass walls separating us from the terrace and an enormous pool beyond.

In the center of the room, two spindly trees sprouted from holes cut in the marble flooring, their branches breaking the sunlight into a shattered glow that drifted over the high-end furniture and the long marble bar in the far corner. I had to admit, the space was impressive, perhaps even ten-million-dollars impressive, if you had the kind of cash to buy a mansion in a dried-out fire zone, followed by energy bills high enough to bankrupt France.

"The foliage is a nice touch," Madeline called over her shoulder as she crossed the space. "It really makes the place reminiscent of Thoreau. I can picture him heading back to a place like this after a refreshing afternoon on Walden Pond."

"Thoreau?" Tiffany said. "Didn't he write a famous book? I don't think I read it."

"Yes," Madeline said, pausing beside one of the trees to shake it. "It was about the need for large swimming pools and backyard helicopter pads and all those other things that make life so spiritually fulfilling."

I wanted to catch Madeline's eye and draw a finger across my neck, tell her to cut it out, but she kept her back to us as she examined the bar.

"If you know this Thoreau guy," Tiffany said, "and he's in the market, I think we have a few select authors purchasing properties here."

"The great intellects represented," I said. "Who else lives here? Anyone famous?"

She graced me with a pricey smile. "We can't reveal ownership, but let's say you'll be very happy with the people around you. It's only the very best. Can I show you the kitchen?"

The kitchen was surprisingly small, given the size of the house, but I supposed the kind of people who bought these properties didn't do much of the cooking themselves. From there, she guided us from the wine cellar to the airy bedrooms on the second floor, barely pausing her scripted prattle about gold fixtures and hand-cut wooden flooring and showers with ten different nozzles. I didn't suspect she doubted our bona fides, especially since I made a point of shouting something about equity and bonuses every few minutes.

"You're very *successful,*" Tiffany said as we examined one of the house's bedrooms, pouring real honey on the last word.

"Yeah, it's been a good year for shorts," I said, echoing what I'd once heard one of Manny's CEO clients say about the markets. "Very short… shorts."

Tiffany's professional façade cracked slightly. "What's a short?"

"They're an instrument," I said, my brain scrambling for any scrap of information. "You're betting against the market. I also do a lot of Bitcoin and crypto, too."

"Okay," she said, her smile snapping back into place. I stepped around her to exit the bedroom, wondering if she was starting to doubt our story. It probably didn't matter so long as she thought we had the cash. Half the buyers in this creepy subdivision were no doubt earning their money through questionable means.

We drifted back to the first floor and onto the terrace with its wraparound views of the hills. Tiffany turned and clapped her hands and smiled expectantly, as if we would whip out a duffel bag filled with hundred-dollar bills and place a down payment right there.

"Thanks," I told her, slipping on my sunglasses against the glare. "We'll think about it."

"We have to really delve into whether it's spiritually fulfilling enough for our tastes," Madeline said. She gripped my elbow and turned me away, calling over her shoulder: "Whether it fits our monk-like need for solitude and contemplation."

"You have my number!" Tiffany shouted, her voice echoing off the house's imposing expanse of brick and glass. "Looking forward to connecting!"

As we climbed into the Mustang, Madeline muttered, "When the revolution hits, her pretty neck's definitely got a date with the guillotine."

"She's just trying to sell a house," I said, starting the engine. "She probably doesn't make that much."

"Sorry, *dear,*" Madeline smirked. "I didn't realize I was supposed to totally prostrate myself in the name of unfettered capitalism and ugly-as-hell furniture."

"I kind of liked the live trees growing in the living room. That was nicely understated." I pulled away, shifting my attention to our real mission: finding the mini-car. Depending on how many paranoid residents were glued to their security cameras, I figured fifty-fifty odds a neighbor would call security to report a vintage Mustang driving in aimless loops. We might only have a few minutes. And if we found our target?

To be honest, I didn't know yet. I was still playing this by ear. Some detective I was making, huh?

We drove up Sunflower Lane and down Waterfall Avenue and around Yellow Rose Circuit. More of the houses back here were custom jobs, the architecture a little more varied, but I was surprised the owners hadn't opted for desert-friendly landscaping of colorful pebbles and shrubs. The grassy lawns were already scorched brown.

"There," Madeline yelled, jabbing a finger against her window.

The mini-car was parked in a short driveway midway down a block. I drove straight. At the next intersection, I turned right and parked at the curb, hoping nobody was home in the nearest house, a three-story monstrosity with a flower garden behind a white picket fence.

I leaned forward and drew my pistol from its holster and

clicked open the cylinder and checked the bullets. "Let's take a walk," I said.

"Don't tell me we're going to walk up, knock on their door."

"Nope."

"Because I'm starting to notice you're impulsive."

"Guilty," I said, returning the gun to its holster. "But I'm not doing my Charles Bronson imitation just yet." I opened the door and stepped out. A cooler air barreled across the grasslands and whistled between the houses, punching back the heat. Above the wind I heard no birds chirping or insects humming, no people chattering, no rumble of traffic. A perfect suburban silence. Against the thrumming blue sky, the houses reminded me of oversized tombstones.

"I hope they put out that dock fire," Madeline said.

"Me, too." I waved for her to follow me to the intersection, where I guided us left, retracing our route. Passing the street with the mini-car, I examined the mansion beyond it: two-story stucco with a sharply angled roof, reminiscent of the houses they built in parts of Beverly Hills in the late 1920s, except even from this distance I could tell the materials in this house were cheap, liable to crumble within a few years. I didn't notice any cameras clipped to the walls or roof.

We walked another block and I nodded for Madeline to turn left again. "You going to illuminate me on your brilliant plan?" she said, pulling out her phone.

"Sure," I said. "Soon as I come up with it."

She opened her browser and typed something in. "The address on that house was five-eight-three." She flicked the screen. "Sold last year for two million, says this real-estate site."

"It say who bought it?"

"No. Maybe we can sneak behind, jump the fence?"

"We'd have to go through someone else's yard, maybe jump another fence or two to get there," I said. "And what if we jump the fence, and those guys are in the back?"

"They'll have words for us," she snorted. "And none of them are gonna be, 'Happy to see you'."

"Wait." I pulled out my phone. "My lone brain cell has an idea."

"Awesome."

"I didn't say it was a good idea," I warned, opening my web browser and searching again for Vonn's website. When it popped up, I tapped on the phone number for the winery's main line.

"Hello?" answered a high-pitched voice.

"Yeah, get me Mike Vonn," I said, slipping into a drawl.

"May I ask who's calling?"

"You may not. You tell him the guys messed up, the guy at the marina ain't dead." Before the woman could reply, I ended the call.

"Subtle."

I almost told her about that night at the comedy club, when I snatched the mic from the second-crappiest comedian in Los Angeles after yours truly and begged the crowd to serve me up Karl for cold, hard cash. "Subtlety is overrated," I said. "But I should have done it from a burner. I used to buy them by the dozen, keep them in my glove compartment. It was a big part of the job."

"Vonn doesn't have your number."

"True. Let's walk this way."

This street ended in a cul-de-sac fronted by houses on steroids, monstrosities with four-car garages and minimalist facades with no symmetry. One glance at them would have driven Frank Lloyd Wright to commit ritual suicide. I guided Madeline into the shade of the lone tree poking from the shared lawn.

"Thank you," she said.

"For what?"

"For everything. You could have done as little as possible."

I nodded. "Yours is a worthy quest. Worthier than anything I've done in a long time."

At the end of the street, the mini-car zipped past, two silhouettes in the front seats. Someone at Vonn must have called those guys and activated them. As we walked back to their house, I tried doing the math: it would take them twenty minutes to reach the burning remains of the dock, maybe another ten to realize they'd been duped, and another twenty back.

Plenty of time.

I hoped.

Much to my relief, our target house lacked a video doorbell. I cut across the lawn, Madeline on my heels, doing my best to stay out of the sightline of any windows as I scuttled down the narrow space between the house's flank and the neighboring fence. We reached the rear, blocked by a waist-high fence with a gate set into it.

I peered around the corner, noting the small pool (with connected hot tub) set into a stone terrace, with steps descending to a narrow strip of lawn. A golf practice net stood against the rear fence, the grass sprinkled with bright golf balls.

I eased the gate open and stepped through. A sliding-glass door separated the terrace from the house's dark interior. I paused, listening for music, conversation, anything to suggest someone was inside. Silence.

I placed my hand on the door handle and glanced at Madeline.

She swallowed and nodded.

I slid the door open a few feet and paused again. What if these pricks owned a guard dog? I didn't need a hundred-fifty pounds of irate canine taking a chunk out of my leg. Or my throat.

No werewolves charged at us. The house's air chilled my sweaty forehead while the day baked my back. I stood on the line between fire and darkness, and it occurred to me that, for the first time in this crazy adventure, I was about to break some real laws. Breaking and entering, for starters. Home invasion with a deadly weapon, if the DA was feeling frisky.

We entered the house, Madeline sliding the door shut behind me. I waited for my eyes to adjust to the gloom. The room was large and spare, with a sectional leather couch pressed against the bare wall. The kitchen area to our right was likewise empty except for a frying pan on the marble countertop. A door beside the refrigerator opened onto a pantry larger than my first apartment in L.A., its shelves barren except for a lone bag of pasta and a canister of sea salt.

I drew the gun as I crept for the doorway leading into the broader house, pausing every few feet to listen. Air hummed from the vents along the ceiling. The doorway opened onto a great room rimmed by a second-floor balcony, connected to our floor by a stairwell to our right. Like the room we'd left, this space was almost free of furniture or art, except for two wooden chairs near the windows overlooking the lawn.

"I–" Madeline whispered.

I raised my hand for quiet and gestured toward another

doorway to our left, which led to a narrow dining room with a long table and no chairs. It connected to a larger room lined with empty bookshelves, every inch painted a glossy white, which made it easy to spot the cardboard box tucked on the lowest shelf in the far corner.

The box looked like it had been re-used to ship things across the country two or three times, its battered sides mummified in packing tape, its top plastered with scuffed labels. I holstered my gun and took my handkerchief from my pocket and wrapped it around my thumb and forefinger before opening the lid, wary of leaving fingerprints. I half-expected to see something horrible, like a severed head. Instead, I found two sets of keys, two wallets, a small pile of gum wrappers, and a smartphone with a cracked screen.

I lifted the first wallet and flipped it open. The driver's license behind the clear plastic window belonged to one Brian Golden. The accompanying photograph captured a fresh-faced hipster in mid-squint. I dangled it before Madeline.

"Our documentarians," I said.

"Oh man," she breathed.

"Yeah," I said, rifling through the wallet's other pockets. I found thirty dollars in ones and fives, a health insurance card, and a plastic credit card.

"That second one's Tommy Dove's?" she asked.

"I'll bet you a pony," I said, dropping Brian's wallet in the box and opening the other one. Tommy's license photo made him look like a high-school football player beginning to soften in the cheeks. His wallet contained a hundred bucks, two credit cards, and a customer-rewards card for a Long Beach coffee shop with nine of the ten slots punched out.

I suspected Tommy wouldn't get the chance to punch that tenth slot for a free latte.

I dropped Tommy's wallet and reached into the box and pressed the phone's power button. The lock screen was an image of the poster for the Ken Ironwood documentary. It would unlock if I presented it with the right face or passcode. I considered trying some combination of Tommy's and Brian's birthdays and addresses, but sometimes these phones locked you out after too many wrong tries.

After a heartbeat of indecision, I pocketed the phone.

"What now?" Madeline asked.

"Rest of the house."

Back to the great room. One door exited the front, another led to a two-bay garage empty of cars. We needed to check the upstairs. I drew the pistol again before we took the stairwell to the second floor, treading on the edges of the risers to minimize creaking. I sniffed for blood or rot, however faint. If they'd killed Tommy and Brian, had they buried the bodies on the property? The strip of grass in the backyard was undisturbed, and I bet planting a couple of corpses in the front lawn would violate the neighborhood's HOA rules.

The second floor had three bedrooms, two with narrow mattresses on the floor. I lifted the mattresses and found nothing. I checked the closets: no clothes on the bars, no bags on the floor. The two marble bathrooms were spotless: no toothbrushes on the sink, no drugs in the cabinets, no shampoo in the tubs or shower stalls.

Nothing anywhere.

Damn.

"Reminds me of a safe house," I said.

"Yeah? You hang out in a lot of those?"

"The Hollywood version, sure."

"I'm intrigued."

"I'll tell you later. There's one more place to check."

We returned to the garage. Against the back wall sat a chest freezer big enough to hold a small cow. It clicked and hummed. I wondered if the coolant was leaking because the garage suddenly felt twenty degrees cooler.

My pulse, stable for so long, started ticking faster, faster, faster.

So much for fending off panic.

This tingle in my skull, I felt it every time Manny asked me to drive over to a young actor's address and verify why they weren't answering their phone. It was a signal from the deepest parts of my brain, trained by a billion years of evolution to sense danger and death. I waved for Madeline to stay in place, but I needed another second to persuade my own feet to step toward the freezer.

I holstered the gun and wrapped my trusty handkerchief around my hand again and lifted the edge of the freezer's lid. It was heavier than I expected, or maybe the dread had weakened my muscles. It rose inch by slow inch, and the weak light played over a paleness crusted with frost – the curve of a cheek, blue lips, an open eye frozen white.

I recognized Brian Golden. I assumed the body crushed beneath him, the hair and clothes furred with ice, belonged to Tommy Dove. True crime documentarians done in by true crime. I wasn't a forensic specialist, but I guessed the large hole in Brian's frozen-stiff shirt was from a bullet.

A metallic thump behind us. I spun as the garage door clattered upward, framing the driveway, where our two friends from the lake, the Lean Man and the Stocky Dude, stood with shiny 9mm pistols tucked against their bodies, the better to hide the weapons from any peeking neighbors.

"You think we're idiots?" the Lean Man said. "You must think we're idiots, because you thought we'd drive back to an active crime scene. Yeah, I think we're about to see who's truly the smart ones here."

25.

"It's *who are* the smart ones here," Madeline said. "Who're. Plural. See, we're smart."

I admired her calm. Most people freeze up when you stick a gun in their face.

From fifteen feet away, the Stocky Dude looked young, maybe Madeline's age, with wild hair and scruffy beard. His Iron Man t-shirt was a size too small, outlining his thick chest and sagging gut, and his jeans needed a wash. He turned to the Lean Man and said, in a curiously high-pitched voice, "She's right. Contraction, 'who is', you know?"

The Lean Man turned to him. He was older, his slicked-back hair gray at the sideburns. He wore a collared shirt with gray and black stripes beneath his nylon jacket. He looked like someone who imagined he was dangerous. "Shut up," he said, baring yellow teeth.

"Guys, I know I'm seconds from death here," Madeline said, "but here's some advice: you really, really need to ask Vonn for a raise."

She tilted her head to me. Her eyes flicked to my holster, then to the pair. *I'm stalling them,* her slight frown said. *Do something.*

She must have watched too many John Woo movies because in the real world, drawing down on two people who already have their guns out is a quick way to end your life. I would need a distraction. If we were very lucky, we might also pry some answers from this gruesome twosome.

My heartbeat was still too fast, my palms moist with sweat. Even if I tried to draw on them as a final kamikaze gesture, the pistol might slip out of my hands. "The whole street can see us," I said, proud of how strong I sounded despite my fear.

"Really? We hadn't noticed," said the Lean Man, stepping into the garage.

The Stocky Dude fished a small plastic fob from his hip pocket and pressed it. He ducked beneath the descending garage door as he followed the Lean Man inside.

The Lean Man flexed his grip on the pistol. "What were you saying about Vonn?"

"He can afford to upgrade your wardrobes." Madeline smiled. "Listen, if we're about to die anyway, can I smoke a last cigarette?"

"No. I got asthma." The Lean Man nodded at the Stocky Dude. "Search them."

If the Stocky Dude stood close to me, I could surprise him with a quick punch to the face, then use him as a shield while I drew my pistol. The Lean Man would aim at Madeline and turn this into a double-hostage, Mexican standoff thing, but I liked the odds of that better than being executed on a garage floor.

"The man has a pistol on him," the Lean Man said. "Holster, left side. He needs to toss it."

So much for that plan.

"Don't talk like I'm not right in front of you," I said. "It's rude."

The Lean Man sighted the pistol on my nose. "Do it."

Moving slowly, I lifted the edge of my shirt, revealing the holster, and used two fingers to pluck the pistol free. I set the weapon on the concrete and kicked it toward the Stocky Dude, who knelt to retrieve it while keeping his own 9mm pointed at my gut.

"Pow," he said, pointing both guns at us. "Gonna shoot you right down. Real cowboy shit."

"Search them," the Lean Man snapped.

The Stocky Dude rolled his eyes and said, "Raise your arms."

We obeyed. Despite his slobby appearance, the Stocky Dude moved like a professional, staying beyond my reach as he circled behind us. Outside of my view, he must have slipped one of the pistols into his waistband, because his hand skimmed beneath my armpits and along my sides before drifting over my crotch, down to my ankles. He stuck his hands in my pockets, pulled out my wallet and both phones and my keys, and tossed everything on the floor. His knees cracked as he stood and circled in front of me, taking two steps back as he did so. His 9mm was in his hand, my pistol shoved down the front of his pants.

"He's clean," the Stocky Dude told the Lean Man.

"Why'd you say that about Vonn?" The Lean Man asked Madeline.

She shrugged as the Stocky Dude slipped behind her, aiming the pistol at the back of her head as his hand slithered across her front and into her pockets. "He pays you well?" she asked.

The Lean Man grinned. "You're fishing, sweetie."

The Stocky Dude tossed Madeline's wallet and keys and cigarettes and lighter onto the concrete. His hand slipped inside Madeline's greatcoat, and she hissed between her teeth. "I'm not armed, you prick," she said. "Stop feeling me up."

"I love the coat," the Stocky Dude whispered in her ear. "It's like you're a sexy Sergeant Pepper."

"Stop being a creep," the Lean Man growled at the Stocky Dude, who bent to feel Madeline's boots. This was the moment of truth. If he detected the faint bulge of the switchblade, we would lose our best hope of getting out of this alive.

"You're a real pair of jerks," I said loudly, hoping to distract him. "Burning the whole county down during fire season?"

The Stocky Dude paused with his hand on Madeline's ankle. "What?"

"That fire you set at the docks," I said. "There's a big wind. It's probably torched half the county."

The Stocky Dude, locked on me, absently brushed his hands over Madeline's boots before pulling back. "Where were you?"

"On the hill," I said, proud of how I pulled his attention. "Watched you the whole time. Took some photos with my phone, too. Guess where those photos are."

"Spoiler alert," Madeline said. "They're in the cloud."

"Protected by a password." I was enjoying our call-and-response routine, our shared vibe in the face of imminent death. "If we disappear…"

"Yeah, yeah, those photos go out to people," the Lean Man said. "You're forgetting we're in a garage. Lots of tools for prying a password out of you."

Even a weirdo thug with a bad haircut is right on occasion. And what's worse than a couple of guys shooting you dead in a garage? A couple of guys pulling out your teeth or breaking your kneecaps before they shoot you dead in a garage.

"You don't have the time," I said.

The Stocky Dude stepped away from Madeline. "Maybe we should call this in," he said. "I mean..."

"What?" The Lean Man's pistol jerked toward his partner. "What?"

The Stocky Dude cringed. "It's the guy's daughter."

"You think I'm an idiot?" The Lean Man shook his head. "Damn, what a mess we have here, people. What a mess."

"I told you," the Stocky Dude said, almost yelling. "We should call it in. We can't mess this up."

"You're right, you're right." The Lean Man sighed. "Okay, see if there's anything in here to tie them up."

The Stocky Dude stuffed his pistol into his waistband and stepped to the racks lining the garage's wall, the shelves loaded with oversized plastic bins. Moving from left to right, he pulled out each bin and checked the contents before sliding it back. At the last one, he grunted and pulled out a bundled length of nylon rope, dark blue with lighter stripes, along with a bright orange box cutter. "Perfect," he said.

"Color of the rope will really match my eyes," Madeline said. "The colors will pop."

The Lean Man waved his pistol. "The balls on you two."

"Big brass ones," Madeline said as the Stocky Man forced her hands behind her back and tied her wrists. Once he finished, he cut the rope's dangling end and walked over to me.

I'd once worked on the periphery of a biopic about Harry Houdini, an action star's misbegotten attempt at scoring his first-ever award nomination. The script had broken down how Houdini had escaped handcuffs, locked chests, jail cells... and rope. I tried to recall the exact details, hoping the screenwriter had done his research before committing to paper.

The Stocky Man slid behind me and gripped my left wrist. His hand was soft enough to make me wonder if he took care moisturizing when he wasn't jabbing guns at people. His grip was strong and he yanked my arm behind me without too much trouble, repeating the action with my right. As he slid the rope over my wrists, I tried angling my hands to generate a bit of slack.

He cinched the rope tight and double-knotted it, yanking my shoulders hard.

The Stocky Dude tugged at his work, testing it. "We're good," he told his partner, stepping around me.

As subtly as I could, I tried rotating my wrists. I had a quarter inch of give. Was that enough to work with? I had no idea.

"Get their stuff," the Lean Man said.

"I only got two hands," the Stocky Dude whined. "Besides, we're coming back in here."

The Lean Man grunted. "Fine, be lazy," he said. "Now we're all walking back into the house. Anyone wants to try anything funny, the bullet's going in your kneecap, okay?"

"Have you always been a thug?" Madeline asked. "Is that something you go to school for?" She turned to me with a smug little smile. "Imagine taking a class called 'Threatening People 101'."

"I was a stuntman," the Lean Man said, a vein in his forehead throbbing. "Then I got injured. You know how many job opportunities there are for a stuntman who can't do stunts?"

"Which movies?" I asked.

"Probably a hundred action films. I really liked working on one titled, 'Get Your Ass in the House'." The Lean Man waved his pistol at the door leading to the living room, his eyes glassy, like he was reliving a bad memory. I imagined a stunt car flipping onto its roof, a broken bone punching through skin, a pile of medical bills. The moment passed. His head lifted, his attention snapping to the present.

"Move," he said quietly, stepping close.

Over his shoulder, through the small windows lining the garage doors, I saw a sheriff's SUV swooping into the driveway.

I did my best to keep my expression neutral as I faced forward. We crossed the living room, the Lean Man pulling the door shut behind us. I felt a burst of elation, dampened instantly by fear. These guys struck me as the types who would shoot cops – and follow that up by shooting us.

26.

Our new friends led us through the house to the kitchen. The Lean Man waved his pistol at the pantry door. The Stocky Dude opened it, smacked on the pantry light, and swept a hand for us to enter. We stepped inside, and they shut the door. A faint scraping on the kitchen tiles, followed by a muffled thump. I guessed they had slotted a chair beneath the doorknob.

I pressed an ear to the door, listening for movement on the other side. Nothing. Stepping back, I moved my wrists clockwise until the rope bit into the skin, then counterclockwise. I hoped the motions would loosen the knots enough to give me more play. If it worked for ol' Harry Houdini, it could work for me.

"What are you doing?" Madeline whispered.

"Magic," I whispered back. Twisting my wrists, I checked the pantry's corners for anything like a camera or a microphone. If they used this room to keep prisoners, they'd want to monitor them.

"Oh, for God's sake," Madeline hissed, crouching low. "I have the switchblade." With her hands behind her back, it was difficult for her to reach her feet. She lowered onto her right knee, her back arching as her fingers scratched the top of her boot. She grunted, puffed out her cheeks, and tried stretching her arms another inch.

"Good thing you learned yoga, huh?" I said.

"Quiet from the peanut gallery." Her fingers squeezed into the tight gap between jean and boot.

"Don't hurt yourself," I said. I kept twisting my wrists, my skin chafing. The rope refused to yield any slack. Maybe I was doing it wrong. Somewhere in the void, I could hear Houdini laughing at me.

"Oh yeah, here we go." The top of the knife poked from her boot. She drew it free with two fingers, found the button on the handle, and snapped it open. Moving slowly, she angled the blade so it rested against the knots. "Am I positioned right?"

I peeked. "Yeah."

But when she tried sawing through the ropes, the blade almost slipped from her hands. She was nervous, her fingers sweaty. "Here," I said, stepping until we stood back-to-back, and wrapped my fist around the handle as she released it. With the knife in my firm grip, it was easier work for her to carefully snag her ropes on the tip of the blade, then twist her body until the nylon strands split apart.

Once she was free, she cut me loose. I tapped the door hinges. They were solid, and I had no tools to knock them free. Just for fun, I tried the doorknob, but it only twisted a fraction before stopping. Aside from Madeline's knife, the only useful item was a box of kosher salt on the pantry's top shelf, which might have left a faint bruise if I tossed it hard at an attacker's head.

I put my ear to the door and caught muffled voices: the Lean Man's low rasp, counterpunched by the Stocky Dude's yapping, and there was also a third person, possibly the cop, who was too low and far away to hear clearly, more of a hum than words:

"...can't do anything without his say-so. His explicit *say-so."*

"...too much riding on..."

"You know he only cares about the money."

A sharp crack, followed by the shuffling of feet. And then the Lean Man's voice, very loud, almost strangled, shouting:

"Oh, we're doing it! You can't stop us!"

Three loud gunshots.

Madeline startled.

Two more gunshots.

I gestured for Madeline to duck before hitting the light switch, plunging us into darkness. I balled my fists. We didn't have much hope against someone with a gun, but we'd make them work for it.

Footsteps in the kitchen, followed by a loud sigh.

"I know you're in there," boomed Deputy Sheriff Reid. "Here's how it's going to go. I'll remove this chair, and then I'm going to leave. You're going to wait a few minutes, and then you're going to come out. You're going to get in your car, and you're going to leave. And by leave, I mean go back to L.A. You're too small for this county."

A metallic click. A scraping as he pulled the chair away from the door.

"And you're welcome, by the way," Reid added. "You don't have to thank me. Don't touch anything as you leave."

His footsteps faded, followed by the hiss of the rear door sliding shut.

27.

I counted to one hundred before placing my hand on the doorknob. I was remembering the more recent night in Hell House when a famous actress pointed a gun in my direction, and I felt too big, too slow, too full of soft things a bullet could slice right through. My breath squeezed through my tightening throat. I told myself now wasn't the time for yet another panic attack.

Madeline placed a hand on my shoulder and squeezed. Maybe she heard me wheezing in the gloom. I placed my hand over hers and squeezed back. If a trap waited on the other side of this door, I would do my best to get her out of the house.

I turned the knob and opened the door slowly.

After the blackness of the pantry, the dim kitchen seemed to throb with light. I crouched, blinking, smelling, looking. The air had the acrid smell of gunpowder, layered atop a funky, putrid odor.

"Reid?" Madeline said. "He killed them?"

"Whatever that meeting was about, didn't seem like it went well," I said. "Hold on."

I returned to the pantry door and wiped the doorknobs with the hem of my shirt, before walking to the door leading to the backyard and doing the same there. If the neighbors heard any gunshots, they would call the police or private security. I had to hope the neighbors were out in the middle of the day, but we couldn't bet on it. We might have a few minutes left. Seconds, even.

"Stay here," I whispered to Madeline.

"Oh, hell no," she said. "You're not doing that."

"Okay." We didn't have time to argue. "Don't touch anything."

I led her into the living room. As I expected, the Lean Man and the Stocky Dude were dead, sprawled against the far wall. Both had their pistols jammed in their waistbands, which told me Reid was as fast on the draw as an old-school gunslinger. The cop had good aim, too, because both men had holes in their foreheads and chests, the wall behind them splattered with blood and brain.

The house's vents whined, the system doing its best to clean the air, but the stink of gore and shit still flipped my stomach as I approached the Stocky Dude and knelt beside him, careful to avoid any blood. I pulled up the corner of his shirt and slipped my pistol from his waistband.

I turned to check on Madeline. She stood in the doorway, swaying on her feet, her breathing ragged. I snapped open the pistol's cylinder to verify all the bullets in their right places. I snapped it closed and returned it to my holster.

Our stuff was still on the floor of the garage. I wondered if Reid had bothered checking the house before we left. I handed Madeline her wallet and phone and cigarettes and lighter.

"Neighborhood's got cameras all over the place," Madeline said. "We're unbelievably hosed."

"Maybe, but we're even more hosed if we panic over it,"

I said, stuffing my own wallet and phone in the appropriate pockets. I took the phone we'd retrieved from the box and returned to the chest freezer. With my fingers tented in my shirt, I hooked the lid open.

"What the hell are you doing?" Madeline asked.

I flicked on the phone and pointed the screen at Brian Golden's icy face, hoping the gray skin and frozen eyeballs would pass muster with the device's facial-recognition system. The screen's tiny lock icon flickered – and popped open. Letting the lid slam shut, I swiped through Brian's apps until I reached Settings, tapped on Security, and reset his lock-screen password to 0111.

"Now let's go," I said, "out the back."

We jogged through the house to the kitchen, pausing to wipe at anything we might have touched, although I suspected it was all useless. The cops have all kinds of tech these days. We were probably depositing flecks of DNA every time we moved.

As we entered the yard, I briefly considered jumping the rear fence and tearing through the adjoining property. Bad idea. For all we knew, the neighbors' yards were entirely fenced in, watched by cameras, guarded by dogs. I forced myself to walk at a regular pace around the side of the house to the driveway, checking nearby windows as subtly as possible.

By the time we reached the Mustang, I heard sirens. A neighbor had dialed 911. They had probably spotted us leaving. We were screwed, so unbelievably screwed. Why hadn't Reid killed us, too? We were witnesses. There was no guarantee we wouldn't tell the police everything we knew if they caught us.

I had an idea about it, but I didn't want to share it

with Madeline. Not until I could examine the dead documentarian's phone.

The Mustang started with a hearty roar. I was so tempted to slam the gas pedal through the floor and tear through the compound's front gate, but the wise play was to mosey out of here like two out-of-touch millionaires on a house-hunting expedition. Shifting into gear, I motored down one street, then took a right, trusting on my internal compass to guide us out.

The compound's gate appeared at the end of the next street. Two police SUVs crouched beside it, ready to pounce on any vehicles entering or exiting.

"That's blown," Madeline said.

"Yep."

"We could Thelma and Louise it," she said. "Charge on through. End in a hail of gunfire. What do you think?"

"I think this has become a very exciting weekend," I said, throwing the Mustang into reverse. I twisted the wheel and bumped us into a random driveway, then shifted into first, motoring the way we'd come.

"There another way out?" Madeline asked.

"If there is, I bet it has a gate," I said.

I took random lefts and rights, working toward the rear of the compound. The McMansions and curated lawns fell away, replaced by a tract of houses under construction. Wooden frames covered in plastic loomed from concrete pads, interspersed with tall piles of gravel. Beyond a maze of chain-link fencing, the grassland sprawled toward the hills, eternal, uncaring about two people trapped in a concrete maze.

"I'm sorry, by the way," I told her.

"Don't worry about it. You had no idea what would

happen." She sighed. "You think they'll give us bail?"

"No, I'm apologizing for what I'm about to do."

"What?"

"Hold on." I judged my best route and twisted the wheel, angling the Mustang toward the nearest house under construction. My plan was to bomb across the concrete pad that would one day become the driveway and garage, soar across the ten feet of gravel beyond, and impact the chain-link fence midway between its posts, punching through with a minimum of fuss. It was a very cinematic vision, something I had witnessed dozens of times during visits to movie sets, but one day it would finally sink into my dense skull that physics in movies has no relation to real life.

All of which is to say, as I piloted the Mustang across the concrete, its right wheels bumped against a rock, and that was enough to edge us left, and I overcorrected, veering between two of the boards supporting the house's wooden frame. With enough luck, we might have slipped effortlessly through the geometries of wood and pallets of drywall and insulation and rebar, but those hopes were dashed like our fender as we plowed through one support and then the next and the next, the wood crunching before our momentum as easily as matchsticks, and I stood on the gas, my dad's most famous words echoing through my head – *the only thing that will save you is speed* – as I tried to ignore Madeline screaming. We rocketed through the rear of the structure in a burst of dust and vaporized wood, airborne over another patch of gravel before ramming into the chain-link fence and plowing it under, roaring into the fields beyond at near-highway speeds. In the rearview mirror, the half-constructed house imploded, its framework toppling, a white cloud drifting into the hot sky.

After a half-mile I slowed, anxious not to hit any hidden ravines or holes as we shuddered across the landscape. The windshield was cracked, the hood dented, and there was a chunk of wood wedged between my side mirror and the door, but we were free and moving. Beside me, Madeline took out her cigarettes.

"So much for a quiet exit," she said, her voice shaking.

"I can be a daredevil, too."

"You're so not funny," she said, lighting her smoke. "Not funny at all."

28.

The designers of this vintage Mustang never expected it to be used for off-roading, but the beast performed well on rough ground, its shocks absorbing the ruts and stones as we plowed through field after field, spraying grass and dirt in our wake. With Madeline navigating on her phone, it took us twenty minutes to find a paved road.

"We're three miles north of Golden Shower, Golden Lake, whatever the hell it's called," she told me as I thumped us back onto blessed asphalt.

"Wonderful. Find us a road back to the lake."

She squinted at her screen. "Go right at the next intersection. In three miles, take a left."

I followed her directions. Beneath the Mustang's confident roar I heard a faint scraping, like something was jammed into the undercarriage. Hopefully it wasn't a cute varmint.

"This solves none of our problems," she said.

"I know."

"I bet lots of cameras got our license plate."

"I know."

"Someone might have seen us coming out of the house."

"I know."

"Do you know why Reid shot those guys? Because I can't figure it out."

"I think they were going to kill us, and he didn't want that to happen."

"Were they? They kept saying I was the guy's daughter. They meant Ken. They were hesitating."

"It just proves Vonn and your Dad were good friends. Vonn must have said he didn't want you hurt. But I bet he said that before we broke into his guys' murder house."

She bumped the back of her skull against the headrest and stared at the Mustang's roof as if it might provide some answers. "Why did the cop care about us?"

"Oh, I bet he couldn't care less. But I think he works for someone who does."

"Who?"

"That's the billion-dollar question, and I bet those documentary guys knew. That's why they ended up in the freezer."

She sighed. "Heading into this weekend, I thought not knowing how my Dad died was the heaviest thing. But this, this is way heavier. We're screwed, aren't we?"

"It's the nature of things to spin out of control," I said. "Everything bends toward chaos."

"Thank you, Cormac McCarthy."

"More like Schopenhauer."

"*Arthur* Schopenhauer? We're getting highfalutin' for folks the cops want to talk to."

"Oh, you're big on your pessimistic philosophers?"

"Buddy, I took three whole classes in philosophy in college. I better have read Schopenhauer, given how I'm paying off those loans until I die."

"We can talk more about eternal justice and the cruelties of the world." I nodded through the windshield. "Take a look at that."

We swept down a winding road through the hills, the lake rising toward us, its shallow waters glowing like lava in the sun's reflected light. To our right, beyond the ridge, black smoke curled like a question mark against the hazy blue.

"Marina's still burning," Madeline said.

"And hopefully not the area around it," I said. We arrived at the lakeside road. To our left, beyond the shoreline's curve, I recognized some of the buildings we passed while pursuing the gruesome twosome. That was two hours and a lifetime ago.

As I aged, I felt like time was always speeding up, slipping away faster than I could remember and absorb what I needed, and so it came as weird relief to have hours and minutes slowing to spacetime syrup, if only for a day or two, and even if it came at the cost of some lives.

I was tempted to tell Madeline about this, and maybe throw in a pretentious warning to wring all she could out of life before time accelerated on her, but I had a more important decision to make: right or left? If the cops were on the lookout for a Mustang, they might have blocked the road in either direction. It was one thing if Madeline wanted to talk philosophical choices, but this was the kind of real-world decision that could end with us jailed or killed.

Instinct told me to take a right, and I listened to it. We drove in silence past the blackened wreckage of the marina, webbed in yellow crime-scene tape flapping in the wind. A police cruiser and a black sedan sat beside the remains of the shack, three officers and two men in suits standing beside it. Two firetrucks had parked on the opposite shoulder, their firefighters standing in the ditch with hoses, spraying down the hillside's smoldering grass.

A car in front of us had slowed to gawk. I resisted tapping the horn. The cops were facing away from us, the larger one gesturing with a pen at the crisped hulk of a boat. One of the uniformed cops turned to survey the road, the toothpick in the corner of his mouth jittering up and down like a seismometer reading an earthquake. His mirrored glasses reflected the greenish blotch of the Mustang. He gripped the walkie-talkie mic clipped to his shoulder and spoke into it.

My fingers tightened on the wheel. The Mustang had a big engine, not that it would do much good against a roadblock.

The cop tilted his head to listen before speaking into the mic again. He turned to the other cops and laughed.

The car ahead of us accelerated. I eased onto the gas, building speed around the next curve. The charred dock disappeared from my mirrors, and I let myself relax a little.

"Damn," Madeline said, craning her head to peer out her window.

"What?"

"The hill's on fire."

I glanced over my shoulder. Gray smoke wisped from the ridge, the grass shimmering in the heat. The whole county was a tinderbox. Hopefully the firefighters had an eye on it.

"I guess we better talk to Vonn, right?" Madeline said.

"Right. We'll wait for night."

"You think the cops are looking for us?"

"Yeah. But I bet the only one who knows where we're staying is Reid, and he seems to want us free."

"I wish we knew why."

"We'll look at the phone. And talk to Vonn. We're not going to ask him nicely."

"I'm fine with that." She bared her teeth. "I've been wanting to kill another person my whole life."

Maybe she meant it as a joke, but her eyes were cold and black as stones.

29.

I parked the Mustang around the far side of our rental house, out of sight even if someone came up the driveway. When I shut down the engine, it rattled like an old man's lungs, white smoke farting from the tailpipe. "I'm sorry I wrecked your car," I told Madeline. "I'd like to help pay for the repairs."

"It was always more trouble than it was worth." She gave the dashboard an affectionate pat. "I should've let it get stolen years ago."

"I can see why they'd want to. It's a real pimpmobile." I climbed out and slammed my door too hard, and something inside the car's body tinkled and thumped. Whoops. From this angle, I could see into the house through one of the living room windows. It looked empty, but I drew my gun anyway, because today's surprises never stopped coming.

I had Madeline wait beside the front door ("Go ahead, caveman," she said) as I entered and swept up to the second floor and down again. The house was deserted. I called for her to come in, then holstered my gun and pulled out Brian Golden's phone and unlocked it. I set the screen on the kitchen counter so Madeline could watch over my shoulder as I swiped through the apps, finding the standard collection of social media and games.

I tapped on the Photos app, revealing image after image of Ken Ironwood at parties, standing on massive concrete piers, perched atop a porch railing with a bottle of champagne in each hand. He looked like the sexy, dangerous friend you tried not to see too often, lest they draw you into something terrible.

"I've seen these before," Madeline said. "But I have no idea how he got them."

There were a few photographs of *Django* tied to the pier, Howard in the background staring angrily into the camera. The timestamp said Brian had shot these a few days ago. So, the boat fit this story.

"Videos next," Madeline said.

"Aye, captain." I tapped on the videos sprinkled amidst the photos. Most of them were clips of newscasts from the 1980s and 90s, all dealing with murders and robberies. The most recent were two panning shots of a vineyard, row upon row of twisted vines reaching for a pale sky…

"It's Vonn's place," Madeline said, reaching past me to pause the clip. She pointed at the left side of the frame, a white triangle jutting from a stand of trees. "That's his house when you drive in."

"Taken a few days ago, too," I said, examining the timestamp. "Next one."

The last clip began in a white room. Whoever shot it – probably Brian – did so surreptitiously, the camera positioned at waist-level. The view swept from left to right, across a marble statue of a torso on a pedestal. It drifted upward, the focus wavering, and locked onto a mask of hammered gold on the wall. I paused and pinched to zoom, the mask's features snapping clear: closed eyes, a thin nose and full lips, a ridged area around the chin that might have been part of a beard.

We heard Vonn's voice: "And you asked–"

A thump, and the clip ended. According to the timestamp, it had been shot the night before we arrived in San Douglas.

"That must be inside Vonn's house," Madeline said. "I didn't see anything like that room in the winery."

"I didn't, either." I closed the Photos app, pulled out my phone, and flicked through my search history. "I'm remembering something."

"What?"

"They think your father robbed some artifacts. Roman and Greek statues, plus a few of those gold masks." I found the true-crime website I'd read the other day. "Yeah, that's it. Gold funeral masks from ancient Greece. Looks like the one in the video, doesn't it?"

Madeline leaned against the counter, a sprinter readying their energy for the last race. "So, my dad is coming up here for years. Becomes friends with Vonn. Maybe does some business with him. They have a falling out, Vonn kills my dad and stuffs him in a barrel? Then takes the artifacts my dad stole?"

"It would make sense. Maybe Vonn gets a bunch of money from your dad, uses it to grow the winery. Maybe he took your dad's boat and put it under his own name, which is why those creepy guys were intent on blowing it up once too many people started sniffing around."

"Okay." She closed her eyes and squeezed the bridge of her nose. "Okay. And we're not sure where Reid fits into all this?"

"He wasn't acting in an official capacity when he gunned those dudes down. Maybe he's making a play on his own, leverage Vonn for money or something like that."

"There are a lot of 'maybes' here."

"Welcome to detective work, I guess. That's why we have to ask Vonn about all this."

"And then what?"

"What do you mean?"

"We'd need to get him to confess directly to the cops. It's not admissible otherwise. Even if we go in there, trick him, tape it, any good lawyer is gonna tear it apart." She imitated a blowhard attorney, her voice loud and sonorous. "'Ladies and gentlemen of the jury, let me tell you about how deepfakes can make my client say literally anything'."

She was right. I knew California was a state with two-party consent, meaning anything taped without one party's knowledge was inadmissible in court. Given how everything was playing out, we had a far likelier chance of ending up in a jail cell than Vonn.

30.

While Madeline took a shower, I stepped onto our front porch. I smelled smoke in the air, and I pulled out my phone to check on any local news about a fire. Several acres were burning along the lake. The fire department believed it had everything under control. I flicked through the news scroll until I saw headlines about a multiple murder in a gated community.

Those stories were scant on details: an unrevealed number of bodies discovered in a mansion. The police were unwilling to reveal causes of death or possible suspects. A random neighbor was quoted as saying the area was usually so safe.

At least our faces weren't splashed all over the web as persons of interest.

I steeled myself and dialed Manny. He answered on the third ring.

"You back yet?" he asked.

"Not yet," I said. "How's everything with you, sunshine?"

"Oh, peachy. I have a pop star who's decided to let a cult move into her guest house. I think they sacrificed a goat on the lawn." He grunted. It might have been his attempt at a laugh. "How could I begin to hate this job?"

"Grab a grenade launcher. Lob some tear gas in the guest house. It'll clear them right out."

"If only it was that simple. I sense you didn't call to hear my lovely voice. What do you need this time?"

"Nothing yet. But I might need a favor tonight."

"I'm telling you for the last time, I don't find you attractive like that."

"And you say I'm bad at comedy. Tonight, if a hypothetical something happened that put me in legal trouble, who would I call?"

"You remember Taylor Valentine? He'd do the job. For every cent you have, of course."

"Who's the bargain version of Taylor Valentine?"

"I can get you Taylor for cheap, Dash. He owes me. You get in hypothetical trouble, you call me, and I'll call him, okay?"

"Okay."

"You want to talk about what's up?"

"There's a local winery owner here. We think he killed Ken Ironwood."

A long pause. "Don't do anything stupid."

"It's stupid, but it's calculated stupidity. There's a difference."

"You consider going to the cops?"

"Sure, but one of the local ones is in on it. Maybe more of them."

"Then come back here. Why risk it?" Did Manny's voice quaver? The big guy had a heart, after all.

The devil on my shoulder reappeared in a cloud of smoke, murmuring his temptations: return to L.A., where it was safe. Where I could order sushi and a beer at three in the morning before retreating to my air-conditioned apartment. Where I could drink and drink until the weekend's troubles softened into an unsettling memory.

Except I didn't want to be that person anymore.

I wanted to tell Manny how this morning, for the first time in ages, I woke up without an urge to slug down a shot of vodka or pop a pill. How my head felt clearer. How I was finally able to control the panic attacks before they ripped through my body and mind like summer storms. Except he would have said none of that was worth losing my life in a nowhere rural county, and maybe he was right.

"Because it's my job," I told him. "If I get in trouble, I'll give you a ring."

He grunted. "Yeah, you do that. Stay frosty."

I ended the call and tilted my head to the sky. I feared cops powering up the driveway. I feared that lunatic Reid blowing my head off. I feared whatever awaited us at Vonn's place. But I also felt alive in a way I hadn't for ages, keenly aware of my pulse in my ears, the warmth of my fingers holding the phone, even the way my knees trembled slightly after all the hours of driving and crouching and running.

I felt good.

Even if these were the last few hours of my life, I felt good.

31.

We waited until dark and took my car to Vonn's. I studied my Maps app's satellite views of the property and found a maintenance road on a far ridge that looped down to the winery. I had my gun, along with a flashlight I retrieved from my car trunk, and Madeline had her switchblade. We could find rope in a winery if we needed to tie someone up.

Before we left, I ransacked the rest of Brian Golden's phone. His inbox had too many emails to sort through properly, but I found a few with screenshots of financial statements. Brian and his partner had gotten their hands on a mountain of Vonn paperwork. Vonn was partners with an entity named "Ouroboros LLC", which owned half the winery and a few other properties sprinkled throughout the valley. I couldn't find any emails indicating who owned the LLC.

We drove past Vonn's front gate, shut for the night. We continued two miles uphill to the ridge and hooked a right onto a gravel road winding through dry scrub and massive boulders. I turned off my headlights and slowed. According to Madeline's phone, we were directly above the winery. We passed the entrance to a maintenance road, blocked by a swinging gate with a 'No Trespassing – Private Property' sign dangling from its steel arm. I drove another few yards before plowing onto the shoulder and shutting off the engine.

"Here are the rules," I said.

"Hit me," she replied.

I studied her as best I could in the dark. Everyone reacts to death and violence in their own way. The first time I saw a dead body (rock star, heroin, bathtub), I almost vomited on the tile, before Manny yelled at me not to leave my DNA everywhere. I wondered if, deep in Madeline's brain, that mansion in the gated community was becoming her personal version of Hell House, a fountain of panic and nightmares threatening to break through. Except she was calm. Maybe too calm.

I realized I knew so little about her.

"We don't kill him," I said. "Even if he killed your father."

She nodded. "Okay."

"I'm serious. When we began this adventure, I told you I wouldn't kill anyone, and I'm sticking to that. If he tells us he killed your father, we'll figure out what to do, but I'm not pulling the trigger on him."

"I said okay, okay?"

"If we must hurt him, I'll be the one doing the hurting. I need you to agree to that, too."

"Why?"

"Because it's less liability for you."

"Okay."

"Okay." I opened my door and stepped into the night. From here, we could see the sprinkled lights of houses against the velvety backdrop of fields and trees, and, in the middle distance, the orange flicker of the fire. The wind snapped and crackled through the brush, and I imagined a firestorm ripping across dry fields and trailer parks and subdivisions faster than someone could run.

Madeline climbed out and shut her door. "We going?" she asked.

"Letting my eyes adjust," I said, keeping the flashlight in my left hand, pressed against my hip.

Once my vision had sharpened enough for me to see the skeletal arm of the gate against the blackness of the shrubs, I said, "Side of the path."

"Why'd you bother bringing the flashlight?"

"It's a good club. Come on." I ducked beneath the gate, grateful for the half-moon reflecting off the white gravel path. Through the gnarled branches I spotted the pale curve of the winery entrance. I had a better view of Vonn's house in its copse of tall trees, its every window blazing orange.

Madeline stumbled behind me, rocks clattering down the incline. "Drat," she wheezed, her voice loud over the soft buzzing of insects.

"Step careful," I whispered.

"I wish," she said, "we had those goggles that let you see in the dark."

I almost stopped in my tracks. Vonn had lost two men under suspicious circumstances. Why wouldn't he prepare his property for an invasion? What if he'd hired more men with guns?

What if those men had night vision?

It wasn't as crazy as it sounded. I knew my share of Hollywood executives who had private security teams drawn from ex-Special Forces and CIA paramilitary, hard men who knew how to crush an esophagus with their pinkie and hit a target from two thousand yards away.

I kept descending the path, scanning the brush for movement, trying not to let my paranoia ride me ragged. If you're in the wrong frame of mind, every shadow becomes an assassin with a rifle.

The insects fell silent.

Pausing again, I raised my left hand for Madeline to stop.

I placed my right hand on my holster, ready to draw.

No, I wasn't totally paranoid. Someone was out here with us.

A white blur against the hills – Mister Skull descending toward us, ready to finish our business.

I blinked, my hand tensing on the pistol.

No, it wasn't Mister Skull – just a rock peeking from the brush midway up the slope.

A warmer wind rustled the branches around us, and the insects began their idiot song again. I sensed a presence moving on.

"What?" Madeline whispered.

"Come on," I said, shaking my head.

We arrived at the winery's earthen flank. I crouched and drew the pistol. Yet again I felt something wrong. Against the black of the parking lot, I spotted two darker splotches, unmoving. I aimed my weapon at the closest one as I approached. It was a body, a young man dressed in black cargo pants and a black t-shirt with the Vonn logo on it, his long hair splayed on the pavement.

The 'hair' shimmered liquidly in the moon.

It was the kid's blood splashed in a wide fan.

His lips were parted, the front teeth cracked. Someone had shot him in the mouth.

I pictured a man lurking in the brush, wearing night-vision goggles that made him look like an insect invader from another world. A professional.

The young man had a pump-action 12-gauge in his grip.

I holstered my pistol, stuffed the flashlight in my other hip pocket, pulled the shotgun free and worked the action to verify the shell in the chamber.

The other shadow belonged to another young man in a Vonn t-shirt and cargo pants, his clean-shaven skull smudged with tattoos, a black hole at the base of his neck, a 9mm on the pavement beside him.

They didn't look like private security. Not the top-dollar kind, in any case. I guessed Vonn had paid a few of his rougher staff members to stand guard around the winery after dark. Whatever their background, they'd proven roughly as effective against this visitor as a kitten versus King Kong.

"We should leave," Madeline whispered.

I shook my head. "We keep going. At least for now."

Instead of marching down the winery road like a pair of idiots, I took us on a wider arc through the vineyards, along a lane between the wired-up rows of scrubby vines. Vonn's people had scattered dry straw that crunched underfoot. Every few yards I paused to listen. No sounds or movement from the house.

The vineyards stopped at a low brick wall, barely waist high. We scrambled over it, keeping low, and alighted on a broad lawn that extended to the house's flank. I waved for Madeline to follow as we sprinted toward the wall like a pair of World War II soldiers and flattened against the stucco. Madeline was almost gasping from the exertion.

"Gotta quit smoking," she whispered.

"That'd be a good idea anyway." I took us left, cornering the house's rear. The lawn flowed to a narrow pool lined on either side with iron tables and chairs. The pool was empty. The dark lump of another body sprawled by one of the tables.

"I can't..."

The voice came from our right, where floor-to-ceiling windows framed an everything-marble kitchen and a lounge area lined with long white-leather couches. Vonn sat at the kitchen's central island, hunched over a MacBook. Reid stood beside him, dressed in a full-body Tyvek suit with the hood down, surgical gloves over his hands.

Reid aimed a cheap silver pistol at Vonn's head.

Both men faced away from us, their attention on the laptop.

A glass door to my right was propped open with a brick.

The heavy flashlight threatened to tumble from my pocket. I set it on the ground beside me and rose, trying to stay on the balls of my feet as I crept toward the door. Fifteen yards, ten.

Reid jabbed the pistol against Vonn's head and said something I couldn't quite hear at this distance. Vonn typed faster.

Nine yards, eight, seven.

I socked the 12-gauge against my shoulder as I slipped through the doorway, aiming at Reid's back.

"This is a shotgun," I told them, my finger tight on the trigger. I'd told Madeline I wouldn't kill, and I intended to keep that promise – unless Reid did something stupid.

"I thought I told you to get out of town," Reid said without turning around. His voice was rushed, manic, his cheeks and sideburns damp with sweat.

"Oops," I said.

Vonn leaned away from the laptop.

"I didn't tell you to stop," Reid told him. "You better obey an officer of the law."

"My hands are tired, so I'm taking a break." Vonn sounded calm, like he was telling one of his workers to hustle with those grapes. He flicked a finger at the glass of red wine beside the keyboard. "May I?"

Reid snorted. "All the big ol' steel balls in the world here. Sure."

Vonn swirled the glass and sipped. His eyes flicked to Reid, then me, then a point beyond my left shoulder. "How's the fire?" he asked.

From behind me, Madeline said, "Still spreading, last I heard."

"Last one almost took this place." He nodded to himself. "I had to get out the garden hose, soak the roof down. To stop the embers."

"Get on with it," Reid said, tapping the pistol's barrel against Vonn's temple.

Vonn's eyes found mine. "I have a deal for you. Shoot this guy and leave, and I'll pay you a million dollars. Cash."

Reid laughed. "Hell, we just transferred your last million. What'll you pay him in, bad wine?"

I stepped to the left for a better view of Vonn's laptop. He had a browser open to a brokerage site. The account totals read zero. "Who's 'we?'" I asked.

Reid snickered. "They don't know."

Vonn craned his head so he could better see Madeline. "Your Daddy never wanted kids," he said. "He thought the world was going to burn, and guess what: he was right. It's all going down."

"Okay, Boomer," Madeline told him.

"Keep that in mind for whatever's next," Vonn said.

"You try to shoot him," I told Reid, "and I'll unload into your back. Stand down."

"Don't try to sound like a cop," Reid said, flexing his grip on the pistol. "You don't have the balls, son. When I finish my business here, I'm going to walk out that door over there, and you're going to leave the county. I'm so generous and kind with you. It's amazing."

Vonn's eyes found mine, his breath fast, his shoulders rising almost to his ears. Waiting for the shot. Or waiting for me to save him. My finger curling on the trigger even as the rest of my body felt paralyzed. Reid was right: I couldn't shoot someone in the back.

"Do you understand?" Reid said, almost screaming.

I considered shooting him in the knee, except his finger would yank the trigger on reflex and kill Vonn anyway, and if Reid didn't pass out from the shock of his lower leg vaporizing to meaty chunks, he would spin and shoot me before I could rack the shotgun's slide again.

"I'll take that as a 'yes'," Reid said, squinting as he aimed. Vonn cringing low, whining loud between his clenched teeth –

A pop, and the window to our left cracked. A bottle shattered on a shelf beyond Vonn's head.

Reid was swiveling when the back of his head exploded, coating Vonn and his laptop red. Reid's knees wobbled as he toppled boneless to the floor, his pistol skittering deeper into the kitchen. I had already dropped to one knee, aiming the shotgun beyond the shattered window. Madeline's hand gripped my ankle and squeezed.

Blinking the blood from his eyes, Vonn raised his quaking hands above his head. "Don't shoot…"

Another pop, and the window's crazed glass burst from

its frame, glittering bits raining on my hands. Vonn's right temple sprung a hole as he slumped sideways, his head smacking the laptop's keyboard.

Madeline moaned. I swiveled and aimed the shotgun at the door. We had some cover, but there were too many windows, too many places to watch at once. I swiveled to lock eyes with Madeline and nodded toward the door to our left, beyond the island. If we could escape deeper into the house, we could find a better position to defend –

"Dash," a familiar voice called from the darkness. "I'm coming in, okay? Don't fire that stupid 12-gauge at me."

"Manny?" I yelled. "What the hell, man?"

"What's going on?" Madeline hissed.

"It's a guy I used to work with," I said. What was Manny doing here? Why did he shoot Reid and Vonn?

Madeline scrambled past me. Grabbing Reid's pistol, she worked the slide like a professional, then rolled onto her back and aimed at the glass door.

I held out a hand. "Don't fire," I told her.

"Oh, I won't," she said. "Not unless he does something dumb." Her eyes were wild.

"Dash," Manny called out. It sounded like he was right outside the house. "I want to come in, but I don't want your friend to shoot me. Can you calm her down?"

"She doesn't trust your intentions," I said. "Sorry."

Something flew through the open door, landing on the couch beside my head: a 9mm magazine. A metallic click, followed by a brass bullet bouncing off the island and onto the tiles on the far side. "I'm empty," Manny called. "Do I pass the test?"

"The gun, too," Madeline said. "I'm not an idiot."

A 9mm pistol sailed through the doorway and onto a couch cushion.

"Happy?" Manny asked.

"Sure," Madeline called. "But no sudden moves."

"Spoken like a real badass." Manny stepped over the threshold, into the light. His choice of attire for a stalk-and-kill was a black suit loose in the jacket, paired with a black shirt and tie. He raised his hands, palms out, and smirked. "I guess we got a lot to talk about."

32.

I set down my shotgun and stood, but Madeline declined to lower her pistol as Manny walked across the kitchen, pulled a bottle of Vonn's wine from a rack, and twisted it open. He poured himself half a glass and swirled it. Seeing him here was weird enough; seeing him act like a wine tourist amidst a massacre was weirder. We should have been fleeing for the hills, not leaving our fingerprints everywhere.

"Why are you here, Manny?" I asked.

"You're welcome." He sipped the wine and winced. "His plonk is still terrible."

"Who the hell are you?" Madeline asked, rising to one knee, still aiming at Manny's head.

Manny waggled a finger at her. "I don't answer questions with a gun in my face."

Madeline lowered the pistol a few inches, pointing the barrel to our left.

"Thank you," he said. "My name's Manny, and I used to be Dash's boss. We kept Hollywood nice and clean for popular consumption. Either of you want wine?"

"Not after you made that face," I said. I plucked a napkin from the island and wrapped it around my hand, hooked two fingers into Vonn's collar and lifted his head from the keyboard. His dead eyes seemed full of reproach. His nose had crushed three keys, filling one of the fields in the brokerage app with a random string of 'gjktgjgkt', but it had kept the laptop awake.

"Finding anything interesting?" Manny asked.

With the napkin around my finger, I stabbed at some keys, revealing more screens. Stocks and bonds sold within the past few hours, transfers of large amounts of cash to accounts with hidden routing numbers. "The money's gone, however much he had."

Manny said, "Our cop buddy was pulling a burn."

Madeline grunted and stood. "Mister Manny, what are you doing here?"

"The million-dollar question." Manny refilled his glass. "Your buddy Dash called me. Said that he'd narrowed down the suspect in your Daddy's killing, and that he'd need me to call a lawyer if anything bad happened. So, I drove up. You're welcome."

"You kill all those people outside?"

"No, that must have been the cop. I was behind you when you were coming down the hill." Manny tugged a handful of black fabric from his jacket pocket. "I was wearing a ski mask."

"I sensed someone there," I said, remembering how the insects had quieted.

"How'd you know Dash meant Vonn?" Madeline asked.

"Vonn and your Dad went way back. It was an open secret."

"Thanks for telling me," I said, settling Vonn's head on the keyboard again. "Could have saved me some time."

"Wanted you to earn your pay," he said, and winked at Madeline. "How's this guy working out? He tell you any jokes?"

"You tell jokes?" Madeline said, cocking an eyebrow at me.

"Oh, he tried to make it as a comedian," Manny said. "I even caught him doing standup."

"That's like making a vegetarian in charge of a slaughterhouse," Madeline grinned at Manny.

"Like asking an arsonist to run a fire department," Manny returned the grin, his shoulders relaxing a bit.

I was fine with everyone calming down, but not at my expense. "You know what's not funny? You two," I said, waving my hands at them. "Go ahead, crush my dreams, Manny."

Madeline's grin dimmed. "Did Vonn kill my father?"

"Maybe it's best to assume that. Digging up the past is never a good thing. And unlike the movies, things don't wrap up with a neat bow." Manny used the ski mask to wipe down his glass before placing it in the sink. "Here's what's going to happen. That pistol I tossed in here? It belonged to one of the guards. I'm going to put it back together – don't freak when I do it – and put it next to his body out there. The cops will think he shot Vonn and the cop, probably after the cop shot all his people."

"Then who shot the guard?" I asked.

"Doesn't matter," Manny said. "We just want to make things hopelessly confused."

"Or we could just leave everything to burn," Madeline said. "We saw that fire from the ridge."

"Yeah, my phone keeps getting alerts." Manny retreated to the couch, where he popped the loose bullet into the magazine before slamming the magazine into the 9mm.

"Then what?" I said. "We're going back to L.A.?"

"Alas, not quite." Manny turned to Madeline. "You drive a vintage Mustang?"

She nodded. "Yeah."

"Then I have bad news for your beautiful car. The cops are onto it. We'll have to dump it." Stuffing the pistol in his armpit, he raised his phone. "Fortunately, I got a local guy. We can drive it to him. Just take me to wherever you've hidden it."

"Manny has people everywhere," I told her.

Madeline stared at Manny, the gears clicking in her head. I could tell she didn't trust him. But she trusted me.

"Okay," she said. "We'll dump the car."

Manny disappeared through the doorway to the outside. I used the napkin to wipe down anything else we might have touched, from the couch cushions to the shotgun on the floor. When I reached Vonn's slumped corpse, I felt for his ankle holster, which was missing.

I spared a glance at Reid, who'd come so prepared in his plastic suit and gloves and booties stretched over his shoes to disguise the tread. Fat lot of good it did him.

"You buy what he's selling?" Madeline whispered.

"Sure," I said. "The worst part is, now I owe him big."

We exited, closing the door behind us. Manny stood at the edge of the lawn, his face floating against the black. "I'm parked at the top of the ridge," he said. "Near you, in fact."

"Lead the way," I told him.

As we walked toward the winery and the scrubland beyond, Madeline said, "You taught Dash everything he knows?"

Manny nodded. "He was like a babe in the woods before I got my hands on him."

"And you did bad stuff for Hollywood pricks?"

I waited to see how Manny would react. Under ordinary circumstances, he didn't suffer fools. But this wasn't the usual Manny – something was off. He remained silent until we reached the tattooed guard's body, where he tossed the 9mm into the drying pool of blood. As he led off again, he said, "You ever hear of Eddie Mannix?"

"Actually, yes." Madeline clapped her hands. "Thank you, procrastinating on Wikipedia. He started out as a bouncer, moved to MGM in the Roaring Twenties, did all their dirty deeds. He killed the guy who originally played Superman, George Reeves, right? Or they think he had something to do with it?"

"Nah, Reeves committed suicide," Manny said. "But the rest of it – yeah, they did it all. Abortions, marriage annulments, dumping the occasional body in the desert. Howard Strickling, too, who was the fixer from hell. No assignment too rough if it kept the big machine rolling."

"And let me guess," Madeline told his massive back as we picked our way up the trail. "You're the modern-day equivalent, right? Is this where you give me a big speech about how morality is a useless construct holding us back? No, that's not it. You're the type who argues that the system is already in place, right, so we might as well profit off it?"

Manny paused and turned. His unblinking eyes reflected the moon. His hands were loose at his sides, but I guessed it took him considerable effort to not curl those huge fingers into fists. Manny had a short fuse. I bet he was imagining what he could slam into her face to wipe the smirk off it.

"It's none of that," he said, almost too controlled, too reasonable. "I did some questionable stuff because it pays, and I have expensive tastes. It's also a thrill. Once you've done certain things, you can't go back to an ordinary life."

"I think I heard a serial killer say something like that once," Madeline said. "In a documentary."

"Manny," I said, quietly, trying to get him to focus on me instead of Madeline. "We have to move."

"Right," he said. "Wasting too much time fielding questions from someone young enough to be my daughter."

We reached the top of the ridge, and I paused to survey the horizon. The fire was closer, a roiling line of orange that left an inky blackness in its wake. A pair of headlights flickered like a firefly along a road close to the inferno, followed by another, then another. Folks were fleeing the area as fast as they could.

"Girl," Manny said quietly. "I'm going to show you something, and you need to promise me not to freak out."

"I promise nothing," Madeline said.

"Here goes," Manny said, and, reaching slowly behind his back, drew a gold-plated pistol, which he pointed at the ground. "This is my personal weapon. John Milius gave it to me. And I had it on me the whole time. I'm putting it back, okay?"

"Okay," Madeline said, and swallowed.

"Just to show you could've trusted me all along." He nodded toward the faint blotch of our car, parked a few yards to our left. "Go back out to the main road. I'll be along in a minute."

I drove us to the road and waited on the shoulder until Manny's headlights emerged from the gravel lane. I didn't recognize his car, a black and totally anonymous sedan, the kind of vehicle you drove on bad business in the countryside. I turned the radio to a local news station, a panicked DJ screaming about evacuations and acres burned and firefighters trying to keep things under control.

The flames might distract law enforcement from hunting us. Small favors.

Madeline sniffed and wiped her nose with the back of her hand. I debated whether to say anything. What comfort could I offer her? You can't fix the past. As cruel as it sounds, maybe it's better to never know what happened.

"I'll tell myself Vonn did it all," she said, swiping at the corners of her eyes. "Killed my dad over a bad business deal or whatever. Killed the documentary guys, too. Because I think we've played this whole thing out, yeah?"

I nodded, but something was bothering me. Something that someone had said – but the details, the timing, slipped away whenever my mind tried to snatch at it.

Manny followed us from Vonn's valley to ours. Speeding cars overtook us, their cargo areas stuffed with baggage. More vehicles screamed past in the opposite lane. Madeline drew a fresh cigarette and zipped down her window an inch, enough to smell the stench of burning acres in our slipstream.

"Vonn was right," she said. "What's the point? It's all burning down. The coral's dead. Forests are gone. We wrecked it all, so what does it matter?"

"It matters," I said.

She pushed the unlit cigarette out the window crack. "There's a word for that kind of philosophy."

"Stoicism?"

She zipped the window up. "Bullshit."

Our part of the valley was shrouded in darkness, still and empty. I rumbled into our driveway. As my headlights swept over the front of our rental house, my paranoia meter jumped from Cautious Green to Nervous Yellow. Nothing seemed amiss, and yet I was seized by an almost overpowering urge to pull my pistol and reverse back down the driveway. Manny was right behind us, though, blocking the way.

I stopped the Mustang.

Manny stepped from his car, his phone in his right hand.

"Something's off," I said, gripping the key in the ignition, hesitating before I shut the engine down.

Manny crossed to the rental's front steps, his phone in his pocket, an odd smile on his face. Like he was waiting for a surprise.

Madeline opened her door. "What's up?" she called to Manny as she climbed out.

He raised a hand for us to wait.

I had just exited the Mustang when headlights played along the low hill blocking our view of the road. The trees above us flared white as a car powered up the driveway's incline.

I reached beneath my shirt for my pistol.

A bright orange Porsche rumbled to a stop behind Manny's car, revving hard before falling silent. The driver's door opened, a tall man rising into view, his face faintly lit by the car's dome light. He was bone-thin and dressed in a nice pair of slacks and a tailored suit jacket that draped perfectly on his sharp-angled shoulders. His gray hair was thinning, and his jaw was covered with a thickening beard, but I knew the face.

I was staring at a dead man.

Except maybe not as dead as we'd thought.

"Hey, squirt," Ken Ironwood said to his daughter. "How goes it?"

33.

How do you react when your father – the man you assumed was planted in a barrel – suddenly reappears, alive and apparently well? Do you scream in his face? Do you wrap your arms around him, hoping to finally make up for the time you've lost? What question do you ask him first?

Madeline's knees wobbled and she leaned against the Mustang's trunk. "Well, shit," she said, low but steady. "Shit."

Ken Ironwood slammed his car's door and bowed at the waist. He was taller than I expected, and I could see why he'd proven so popular at all those Hollywood parties back in the day. Like movie stars and rock gods, he glowed with an inner light. "Look," he said. "There's so much to say."

"Shit," Madeline said. "Oh, shit."

"I can't begin to know how you feel," Ken said, walking toward us. I snapped out of my trance, realizing Manny had drifted up the stairs and along the front porch until he was almost beyond my line of sight. I took three big steps away from the car, turning so I could see Manny and Ken at the same time. What the hell was going on here?

Ken's eyes shifted to me. "You're Madeline's friend. The one she paid to find my killer," he said, and laughed.

"That's right," I said.

Ken nodded. "You worked for Manny."

"Also correct." I was thankful for the gun. "Manny, what the hell?"

Manny grimaced. "Angie, man. She was helping keep him hidden."

With a banshee scream, Madeline charged across the gravel, throwing her left fist in a loose haymaker that connected with Ken's jaw. He staggered, arms flailing, almost toppling over. I gripped my pistol, ready to draw, but Manny clicked his tongue – he already had his pistol out, aimed at my head.

What a way to ruin a friendship.

"Manny," I said. "Manny, what the hell is this?"

Ken tried to rise, and Madeline hit him again, plowing her right fist into the side of his neck. He stumbled, his knee slamming the gravel, only saving himself from an epic faceplant by throwing out both hands. "Kid," he hissed. "Fucking quit it."

"Asshole," Madeline said, rearing back a foot to kick him in the ribs.

Manny adjusted his aim and fired off a shot over their heads.

Madeline jumped back, startled, her hands raised. Ken spat and rose on shaky knees, brushing off his lapels.

"Dash, toss that pistol and let's all go inside," Manny said. "There's lots to discuss."

34.

"I'm sorry," Manny said as he flicked on the overhead lights and pushed two chairs into the center of the living room. "It's been a long night for everyone, and it's not even eleven. Sit down."

"We say no, you'll shoot us?" Madeline said, her cheeks flushed.

"Maybe in the knee," Manny said, angling the pistol.

"Come on," I said, taking a seat. "I don't think we have a choice."

"There's always a choice," she said, but plopped next to me.

Ken paced the first floor, opening doors and drawers, checking behind the television.

"What are you looking for?" I asked.

"Cameras, microphones, all that good stuff," he said. "You know how it goes. Manny said you were the best operator he ever worked with."

Manny glanced at me and winked, like he hadn't pointed a gun at my head outside. His cheeks were shiny with sweat despite the cool air leaking from the vents. "Now put your hands behind your back," he said, pulling a handful of plastic zip-ties from his jacket pocket. "It's for your own protection."

I shook my head. "No. We're fine. We're just talking, okay?"

"Kneecap," Manny said, raising the gun an inch.

"There's no need," I said, except when I glanced at Madeline, she looked like she wanted to fly across the room and rip out Manny's throat with her fingers.

"There's plenty of need," Ken shouted from the far side of the house. "When you calm down, we'll cut you free, pinkie swear."

"You don't have a choice," Manny said, his gaze lasering into me. "I'll do anything for a client."

"Especially your best client," Ken said, jabbing both thumbs at his own chest as he circled toward us.

"And Angie knows about all this," I said.

"Yes," Manny said. "She and Ken go way back. But she's untouchable. Folks like her always are."

I sighed theatrically, as if the whole thing bored me, but inside I was scared, the kind of fear that quakes your insides and makes your knees weak. I put my hands behind the chair's back. Manny dipped behind me. The zip-ties slipped over my wrists and tightened, biting into my skin. Another snap, and my wrists tugged to the left as Manny used another pair of zip-ties to bind me to the chair back.

"I'll fucking kill you," Madeline informed him, but her anger had burned away to ash, leaving her pale and weak. She looked like a little girl in an oversized coat, all red hair and gangly limbs and big eyes.

"I know, darling," Manny said, and bound her, too.

Ken stepped before us, palms out. "Look. I can't put into words how bad I feel. How I wish things had gone differently. I did it all to protect you, okay?"

Madeline snorted. "Explain."

"What's your last memory of me?"

Madeline swallowed and shook her head. "I don't remember. You playing with me at the beach, maybe? I would have been two."

"Yeah." Ken smiled slightly. "You always loved the beach. And I loved taking you there. I regret so much that I couldn't stick around, but I went to this party and this guy challenged me to a duel. Russian prick, real connected guy. He messed up, because he was too slow and I shot his dumb ass between the eyes, but it also meant I had to run. Otherwise, his friends would have chopped me into shark chum."

"Who's in the barrel?" I asked.

He cocked his head to study me, as if I were an interesting insect pinned to a board. "Does it matter?"

"I've been running around this damn county trying to get to the bottom of it," I said. "I've had a bunch of guns pointed at me, so yeah, I'd say it matters."

"An associate of mine. Just a lowlife who would've gone to the cops, sooner or later." He shrugged. "He said the wrong thing one night, and hey presto, we needed to get rid of a body. Then I had a flash of genius. I thought, why not smash out his teeth, throw my old wallet in there with him? By the time anyone found the barrel, he'd be a skeleton, and everyone would think they solved the mystery of my disappearance. Heck, if it wasn't for climate change, they might have never found it at all."

"Do you have any idea what you put me through?" Madeline said, fists clenching. "What you put mom through?"

"Hey." His voice was quiet, almost gentle, but his gaze was hard. Here was the gangster who smuggled enough drugs to poison a city, who shot other men in the back, who abandoned his daughter to save his own skin. "These men, they would have killed you, too. They would have killed your mother, my friends, anyone I'd ever known. By disappearing, I cauterized the wound, do you understand?"

Madeline snorted.

"You got into business with Vonn?" I said.

"Yeah, we had a friendship going way back. I paid him a lot of money, and he set up all kinds of shell companies for me, a piece of the winery, a house not too far from here. I wasn't hurting anyone, you understand? Well, not anyone who mattered."

"*Django* was your boat," I said.

"Yes. Yes, it was. I kept moving it between shell companies."

"Sorry Vonn's guys blew it up."

"I had Reid settle it."

"You had him kill those guys, plus Vonn."

"I had him take care of those documentary guys, too." Ken grinned ruefully and shook his head. "I told him to do those two quietly, and you know what that knucklehead did? Killed them right in the station when nobody else was around. He was losing it. I had to call Vonn's guys, get them to help him hide the bodies. Embarrassing."

Madeline shook her head. "God, you're such a chump."

He spun on her. "I did what I had to do. You understand?"

Madeline muttered something under her breath.

"I said," he leaned in closer, until they were almost nose-to-nose. "Do you fucking understand, dear daughter?"

Madeline bit him.

It was more of a gesture than an attack. Her head darted forward, jaw snapping, and her teeth grazed his nose, barely breaking the skin. He darted back, hissing in anger, and raised a hand, as if about to strike her. She smiled back, her eyes twinkling with feral glee.

Ken rubbed his nose and squinted at his fingers for any blood. He grunted, satisfied, and turned to me.

"Stick anything close to me, I'll bite it clean off," I said. "I bet it tastes like chicken."

Leaning against the kitchen counter, Manny barked laughter.

Ken shot him an irate look before swiveling back to me. "How'd you find out?"

"Find out what? The recipe for a better pancake?"

He punched me.

He put enough hip behind it to crack something in my jaw. Pain screamed down my face to my collarbone. For an older man, he had a lot of force. I twisted my aching head to the side and spat red.

"Thank you for not spitting that on me," he said, rubbing his knuckles.

"Thought about it."

"I have no doubt. And if you had, I would've chopped your balls off." He smiled. It was a gorgeous smile, the kind that opens all kinds of doors in life. "You know about ball-chopping, don't you? Manny taught you well, from what I heard."

Manny looked at his feet.

"Honestly, after ten years or so, I never expected anyone to look for me," Ken said. "But then I heard about that damn streaming series. Suddenly the internet is full of these creeps with their websites, trying to crack the case. Like, get a life. Don't they have anything better to do?"

I shook my head. "True crime is big. You have all these

series and podcasts, and they're grabbing any crime they can find. Once they tackled all the big serial killers and Jim Jones and whoever else, I guess they were stuck with you."

"Bottom of the barrel," Madeline said, and laughed. "Pun definitely intended."

A fresh burst of wind rattled the sliding-glass door in its frame, and I smelled – or imagined I smelled – a hint of smoke. How far away was the fire? I tried to meet Manny's eyes again, but he was still focused on the floor like it was the most interesting thing he'd ever seen.

"I kept tabs on you," Ken told his daughter. "I cared, even if I couldn't talk to you. I even listened to the music you put out. Not my thing, but I guess you had a few fans. And the movies you were in – I watched them, at least for the half-second you were onscreen. Then you got into drugs, and I guess you didn't really do anything after that, did you?"

"I was the life of the party," she said, her jaw tight.

"I bet you were. I always doubted you were really my kid. Your mother, she got around."

"That'd be fine with me. You suck."

Manny looked up, locked on something beyond the glass door. "Ken," he said. "I saw an ember. We better go."

"How close?" Ken asked, looming over Madeline.

"Way back in the trees. We got to move."

"You're leaving us here?" Madeline said. "You'll let us burn up? What kind of sick fuck are you?"

"I'm not totally cruel," Ken said, "but you didn't give me a choice. This is your fault. You would've told the cops. Would have ruined my life again, just because I'm living like I want to live. But here we are. I'm leaving after I get my stuff."

"Stuff?" I asked.

Ken straightened his lapels and ran a hand through his hair, like he was fine-tuning his appearance before stepping out of the bathroom at a swank Hollywood gathering. He turned to the door. As he passed Manny, he dipped his head and said, at a near-whisper: "Make sure it gets done."

Manny made a face like he was sucking on a lemon.

When Ken opened the front door, I smelled a stronger whiff of smoke, acidic and pungent, as if the fire was eating plastic. He stepped onto the front porch and closed the door behind him and walked to his car. Opening the driver's door, he reached inside to flick the headlights on. Next, he popped his trunk and removed a pry bar.

Madeline had let her head slump forward, her thick hair hiding her face. Her shoulders hitched, and I heard a faint sob.

"Manny," I said. "You don't have to do this."

Manny puffed his cheeks, his shoulders slumping.

"We go back," I said. "You can't let it go down like this."

Tossing the pry bar from hand to hand, Ken walked to the Mustang, its flank visible through a window. He notched the pry bar into the narrow space between the driver's door and the fender, and, bracing his feet, yanked hard. With a loud screech, the door shell peeled back a few inches.

Ken tossed the bar aside, knelt, and reached carefully into the sharp gap. His hand emerged again with a small canvas bag, which he tucked into his jacket before standing.

"What was that?" I asked.

Madeline's head rose. Her eyes were wet. "My mom always said people were trying to steal the Mustang. She got great at hiding it. Even shot a guy who tried to take it." She laughed without humor. "My Dad, the bigshot famous criminal, and he couldn't even snatch a car back from his wife. What a loser."

"Technically, it was always his car," Manny said quietly. "Your mom had no right to take it after he disappeared."

"He didn't leave them much, you dumbass," I said. "What's in the bag? Gold? Diamonds?"

Ken had crossed the yard and climbed into his car without another look at the house.

Manny tossed up his hands. "Look, I'm sorry. Like Ken said, if things could've been another way. But there's too much at stake."

The Porsche's engine roared, the headlights sweeping the yard as Ken backed down the driveway, ready for whatever glorious criminal future awaited him.

"C'mon, Manny," I said, trying to meet his eyes. "You know me. We go back."

"We do, we do, we do, and I'm so sorry." His voice warbled as he strode across the open space, whipped a cute yellow dish towel from the kitchen counter, and spun it into a loose rope. "You should have come back into the fold, man. We would have let you in."

"Not if you're doing this kind of shit," I said. "This is low, even by our standards."

"You don't get it," Madeline said to me. "You keep clinging to this thing called morality, which doesn't really exist. Manny's just an animal looking to get by."

"Okay." Manny stopped in the middle of the space, roughly equidistant between us, the towel-rope tightening in his grip. "Please don't plead. It won't work. Which one of you wants to go first? I swear I'll make it as quick as I can. The fire's coming this way, I won't let you burn."

"You know what's mercy?" Madeline said. "First, turn

me the other way so I don't have that 'Live Love Laugh' sign in my face. Second, just shoot me in the head. Quick, painless."

"No. Not with my gun." The towel trembled slightly in Manny's grip.

"You'll have to choose which one of us to do first," Madeline said. "We're not giving you the least inch here."

"Damnit." Manny swayed from foot to foot, his hands flexing on the soft towel. "Damnit."

"C'mon," I said, trying to make my voice as soothing as possible, too aware of the warm breath hissing up my throat, the pounding of blood in my ears. It was so hard to keep my fear tamped down. "I'm your guy, Manny. Remember that? I'm not some rando."

"Yeah," Manny said. "I know."

"I remember you telling me once that murder was a permanent solution to a temporary problem." Our eyes finally met, and I tried to fill him telepathically with our shared history. If he saw me as a human being, a friend, he'd waver. I was sure of it. "That's still true. We can figure something out."

Manny groaned.

I glanced at Madeline, her eyes darting around the room for anything that could give us an advantage.

As subtly as I could, I tried lifting my arms. The plastic around my wrists had maybe a half-inch of give. Not enough to slip free.

Manny closed his eyes. When he opened him again, his gaze was hard, merciless. He'd crossed his mental Rubicon.

"I'm sorry," he said, and there was no weakness in his voice now. Tightening the towel-rope, he stepped behind Madeline, who growled and thrashed like she was attempting to headbutt him. She tried throwing herself forward, but he grabbed the chair with one huge hand and dragged her back. Her growling rose into an angry whine, like an animal pleading for mercy, her eyes hot with panic.

She tucked her chin, blocking her neck, as if that would save her. Manny wove his fingers into her hair and yanked her head back, then dropped the towel-rope across her throat. He pulled, bracing a knee against the back of the chair. Her eyes bulged. Her tongue burst from between her lips.

35.

I yelled my head off.

Madeline had also given me an idea. I braced my feet and stood as best I could. The seat of the chair banged against the back of my knees and the flex-cuffs bit into my flesh and I almost toppled over, but I was upright, my tethered hands flapping behind me like penguin wings, hilariously useless.

Manny was so intent on strangling her that it took him another instant to realize I was trying something. He looked up, startled, then confused, as I hopped toward him.

"Dash," he said, in the indignant tone of someone arguing over a bar tab. *"Stop it."*

His hands slackened on the towel-rope, and Madeline gulped oxygen before coughing a spray of bile. I hopped again, and Manny stepped backward, using Madeline's chair as a shield, his confused look softening into pity. Maybe he thought I was trying to attack him, but he made no move for the gun in his jacket. To him, I was a sad joke.

And that might have been true, if I'd intended to leap at him with tethered limbs and a heart full of moxie. Instead, I bent my knees and pushed, tackling Madeline at the waist, my weight crashing her sideways onto the floor. Two of the legs on her cheap, flimsy chair – *cheap IKEA crap*, she'd called it when we first arrived – snapped off at the base, along with a satisfying crack as the back separated from the seat. Her hands were flex-cuffed, but she was free of the chair.

I tried rolling off her, but my chair had survived the impact in fine form. Pinned on my side, I could only watch as Manny approached, shaking his head sadly, torquing the towel-rope again.

"You idiot," Manny said. "But you always had heart. A little too much, in fact."

Madeline slithered under me, grunting. I tried shifting my weight so she could scramble free, but she had no interest in that. Her hands brushed my side, her legs, scrambling inside her left boot –

Manny gripped my shoulder, his fingers like iron, and heaved. The world tilted crazily as I flopped in the opposite direction, my chair squealing against the floorboards. I twisted against the flex-cuffs, hoping the impact had loosened something. No, I was trapped.

Manny knew it, too. He puffed his cheeks and blasted air between clenched teeth before tweaking his lapels, because first and foremost he was a fashion horse, the kind of guy who liked to look perfect even when trying to strangle two people to death. He turned to Madeline, ready to finish the job. He still wasn't reaching for his gun, still didn't see us as anything more than an annoyance.

That was his one big mistake, because Madeline pulled Ken's antique switchblade from her boot and swung the blade in a short, sharp arc that ended with Manny's ultra-expensive shoe, the steel punching through fine leather into flesh and bone.

Manny squealed and tried to kick her with his other foot, but she rolled to the side, dodging the sole, before yanking the knife free and stabbing again, sinking the blade into

Manny's calf. Manny unleashed a full-throated roar and stumbled away, the backs of his knees smacking into the legs of my chair. He fell.

I started laughing.

Yes, as my former boss tried to murder me and my friend, in a house about to burn in a wildfire, hysterical laughter boiled up my throat. I never expected the day of my possible death to play like a slapstick comedy routine.

Beside me, Manny bellowed again and struggled to rise, his hand slipping past his lapel like he meant to draw the gun. I levered my legs and rolled on top of him, pinning his arms to his sides. I laughed in his face, and a saner annex of my brain heard the lunatic note in it, like all the years of tension and drinking and anger were pouring out of me.

"Let me up, you shit," Manny wheezed.

Madeline rose onto one knee and pulled the knife from Manny's calf. He yelped. She performed a cute trick with the bloody blade, flipping it backwards to snag and split the flex-cuffs binding her wrists. She stood, shaking her arms loose. Her throat was red and raw. The light glittered on the tear-trails coursing down her cheeks, which at first I mistook for trauma from the near-death experience, an onrushing breakdown. Then I caught the fury in her gaze. She was crying with anger.

She charged forward, lashing out her right leg like Messi going for a goal, and drove her heel into Manny's jaw. With a satisfying crunch, his head snapped back, one eye closed and the other open but staring at nothing.

"Help me," I told her.

Kneeling, she sawed through my flex-cuffs. Freed, I rolled off Manny and reached into his jacket, drawing his gold pistol.

She presented me with the knife, handle-first.

"You do the honors," she said. "He was your boss."

"What?" I slipped the pistol into my waistband, the grip jutting awkwardly against my hip. I hated its weight and flashy color, but it would do until I retrieved my own weapon from outside.

"Kill him," she said, pushing the handle against the back of my hand. "I'm not going to do it, even if the fucker tried to strangle me. I don't want his grubby little soul on my ledger."

I gripped the handle, slick and warm from Madeline's palm.

I could kill him. I knew that. It wouldn't even take that long – a second to kneel and another to slice his neck from ear to ear. Madeline's boot had knocked him out. He wouldn't feel it. And if that was too grisly, I could always use his gun: a quick tap to the temple, bam.

And yet.

And yet.

"No," I said, stepping away.

I expected an argument, maybe an indignant snort, but Madeline nodded and said, "Okay. Then what?"

"Then nothing," I said, tossing the knife overhand into the kitchen. I was hoping the blade would twirl effortlessly though the air before sinking into the wall, but it bounced off the edge of the sink before clattering to the floor.

"We're leaving," I added, turning to her. "Maybe Manny will burn or maybe he'll live, but we'll deal with it later."

Madeline rolled her eyes and said, "That was my knife, you idiot." Trotting into the kitchen, she retrieved the blade and wiped Manny's blood on a towel.

"Sorry," I said.

"You know when you'll be sorry?" she said, returning the knife to her boot. "When he shows up later and tries to kill us again, because you didn't do it the first time."

"If you feel that strongly about it, you should do it. And I'm not calling the cops, either." I grabbed my duffel bag and slung it over my shoulder. I felt sorry for whoever owned this place. At least the fire would spare them from ever knowing it was a crime scene.

"Why? What part of 'he might kill us later' do you not understand?" Her voice rose, raspy over bruised vocal cords.

"Maybe I don't want it on my ledger, either," I said, stepping outside. "We'll deal with it. You coming?"

"Meh," she said, circling toward Manny's unconscious form. She raised her foot like she meant to slam it again into his face, before thinking better of it and stepping away. "I have no words for my disgust."

"Or you could be thankful you don't have that killer instinct. Let's take the Mustang. More horsepower." I held the door open and waved her through. A red-hot ember settled on the porch outside, sizzling the varnished wood, and the trees on the far ledge flashed with hellish light. The wind was blowing in our direction. The flames would only need a few more minutes to reach the house.

Madeline jogged past me, her car key already in her hand. I considered heading back inside, binding Manny's wrists, and taking him with us. Yes, we had a lot of history. Manny had taught me almost everything I knew about surviving life's underbelly. He had been a friend, in the weirdest possible way.

But Madeline was right. He'd tried to kill us both, and if he lived, he would certainly try again. I shut the front door and sprinted down the steps after Madeline, who was already behind the wheel, seatbelt fastened, gunning the engine. I had no time to search for my gun in the yard as she reversed toward the driveway, forcing me to tear open the passenger door and leap in, slotting the duffel bag between my legs. She twisted the wheel and stood on the gas, catching air on the driveway, embers swirling in our path. I had a last look at my broken-down Nissan in the yard. A Viking funeral was exactly what my trusty steed deserved.

On the main road, the horizon dissolved into a flickering red line.

"Right or left?" she asked.

"Right," I said. "Road out of the valley's that way."

She twisted the wheel in that direction and stomped the gas. The two-lane was empty and the Mustang gleefully consumed miles despite its rattling engine, the odometer clicking toward eighty. Whenever she took a curve, loose bits of metal tinkled musically inside the torn door. Gray ash salted the windshield, the wipers leaving ghostly streaks.

She rubbed her neck. "I think I died back there."

"Yeah? Your life flash before your eyes?" I pulled out Manny's weapon and popped the clip. It was fully loaded.

"I think so." She coughed. "Lots of regrets. Should have done that naked skydiving thing when I had the chance."

"I don't even want to know."

"Yeah, you do. In your heart of hearts, you do." Her hands flexed on the wheel. "Where do you think my dad is?"

"Let's focus on getting out of here alive." I placed the golden gun between my legs on the seat, barrel pointed ahead. "After that, we can talk about whether to call the cops, FBI, whatever."

"Or a hitman. That'll make things nice and simple." The road dipped into a shallow curve. My side mirror filled with seething fire, hell on our heels. I twisted in my seat for a better view out the rear window. Another flame-snake swallowed the edge of the field on our left. The whole county was burning up.

"Oh, shit," Madeline said.

I shifted forward. Beyond the curve, the glare of red lights: two lanes of bumper-to-bumper traffic stretching into infinity. A faint chorus of honking as people pounded their steering wheels in fear and frustration. Madeline hit the brakes, bringing us to a screeching halt.

36.

"Maybe we should find a way around, huh?" Madeline said, fast and panicked. "No sense in waiting to get cooked, right?"

"Right," I said, guessing that all the roads behind us were tunnels of fire. And what if we ran into an obstacle? The smoke would choke our engine, then our lungs, before the fire turned the Mustang into a funeral pyre.

"Okay," she said, throwing the Mustang into reverse.

"Wait," I said.

"What?"

I pointed through the speckled windshield at the cars ahead of us. "That car, it belongs to Ken, right?"

She leaned over the wheel, squinting. "Unless there are two people driving obnoxious Porsches, which isn't outside the realm of possibility in this part of the world."

"Yeah, but that color? It's him." The Porsche was in the left lane, bracketed by a junky Toyota and a brown RV that looked like a serial killer's rolling hideout. Had he seen us?

"No point in calling the cops, right?" she asked.

"Cops are probably running for their lives," I said, craning my head for a better view of the road ahead. The line of red lights glowed like evil eyes for a mile or two ahead. If an accident blocked both lanes, we'd be jammed here as a wave of smoke and fire swept over us.

"I don't have signal," she said, tossing the phone onto the dashboard. "Let's reverse out of here. We can get his license plate, we can track him down, right?"

"Right."

"Okay." She twisted around in her seat for a better look out the rear window as she eased on the gas, the Mustang's damaged joints creaking. "Oh shit."

A fresh wave of cars slammed to a halt behind us, honking and flashing their lights. Madeline cursed.

The Porsche's door eased open, and Ken slipped out.

I thought he was going to run. Why not? He would move faster on foot than any car on this road. If he could jog a few miles ahead, he might steal or carjack a new vehicle and continue his merry way. But Ken had other plans in mind. He strode onto the narrow shoulder, working his shoulders, flapping his hands, like he was a concert pianist warming up for a big night at the keys.

"What's he doing?" Madeline asked.

"Maybe he's got another bullshit speech for us."

"What should we do?"

"Get out," I said, slipping Manny's pistol into my waistband again. "We're sitting ducks here."

"The fuck will we do out there?"

"That's up to him." I already had my door open. Ken watched me emerge with a smile on his face, like he'd been waiting for this moment his entire life. The smoke made the back of my throat itch. I didn't want to think about how many minutes we might have left before the wildfire crisped us all.

I stepped onto the shoulder and Ken squared himself to

me, his thumbs hooked into his belt-loops. "Growing up, I was always a huge fan of Spaghetti Westerns. Listened to Morricone all the time, that sort of thing," he said.

"Any other day, I'd bullshit with you for hours about 'The Good, the Bad, and the Ugly'," I said, trying not to cough as ash tickled my throat. "But today is definitely not that day." In my peripheral vision, the closest drivers gawped at us.

"No, I guess not." He shook his head. "I'm not going to let them arrest me, okay? I'm not built for prison."

"Nobody is."

"Makes sense." He shifted his feet, his hands dropping to his sides. "I have an idea: Eastwood and Van Cleef."

"You want a duel?" I said. "Fast draw at ten paces, all that bullshit?"

He nodded. "You're on my wavelength. Yeah, how cool would that be?"

"Not cool at all." I clenched my hands into fists. "Look, this is stupid. In case you didn't notice, there's a giant-ass fire–"

"It's not stupid." He whisked his jacket back. A pistol grip poked from his waistband. "It's how real men die. You ready?"

"No." But I pulled my own jacket away from my waistline and hooked my thumb into my belt an inch from Manny's weapon. My heart hammered against my sternum like it wanted to break free and sprint across the fields, leaving my body to whatever was coming. This was fucking absurd. Who did this kind of thing?

Crazy dudes like Ken, that's who.

His eyes blazed. "On three, we draw down, okay? Best man wins."

"Dad," Madeline said from somewhere behind me. "Please don't fucking do this."

Ken's eyes shifted to a spot over my right shoulder. His left hand twitched. "Sorry, kiddo. It's pretty unfixable at this point, isn't it?"

"You said it," she said, her voice hard.

Ken was serious about drawing down. If he killed me, he would shoot her next. After that, he would likely blast any random driver who looked at him funny.

"Then let's get on with it," Ken said, his hands tensing. "On three, okay? It'll be like the old days..."

The fear was a live thing in my head, screaming orders that made no sense. The fear wanted me to dive behind the nearest car for cover. The fear wanted me to turn and run as fast as I could for the burning hills. The fear saw the lunacy in Ken's eyes and thought I had no chance.

"One," Ken said, but his hand was already in motion, a blur darting for the pistol's grip, damn he was fast –

A loud crack echoed off the stalled cars. Someone screamed, muffled by glass.

Ken stood tall, smiling at me, but his eyes were already losing focus, his grin fading at the edges. His shirt wet and red a few inches above the belt.

"That you?" I said, not daring to turn around.

"Yeah," Madeline called out. "I forgot to tell you: I picked up your gun in the yard."

Ken spat thick blood down his chin.

"How's that for a big twist?" I told him.

Ken gurgled and fell to his knees. He swayed there, his hands clutching the right side of his chest, before falling onto his face. I walked over and knelt and reached under his body for his pistol. He might have groaned, but it was hard to tell over a fresh blast of horns. I thought the closest drivers were alerting everyone to the gunfight on the left, but as I stood again, I saw the source of their fear: behind us, the fields seethed with black smoke, bright tongues of flame within a hundred yards of the road. I could feel the heat.

Madeline was behind me, my pistol in her hand. Her face was a blank mask, no tears. "We need to get out of here," she said, and coughed.

"Yeah," but as I moved toward her, something snagged my left foot. Ken's bloody hand wrapped around my ankle. His head turned slowly so he could fix me with a pleading stare.

"Check him for that bag," she said.

I kicked Ken's hand loose and knelt and tapped his left jacket pocket, then the right, feeling metal beneath the fabric. I pulled the bag free and opened it, the nearest headlights glinting off gold, the hard sparkle of diamonds, a thumb-sized book with black leather covers. I pocketed the bag and stood. Ken was gone by then, tiny flames dancing in his eyes.

I returned to the Mustang. Around us, drivers were deciding to make a last-ditch power drive for safety, plowing off the road and into the fields. A tiny Fiat rolled past, bouncing over ruts and bumps like a porpoise through waves, followed by a heavy SUV. I remembered it was only two or three miles in that direction until you hit the intersection, and if you went left you would reach the bridge crossing the dry riverbed, an excellent firebreak.

"I'll drive," I told Madeline. "Ready for another bit of off-roading?"

37.

We survived.

I pointed our headlights into the darkness and mashed the gas pedal and tried to ignore the rocks and dirt and small animals thumping into our windshield, cracking it in places. The Mustang's shocks absorbed the worst of the bumps, but my spine jangled, my skull rattled, and my hands were quaking on the wheel by the time we returned to smooth asphalt.

We sped from the valley, barreling past a dozen cars that had stopped on the shoulder so their owners could capture the destruction on their phones. San Douglas looked like a newly built level of Hell, the ridges crackling with flame, the smoke blotting out the moon. The Mustang's engine whined and clanked, and the swinging needles on the dashboard dials promised a fortune in repair bills, but we were alive.

Neither of us said a word until we reached the coast. The highway sign for Santa Barbara flashed past, and I briefly considered taking the exit. I knew if I stopped moving for more than a few minutes, I was liable to pass out until morning. Instead, I steered us into the left lane and let the Mustang find its speed, its body shuddering harder with every passing mile.

We were still on CA-1, roughly ten miles from Santa

Monica, when the Mustang finally wheezed and died. With the last of our momentum, I piloted us into a parking lot above the beach. We were alone except for a few kids sitting on a jeep's hood at the far end of the lot.

"Fuck," Madeline said.

"That's one word for it."

"I shot my father." Her voice quavered.

"He had it coming."

"Yeah. But I couldn't have done it if he hadn't pointed the gun at you. Kicked in that killer instinct like," she snapped her fingers. "Are we in trouble?"

I tapped the wheel. "Thank you again for saving my life," I said. "And to answer your question: I think we're good. The winery probably burned. Our rental house definitely burned. Your dad's gone, Manny's gone, Reid's gone. Angie–"

"Yeah, who's that again?"

"Queen of the Underworld, and this isn't something she'll concern herself over." I wasn't sure about that, but I didn't want Madeline to panic. Not yet.

"I thought the cops were looking for this car. Isn't that what Manny said?"

"Might have been bullshit. There's no evidence tying us to anything." I gave her my best imitation of a reassuring smile. "And I bet there's more than one Mustang in California."

"I don't feel soothed."

"That's why we're going to leave the car here. Keys in the ignition."

"And someone can steal it?"

I laughed. "Hey, you don't know what happened to it. You spent the whole weekend in your apartment, smoking weed or whatever it is you do. I'm the one who rented the house. Nobody's alive who can put you in San Douglas."

"Except those nice people at the vegetarian place. And those people in the other cars who saw Ken die."

"Damnit, you're right. We'll have to go back and kill them all."

"Nah, not the restaurant folks. They made pretty good food."

"I wouldn't worry about the other drivers, either," I said. "Everything was on fire, everybody was freaked. It doesn't make for reliable witnesses." I climbed out of the Mustang, my muscles throbbing from the drive and the weekend's abuse. I raised my arms above my head, and executed a quick tree pose, bending my left leg and slotting my sooty foot against my knee. I did it flawlessly.

"Good job, yoga master," she said.

I stretched against the railing that separated the lot from the dunes, which descended thirty feet to a strip of pale boulders and the roaring Pacific beyond. It was high tide, the breakers thumping a narrow strip of sand like a titanic heart, a soothing sound as old as time. If you were a first-time visitor to Earth and saw the ocean, you'd think: perfection. And then you'd turn to look at the coast with its endless concrete and burning lights and machines belching smog, and think: why did they go so wrong?

Beside me, Madeline shrugged off her greatcoat, revealing her sweatshirt stained with drying sweat and, along the hem, a black spray that might have been dried blood. "I remember going on a date with a costume designer for this zombie show," she said, carefully folding the coat over her left forearm. "And he described clothing as a suit of armor. You wear it because it gives you strength, gets you through the day. That's why I always wore this thing – it sets everyone on their back foot."

"I didn't figure it was because you wanted to look like a member of the Politburo."

"I think it's lost its magic," she said, and tossed the coat over the railing. It flopped down the dune like a broken raven and settled on the distant rocks.

Before I could say anything, she yanked her cigarettes and lighter out of her pocket and hurled them at the ocean. "Reset," she said. "Total fucking reset."

"I get it," I said.

She leaned against the railing, her hair a curtain over her face. "Can I ask you something?"

"Anything."

"Why comedy? Once you escaped from your old life, you could have done whatever you wanted."

I shook my head. "I'd always been a fan of standup. No matter who's in front of the mic, they're all trying to do the same thing: work out their issues. They're trying to heal a little of what's broken inside of them, and I hope they're trying to help the audience do the same. I felt like I wanted that. Needed that. Except..."

"You're not funny," she said.

"I'm not funny. But it's not even that. I wasn't willing to dig deep. I couldn't be honest enough with myself." I laughed. "I should have just opted for therapy."

The ocean hammered the coast. At the other end of the lot, the teenagers broke into fierce laughter, smoke blasting from their mouths. Their weed smelled like a dead skunk.

"Thank you for everything," Madeline said. "The therapists, they'd call it 'closure' or whatever."

"You're welcome."

"I'll pay whatever your fee is. Let's ignore how you wrecked my car."

"No fee," I said, and pulled the heavy bag from my jacket pocket. "There's gold and diamonds in here, plus a little black book. I'll take a few pieces and the book for my troubles, but the rest of it's yours."

"Yeah?" She took the bag and opened it. "You're sure this stuff's legit? Because you wouldn't exactly describe my dad as an honest guy."

"Yeah, I am. Otherwise, why chase after the Mustang so hard?"

"Good point. What's in the book?"

"I'm guessing blackmail stuff. I know how to use it. Do me a favor?"

"What?"

"Lie low for a few days. And spend the money well." I nodded at the road above. "You should call an Uber, get out of here. We'll stay in touch, yeah?"

Before I could react, she locked me in a crushing bear hug, her face against my chest, her hands locked over my spine. She squeezed like she wanted to crush the air from my lungs and absorb whatever was left of me. I wrapped my arms around her shoulders, lightly.

After what felt like an eternity, she loosened her grip and stepped back. I had two warm, wet spots over my sternum. She wiped her eyes and opened her mouth as if to say something before shutting it again. Instead, she smiled and shot off a quick salute, then spun on her heel like a dancer, hands over her head, and walked up the incline to the road.

I leaned against the railing and tried to time the crashing of the waves to my breath. I felt good for someone who'd survived a couple of shootings, left his mentor to die, and outrun a firestorm. I told myself I'd balanced the world's scales a fraction.

My phone buzzed. I checked the lock screen: unknown number. I answered it anyway.

"You asshole," Manny wheezed.

"You made it," I said, feeling good.

"I'm going to fucking kill you and the girl," he said. "Expect it."

"I'll make it easy on you," I said. "Let me tell you where I'll be tomorrow at midnight. I have Ken's little black book."

I gave him a familiar address, and he ended the call without a word. I returned to the ocean, the breakers silvery in the moonlight, the fish tearing each other apart beneath that placid surface. I remembered one time when Manny and I cleaned up a starlet's messy suicide attempt, and afterwards we sat on the beach not far from here, swigging from a bottle of rum as the sun came up, laughing at the absurdity of our lives. That memory should have sparked the warmth of nostalgia in my gut, but instead I felt nothing. Perhaps that was a good thing, considering what was coming next.

38.

The police had left the front gate of Hell House unlocked. I snatched the yellow tape away from the front door and used my rusty lockpicking skills to open it. It was two hours past dusk and the air was crisp and cool, courtesy of the wind blasting through the canyons.

During my day at home, I had dusted off my bespoke blue suit, the one I'd purchased with my first big bonus from working with Manny. I paired it with a crisp white shirt and my favorite pair of shoes, a hand-stitched pair in brown leather. For a bit of whimsy, I slipped on a pair of black socks patterned with orange cats. It was hard to believe I used to dress like this every day. I figured I had a fifty percent chance of dying tonight, maybe higher, and I wanted to look my best.

I walked through Hell House, turning on lights and shutting windows. The kitchen was still buried under a mountain of debris, moldy pizza boxes and cartons of takeout Chinese that smelled like death, bottles half-filled with warm beer and dried crusts of wine. Nobody had cleaned the bloodstain on the tiles beside the sink.

I poured a glass of water from the filter in the fridge before venturing onto the patio. In the pool, medical gloves floated like exploded jellyfish; the bottom was littered with glass and glittery bits of trash. It was a billion-dollar view beyond the far wall, the city a blanket of lights. I unlocked the back gate, which opened onto a dirt path winding its way through the hills, before returning to the kitchen.

I left the house's front door open, so I heard the gate's hinges creak as I stood at the kitchen island. Cautious footsteps on the front walk – at least three people, maybe more.

I took Ken's little black book from my suit pocket and set it on the marble in front of me, visible from the door. I was confident in my plan, but there was always room for error, wasn't there? You could never account for someone doing something impulsive and stupid.

A large man with a shaved head appeared in the kitchen doorway. He looked stouter than a brick outhouse, dressed in his tactical best: a black nylon jacket loose enough to hide significant firepower, paired with roomy jeans and combat boots.

"I'm not armed," I told him.

He nodded and stepped into the room. "Gonna search you anyway, buddy."

I backed away from the counter and raised my hands. As he patted me down, a second man appeared in the doorway, older and smaller than the first, his gray hair cropped hard against his skull. He was dressed almost identically to his partner, in a nylon jacket and jeans.

"He's clean," the first man told the second.

The second man touched the black bud in his left ear and said, "We're set."

Manny slid into view. The left side of his face was red, the cheek slightly blistered, the hair around his temple scorched away. His left hand was wrapped in a thick bandage. In place of his usual suit, he wore a loose blue shirt and expensive jeans. He tried giving me the same hard stare he used on paparazzi and other scumbags.

It should have sent a paralyzing burst of fear through me.

Instead, I smiled. "You look good for someone who almost burned to death," I said.

He surged forward, his good hand crimping into a fist, no doubt ready to beat me to a pulp – until he spotted the little black book by my hand.

He stopped. "That's it?" he said.

"I read it today," I said. "It's got everything you'd expect. Names, imports, amounts. You'd never believe who's in there, or maybe you would."

He sighed and nodded. "And let me guess, you took photos of every page, right? You've uploaded them to the cloud? It'll go to the press if you disappear?"

I pointed at him and winked. "Exactly. Why don't you bring her in?"

He played dumb. "Bring who in?"

"These big guys, they're not here to protect you. Remember what she said at her house? That she only leaves her fortress of solitude when her ass is on the line?" I tapped the cover of Ken's book. "She's all over this. Murder, major larceny, blackmail, all that good stuff there's no statute of limitations for."

Manny peered at me. "You finally took my advice about dressing up."

"I did some thinking this weekend," I said. "Now get her in here."

Manny nodded to the second man, who touched his ear again and murmured a few words. I remembered the first time I'd been in this house, with Manny ordering around the cops like he paid their salaries, and an innocent woman choking her last on the cold floor of the garage. I spent so many years trying to drown that memory in alcohol and pills, but now I forced myself to lean into it, to remember the astringent stink of bleach and the feel of skin cooling to my touch. I could bear that burden.

The house's front door creaked, followed by a rhythm of soft footsteps and hard thumps. I was confused by the thumping until Angie shuffled into the kitchen doorway, dressed in a black pantsuit and a white shirt, a lacquered cane in her hand. The cane was topped by an ivory skull. The two purple jewels in the skull's eye sockets caught the light and gleamed.

"Hello, Dash," she said.

"Nice to see you," I replied.

"Wish I could say likewise." She turned to Manny. "Have the guys go outside."

Manny nodded to the security dudes, who exited the door to the rear patio. The one with the shaved head took a vape from his pocket and blasted a cloud of vapor into the hot air, while his partner settled into one of the chairs beside the pool.

"He's got Ken's book," Manny said. "He says he took photos of the pages, uploaded them to the cloud. If he's killed..."

"Yeah, yeah, the press and a bunch of bloggers will get an interesting email, blah blah. I practically invented this setup." Angie leaned her cane against the counter and sorted through the nearest cluster of bottles. "Did Karl ever drink anything of quality?"

"I think he was more of a drugs guy," I said. "But then again, I only knew him for a few seconds before he got shot."

"You're a dark soul, Dash," Angie said, examining the label on a half-empty bottle of whiskey before uncorking it and pouring two fingers' worth into a red Solo cup. "Any port in a storm, huh?"

Manny trembled, his intact cheek reddening until it almost matched the color of his burnt skin. "Angie, I hate to rush you…"

"Ah, right. Okay, let's cut to the point." Angie slugged the liquor. "Dash, what do you want? Money? A job?"

"Accountability," I said.

"Oh, you poor, lost soul." She snorted. "There's no such thing. You used to not be this naïve. What happened to you?"

"Angie," Manny said, shifting his weight from foot to foot. "We have to wrap this up."

She jabbed a finger at him. "We move at my pace," she said. "Yet again, you've failed to contain a situation spinning out of control. It's not the first time I've had doubts about your competence, Manny, but God help you if I think it should be your last."

She punctuated the threat by tossing the Solo cup at the sink – and missed. It clattered onto the tiles beside Karl's bloodstain. "The daughter get what she needed out of your little weekend?" she asked me.

"I'm cheaper than a shrink," I said.

She smirked. "Now that's funny. We're going to have to kill her, you realize. Even if you're not lying about emailing the press, it'll never get any traction. We'll flood the zone with shit."

I was sweating, trying not to side-eye the patio, where the security men lurked beside the pool, their faces bathed in blue light. I checked my watch and the slightly crooked second hand inching so slowly toward the top of the hour. When I looked up again, Manny had drawn a .25 automatic and pressed it against his hip, barrel pointed at the floor.

I chuckled.

"What's so fucking funny?" Manny asked.

"When I first saw this little book, I thought I'd trade it for my safety. That's how I would've done it before." I shrugged. "But when I got back to my apartment last night, someone was waiting for me. They'd been waiting there since I'd driven up to San Douglas. They figured I'd have to come home at some point."

I checked the patio. The security guys were gone.

Manny followed my gaze. It took him a heartbeat to realize the situation, and when he did, he startled, his .25 shifting toward the window. He was fast for a big guy, but he was too late.

The window exploded along with Manny's throat. He dropped his pistol and scratched at his collar and slid against the counter, blood pouring over his fingers. He flopped onto his back, his feet kicking the nearest cabinet, bottles and plates raining onto him. Maybe he'd have time to appreciate the irony of dying the same way as Vonn and Reid.

Manny shuddered and went still.

Maybe not.

Manny's .25 landed beside the counter. Angie eyed it, gauging distances and angles.

"I wouldn't," I said.

She grunted and grabbed a plastic bottle of vodka. "So much for going out in a blaze of glory."

"This isn't a movie."

She unscrewed the bottle and took a sip, winced. "Who's the shooter?"

"Remember what I said about accountability?"

The door to the patio opened and Mister Skull walked in. It was the second time I'd seen my stalker in full lighting, and I was jolted yet again by the difference between the shadowy monster of my dreams and this short figure in loose black clothes, surgical gloves, and a cheap Halloween mask. Mister Skull held a pistol with a comically oversized silencer screwed onto the barrel.

"Who the hell are you?" Angie asked.

The visitor stripped off the mask, revealing a familiar shock of blonde hair, merciless blue eyes.

Mister Skull? Shame on me: as I'd learned last night, it had always been Miss Skull, and she was pissed.

"Her name's Natalia," I said.

I waited to see if Natalia wanted to say something, but she remained locked on Angie, her hand squeezing the pistol's grip like it was a throat she wanted to crush. "You remember a couple of years back, what happened in this house?" I asked.

Angie stiffened. "No, I don't."

"My sister was killed," Natalia said, so softly I had to strain to hear her. "And you – your people – you tossed her away like trash."

"He did it." Angie pointed a quaking finger at me. "He did that thing."

"Yes, I did. And I tried calling her a long time ago, to tell her." I turned my gaze to Natalia and dipped my head, a penitent praying before the altar. "I even visited her house a few days ago, after Karl died, and I still couldn't do it. I was too weak. But right after I came back from San Douglas, I suddenly had the strength. I guess that's the upside to surviving a wildfire and a shootout. So, I called her again, meaning to tell her everything about what happened to her sister. And you know what she told me?"

"I told him, 'I'm sitting in your apartment'," Natalia said, an impish grin twitching the corner of her mouth.

"She'd been tracking me for a long time," I said. "Ever since she saw me in the police station, after her sister died. She paid people for information. Hurt some others. Good detective work. When I finally spotted her, I thought she was some rando who was after Karl – she was right by the pool there, she'd come through the back – but she was really after me. And later, after I went to her house, she followed me home. When I went to San Douglas, she broke into my apartment and waited there, figuring I'd have to come back at some point. I told her the truth, Angie. The whole truth."

"For a long time, I blamed Dash. I was wrong about that. He was just a blunt instrument," Natalia told Angie, her voice rising from a raspy whisper to something deep and ancient and terrible, a god's voice in the desert darkness. "You were the brain. My sister – who never hurt anyone, who was too fucking soft – she was a fucking person, not some *thing* to be dealt with, tossed away, forgotten about. Now go ahead, give me your bullshit excuses."

Angie placed the vodka bottle on the counter and stiffened her spine. "There are a lot of things I could say, but why don't you just–"

Natalia's rising hand was a blur, the pistol making a loud thump like a dictionary hitting the floor. The bullet struck Angie in the forehead and she dropped like a trapdoor had opened beneath her, taking her cane with her on the way down. For someone who'd once possessed so much power in this town, it was an ignoble death. Which made it sort of perfect.

"We good?" I asked Natalia.

"No," she said, dropping the silenced pistol on Manny's chest. "But we're even."

"What now?"

"We live." She kicked aside the skull mask. "Or try to."

She disappeared through the open doorway to the patio without another word, her footsteps lost in the lapping of water against concrete, the distant hum of traffic, the ticking of my watch. I wiped down the counter where I'd leaned on it. I dropped Ken's little black book beside Angie's body. I hoped the cops would treat it like a confession.

Leaving through the backyard, I passed the security guys' bodies sprawled behind a bush. How had she killed them so quietly? Natalia had said almost nothing about her background when I found her in the apartment, but she'd alluded to a gangster father and a short childhood. However that translated into the ability to snuff out a pair of trained guys, I didn't want to know. I was finished here.

The door in the rear wall opened onto a dirt path winding its way through the hills. The road curved below, lined by houses teetering on the edge of cliffs, the darkness broken in places by the luminescent squares of pools. As I worked my way to a lower elevation, the path dipped behind thick scrub, hiding civilization momentarily from sight, and the scent of jasmine teased my nostrils. I could imagine I was walking through the land as it had existed long before humanity had set foot on it, a perfect canvas for life, all elements in balance.

I elbowed through a screen of bushes and emerged again onto the pavement, the rumble and honking of the city slamming back onto the soundtrack. I liked to think I had the solution to everything, and that wasn't true: like everyone else, I was along for the ride. But even if I couldn't save the world, maybe I could fix myself.

39.

It took me another two hours to walk home, and by the time I unlocked my front door, my beautiful shirt was sticky with sweat and my pant legs were coated with a fine layer of dust. I stripped off my suit in the bedroom and changed into a pair of jeans and a t-shirt and retrieved my phone from where I left it in my desk drawer. If the cops tried to tie me to the killings in the hills, they would ping my phone and see it was sitting in my apartment for most of the night.

I texted Madeline:

We're all settled here.

A few minutes later, she replied:

All's right with the world. Going to bed. I think I'll sleep.

I hoped Madeline would be okay. The movies teach us that all you need to escape your generational trauma is a dramatic event, preferably with a couple of explosions and quirky characters. Too bad it never works that way. If she ever wanted to talk it out over a burrito, I would be there.

Next, I texted Ellie James and asked what she was doing. She replied that she had finished a delivery run to downtown, did I want to grab a drink? I told her I had quit alcohol for the time being, but I could use some food, and there was a pretty good place, *The Frying Pan*, that I wanted to try.

The Frying Pan had a counter open to the sidewalk. You could sit on a stool and watch the chefs on the other side of the window fry and broil the fullest range of nature's bounty. Ellie was already there when I arrived, pouring hot sauce onto a deep-fried octopus on a skewer, and when she saw me, her face lit up. It had been a long time since anyone looked at me like that.

"How goes it?" she said when I sat down.

"I'm good," I said. "Long weekend, though."

"You go somewhere?" She squeezed my knee. "You got a little color."

"Went up the coast a bit," I said. "Gave me some time to think."

She bit into the octopus and held out the skewer, offering me the other half. I took it and crunched down. The fried flesh and napalm sauce were overwhelming, crackling down my tongue, reminding me that I was a creature no better than any other in this world, a thin envelope of skin and bone, nerves and muscles, hopes and fears. I swallowed and felt like everything might be all right.

"Yeah?" she asked. "What'd you think about?"

Her pupils reflected the *Frying Pan*'s lights as twin galaxies. I wanted to tumble into them and forget the past fifteen years of my life. She was a fresh start, a glorious chance, and although so much could go wrong if we took this further, my thundering heart told me I had to try.

"I'm thinking of starting a detective business," I said.

ACKNOWLEDGEMENTS

I spent years bouncing between New York, Los Angeles and Las Vegas as a journalist for a handful of glossy magazines, which meant many late-night conversations with the fixers, PR experts, and other folks who work behind the shiny edifice of our pop culture. I'm thankful for their stories, some of which (in heavily modified form) found their way into this book; Dash wouldn't be a fully realized creature without you.

A massive thank you to Daniel Culver, my incredible editor at Datura, whose sharp edits helped turn the manuscript into a finely honed blade. I'm also grateful for the rest of the Datura crew, including Gemma Creffield and Caroline Lambe.

I'd be remiss if I didn't thank my author friends who helped push me through the writing and editing process, sometimes in fits and starts. Libby Cudmore helped turn this manuscript into a book. Steve Weddle, S.A. Cosby, Todd Robinson, Eryk Pruitt, Rob Hart, and Paul Garth all provided crucial advice and edits.

And, as always, to G and M: my two hearts.

ABOUT THE AUTHOR

Nick Kolakowski is the author of several crime novels, including *Love & Bullets* (Shotgun Honey) and *Absolute Unit* (Crystal Lake Publishing). His work has been nominated for the Anthony and Derringer awards, and his short story *Scorpions* appeared in *The Best Mystery and Suspense 2024*. His short fiction has appeared in numerous anthologies and magazines, including *Mystery Weekly, Dark Yonder, Rock and a Hard Place Press,* and more.

One

September 9, 2000
Gillian Charles, Age 12

A long white panel snapped into place, blocking the hall. From above, an image projected against the surface.

Four Contestants occupy a room.

Tommy solves a maze.

Ellsberg plays chess.

Leah bedazzles a pair of jeans.

What is Gillian doing?

Gillian Charles read the riddle three times. The intricate braids her mother painstakingly constructed frayed and dangling in her face. Her green-and-black flannel full of holes, her bell-bottom jeans torn open at her bloodied knees. And she was barefoot, her Keds lost somewhere in the maze behind. Today appearances didn't matter. Not hers, anyway.

What is Gillian doing?

A moment of panic. The question asked more of her than she expected. Every decision she'd made in the Contest up to now – each riddle solved and puzzle cracked. Maybe she'd misinterpreted the answers? Mom always said she acted too fast, didn't think things through. Maybe she'd jumped down a rabbit hole to a dead end.

No. This was the Puzzle Man at his best. Sebastian, testing

if Gillian would doubt herself. The answer was obvious.

"Playing chess with Ellsberg," she said.

The panel raised and she advanced.

Another panel blocked her way.

What goes through your neighborhood and past the airport and brought you here, yet never moves?

"The road," she said.

Gillian faces south.

Leah faces north.

They can see each other without mirrors.

How?

"They're face to face."

More obstacles. Sign after sign.

"The letter M."

"The door with the lion."

"Pull out the plug."

The assault continued. Each question making Gillian stronger. Sharper.

More likely to win the Contest Extraordinaire.

The hallway became a scummy cast-iron pipe, the top a good six feet above Gillian's head. Water streamed from grated downspouts, rising almost to ankle height. She found herself not alone. Ahead sloshed a tow-headed spindly white boy, clad in a blazer, polo, and shorts, a purplish birthmark splotch visible through his thin hair. Mr Peanut brought to life.

Martin Ellsberg lived in a trailer park outside Mobile, Alabama, where his fussy appearance had earned him his fair share of bruises. But he was tough – despite the Contest's rigors, he'd managed to retain his leather Oxfords, the most ridiculous footwear Gillian could have imagined. He'd decoded his last puzzle a full three seconds before her. Underestimate Ells and his affected hint of a German accent and you'd find yourself wheeled out of the Contest on a gurney.

Still, with no sign of the other Contestants, Gillian relaxed. She was comfortably ahead, and could easily beat Ellsberg in a foot race. He startled as she ran up, but quickly regained his composure. They exchanged the secret handshake – Slap. Backslap. Elbows. Fistbump – then walked side-by-side down the tunnel.

"On that last puzzle," he said. "You should have been quicker up the ladder."

"You took the ladder? Interesting."

He frowned. "What did you do?"

Gillian didn't answer. She pulled loose peanut M&Ms from her pocket. She'd never eaten the peanut ones until the Contest. Until Tommy. She popped a few into her mouth.

"What happened to Leah?" Ellsberg asked.

"She blew it on the Drink Me challenge. I saw her barfing everywhere."

Ellsberg nodded. *Of course.* "Food poisoning, I'll bet." He rubbed his birthmark. "Have you seen Tomas?"

The sudden memory of Tommy's stare: Gillian and he alone in the room. "Not since the beginning. He got stuck on the deduction puzzle."

"Probably out of it, then." Ellsberg's gaze lingered on her bare feet, maybe wondering how close she'd come to *out of it.* "Where do you think they go? When they lose?"

"Nobody gets hurt, remember? That's what Sebastian said."

Sebastian Luna had created the Contest Extraordinaire. He was an entertainer, a mogul, and a savant. His Bazaar – the puzzle palace above and the tunnels below – was a winner-takes-all opportunity for the first to escape. The prize gargantuan – a house, a new car, more money than their families had ever dreamed. But for Gillian, the Contest offered more. A chance for a life spent at Sebastian's side.

Ellsberg made a dubious noise. Looking at him, so full of himself, Gillian couldn't help but like him. She offered him the rest of her candy. He eyed the gift suspiciously.

"Are those the M&Ms Tomas gave you on the first day?"

"His mom sent him with a huge bag. She gets donations at the dentist where she works."

"I know. But you shouldn't accept gifts. You already spend too much time together."

She shrugged. *Do you want them, or not?* Ellsberg turned up his nose.

"Peanut are the best ones," she insisted.

"They stick to your teeth."

She smiled at him, her teeth nasty brown from chocolate and peanut fragments. Ellsberg grimaced but couldn't maintain his disgust. He burst out laughing, which got Gillian going, the pair in giggles when a new voice echoed down the tunnel.

"Hurry up. You guys are missing it."

All the humor drained from Gillian's body. She'd let friendship lull competition, and assumed she couldn't be beat. She was losing right now.

They ran up the tunnel.

He stood at the lip of the pipe, water cascading around him and plummeting over a thirty-foot drop. Tommy Kundojjala was cocky. Short and solid and no reason to be cool, yet somehow cool nonetheless. His voice was high-pitched and cringey. His right eye lazy. His Hannah

Montana T-shirt practically spotless, even now. But he made friends with ease. Shook hands like the president, or someone famous. And he was smart – his Contest qualifying time the fastest among them. Motivation ran in the family. His parents had chased opportunity from Odisha to London, then finally to the US. They and Tommy lived with his six siblings and two aunts in a crappy apartment outside Chicago. He needed to win the Contest as badly as Gillian. But she meant to win, nonetheless.

Gillian approached and performed the handshake dance with Tommy. Then she stood as close to the edge as possible, as still as she could with the arctic cascade frothing at her naked ankles. The pipe was one of many in a vast cavern, each dumping water into the dark blue lake far below. Across the water, at the foot of a sheer cliff, she saw a sliver of beach. Above that, the sinister mouth of a cave. No ladder, no bridge, only one way down. This was the finish line, or close to it. She could feel it. But Tommy hadn't jumped yet, which made her nervous. His actions in the Contest so far were a mystery she couldn't solve.

On her left, the boy himself grinned, his teeth blinding white. "You ready for this, Gil?" His voice suggested she wasn't. "Long way down."

"I'm ready."

They stood side by side. Ellsberg shuffled nervously behind. Tommy cast a sidelong look at her bare feet.

"Won't your mom be pissed about the shoes?"

"Those were lost and found from the rec center. My real shoes are at home."

"Lucky you."

"Are you kidding? They're used. Mom lost her mind

when I bought them – not enough ankle support." Gillian adopted her Mom voice. *"I would have bought you new shoes."* She sighed. "And she would have. So, no way."

"I like your mom. I'll apologize to her after I beat you."

He thought he was cute. And he was, kind of, but Gillian wasn't about to tell him. Instead, she pulled another M&M from her pocket and chewed obnoxiously. A slow smile crept over Tommy's face as he recognized his candy.

"A lot of talk," Ellsberg piped up from the back, "for someone who hasn't jumped."

"You in a hurry to get rid of me, Ells?"

"No." Ellsberg was strangely intense. "I'm suggesting you're frightened."

The boys had butted heads at the start – more Ellsberg's doing than Tommy's – but they'd grown friendly throughout the qualifiers, as had Gillian and Leah. Having survived the same puzzles, and come from similar struggling backgrounds, they'd found friends as much as competitors. The handshakes, the matching jelly bracelets. Fun, so long as no one mentioned what would happen on the last day. When only one of them would remain.

Tommy played it cool. "Am not."

"Yes, you are, you're scared to death. I can tell. You'll never jump."

"I can jump any time I want. Just give me a second."

"Ridiculous. You'll still be standing right here when I win."

Tommy got louder, "I'm not scared."

Neither of them moved. As Gillian reconsidered Tommy's behavior, she understood. The drift in his right eye. His terrible depth perception, his fear of heights. But Ellsberg she couldn't figure. His voice wavered. He breathed quicker.

It wasn't Tommy stopping him – Ellsberg was also afraid. Afraid of whatever waited for them down below.

Their fears held them back. They hesitated, with everything on the line.

Gillian threw herself over the edge.

Frigid water raked her skin, the cold claws of a witch. The shock almost sent her to the bottom, a dark gloom she couldn't see. She kicked toward the light, her lungs straining, and quickly broke through. Once she got her bearings she stroked toward shore, eventually clawing her way onto the small sandy peninsula. She rolled over to see what she'd left behind. A world of water. PVC of various widths sucked water from the lake and routed it throughout the vascular system feeding the sprawling complex, only to dump it back here again via the many open drainpipes. Gillian wondered where the pipes went, but figured she'd have an eternity to explore when she won.

She stood and faced front. Before her lay the only visible exit. Stakes pinned a large cargo net to the sand, the rope rising toward the dark cave fifteen feet above. The mesh course resembled a giant's hammock, the cave a hungry, gaping mouth. Over the entrance a message had been engraved in plate steel: VICTORY.

This was it. This was the last challenge. Gillian looked around quickly, but the boys had yet to appear.

She ran for the rope course.

The braided coils scraped her skin. Each rope square just large enough that her knees plunged through the gaps, the course ensnaring her like some feral animal. But she learned to spread her stance, aiming for the thick knots where the ropes met. She was going to leave the beach behind.

A desperate choking cry, from over her shoulder. Every fiber in her being cried out to continue, to scale the path ahead and blaze down the yellow brick road, but despite herself, she turned. Ellsberg flailed in the dark lake. His chin frantically jerked above the surface. He couldn't swim.

From somewhere in her head, her mother's soft yet firm tone reached her. Mom towering, despite her short stature. *Gillian Charles, you intend to leave that boy? What kind of person does that make you?*

She froze. Her hands locked around the rope coils. Ahead lay everything. The way out of hand-me-downs. Prize money to afford treatment for Mom's lupus. The unfettered life she was owed, and not the trap she lived in. She pictured the couch she shared with her sister, their dumpy apartment so close to I45 you could hear the 18-wheelers running day and night. Winning promised access and money and everything she'd ever want.

Ellsberg gurgled. He disappeared under the water.

She wanted Ellsberg to be OK.

Throwing caution to the wind, she turned around. Crawled headfirst back to the sand. She hit the beach, keeping her head on a swivel. She stretched her peripheral as far as possible. There was no sign of Tommy.

She could do this. She could pull Ellsberg to safety and still win the Contest. Be cutthroat yet kind.

Into the water she went, bracing herself for the skin-stripping cold. With strong strokes she lanced toward the spot where Ells had vanished. The water thundered in her ears, and she realized only gradually it was the sound of her own heart. Every beat a ticking clock. The sound of Tommy drawing closer.

Looking down, she opened her eyes. She couldn't see the bottom, but she identified the dark thrashing form of a boy in leather dress shoes. Futilely scraping at the water as if trapped in amber.

Ellsberg, you dummy, you should have known. Sebastian knew everything about the Contestants. Their strengths, their fears, their weaknesses. *He'd have known you couldn't swim.*

Down she plunged.

She kicked hard. Water sluiced around her body. With arms extended, she torpedoed toward Ellsberg. Her fingers locked around his heavy blazer, the boy a sagging dead weight. She angled back, but drew no closer to the surface. Her lungs heated up. The water became a presence, a monster indifferent to her Contest victory, indifferent to her life in every way. She pulled. Her muscles stretched, her bones separating from the sockets. Ellsberg squirmed in her grasp, his every movement conspiring to send them deeper.

This idiot. This dumb kid with no chance. He was going to kill them both.

Ellsberg popped free of the jacket.

He hovered there, strangely weightless for a moment, buoyant with enthusiasm. Gillian grabbed his waving arm and again reached for the light above. Pressure drove her toward the surface, the urge for air and the urge to win. She'd seized this chance and spent months training and proving herself smarter than every genius in the room. Ellsberg wasn't going to stop her. Nothing was.

They broke the surface, gasping for air. Ellsberg clung to her, a torpid seal needing to be beached. With her muscles burning, Gillian tugged him to the sand. Together they stumbled ashore. Ellsberg collapsed immediately, coughing and spitting, but Gillian stayed on her feet, something more powerful than exhaustion driving her back to the rope course.

"I'm sorry," Ellsberg gurgled.

His words were cold comfort. She told herself she'd done the right thing. Told herself that now Ellsberg was safe, she could stop thinking about him. He wasn't the problem. The problem was someone she couldn't see.

Up the course she went. Her previous experience prepared her for another go. In no time she crested the rise and left the tenuous footing of the rope course behind. Without hesitation, she ran into the cave. Multicolored lights strobed in deep wall sockets, the tunnel a psychedelic whirlwind. The wind howled. Shapes twisted in the dark. Nevertheless, she ran. Her muscles burning, her feet bruised, she ran.

And then she stopped.

Ahead, the tunnel forked. At the end of each path stood a door, smooth and unmarked, the choices identical. No tracks to tell if anyone had passed, the tunnel floor swept clean. On the ground at the split, three somethings glimmered. Three boxes, labelled with nonsense phrases.

GOTH REF

FILTHIEST CULT LET

GEARHEAD TENT

Word scrambles. They weren't difficult, almost to Gillian's chagrin. The answers overly reliant on the word *the*. Gillian carved answers from the muddle, and her expression soured. Sebastian thought he was being clever when he bestowed terms of endearment on each of the Contestants. Ellsberg,

The Frog. Tommy, The Great Dane. As for Gillian, Sebastian sometimes called her his *little cuttlefish*. The fish a chameleon. A creature that saw everything, some scientists thought from before birth. Gillian hated the term.

She knelt and opened her box. Inside were two fox-eared skeleton keys. The bits of the left key enclosed, creating a square with the shaft. The right key bits hooked over that square, the bits open, but the gap not sufficient to pull the keys apart without manipulation. Devil's Keys. A chill went through her body, and not from the dampness seeping into her bones.

Sebastian knew their weaknesses. Gillian had never tested well on disentanglement puzzles. Mechanical frustrations with pieces that were difficult to both take apart and reassemble. But she spotted the two keyholes in the false bottom of the box. Quick experimentation revealed she couldn't turn one key at a time, but only both simultaneously. Behind these locks would lie the answer she needed. Which tunnel should she take?

She straightened and cocked her head toward a sound from behind her. She couldn't make out the words, but she thought she heard conversation.

Tommy would have hit the beach by now. She didn't have a lot of time.

She returned her attention to the puzzle. The left key – the left fox – had a groove toward the end of the shaft, narrow enough the gap in the right key bits would slide over. But that narrowed section lay outside the left key's square, the square the right key was trapped within. She'd have to move one around the other. But move which key, and which way? Given the right one held the gap, she started there. Turning the key toward the end of the left key's shaft, toward the groove. But the enclosed bits of the left key prevented her from reaching her destination. She tried going around the other direction, away from the groove, but fared no better. The square of the left key was enclosed with thick metal. How could she ever separate them?

Her hands trembled. She knew she relied too much on gut instinct. Twisting and turning and bullheading her way, finding answers through constant trial and error. Eventually she'd solve the puzzle, but through such a convoluted process entire nations could rise and fall. She didn't have that kind of time. It killed her to just sit here, but she needed to think. To plan.

A laugh sounded out on the beach. The noise of rope tendons stretching as someone threw themselves at the web leading to where Gillian stood with her thumb up her butt.

Hold the puzzle in your mind, Gillian. You can do this. Show him.

She could always guess which tunnel, but maybe neither tunnel was correct.

Slowly, she rotated the entanglement. Her brown eyes darted over the length of the keys. *Think in three dimensions, not two. Absorb every detail. Imagine the end state.* And then she smiled. There. The groove at the end of the left key wasn't the endpoint, it was only a stop along the solution path. On the loop of the same key, at the fox's cheek, another groove that she'd missed. Guide the right one there and the foxes could detach. The keys could then be inserted into the false bottom.

Again she brought the right key toward the end groove, but kept the length at a ninety-degree angle, on a z-axis relative to the left key. In this arrangement the gap in the right swung over the groove, putting the onetime right key on the left. Then she flipped it such that the bow was on top. Breathing slow, she moved the key down the length of its mate, toward her chest, toward the left fox's head.

The bits of the right key passed over the cheek groove and put it inside the fox's head, inside the bow. She moved the right one clockwise, around the circumference. The right key again reached the groove, and she slid it out. The fox-eared keys separated in her hands.

Bare footsteps scuffed against the rock behind her.

Gillian jammed the keys into their respective locks. She turned, the bottom unlocked and popped open, and she found a tiny slip of paper lying underneath. She read the words without retrieving the paper.

TWO WRONGS.

Don't make a right.

The left tunnel.

She abandoned the box. Ran full tilt down the left tunnel, her arms pumping, her braids slapping against her face. When she hit the door, it opened without resistance. Ahead lay only darkness. She didn't slow, didn't hesitate. Behind her the door clicked shut and she knew there would be no turning back. She felt the first curtain as she ran, a simple gauze veil designed to filter light. There were more curtains ahead, each layer heavier than the last, requiring her to push the fabric aside with exhausted muscles. She barreled through chiffon and linen. Fought through cheesecloth and velvet. She heard voices. Muffled at first but growing stronger. She pushed and shoved and muscled through. She heard cheering. The tunnel grew brighter and brighter.

She burst free of the passageway and stumbled into bedlam. A giant tent unfolded around her, the canvas sheltering row after row of packed bleachers. The big top crowd thundered. The air smelled like popcorn and cotton candy. One sawdust-covered ring dominated the floor, and a man stood in the center. Dominated it, despite his stature. He was small and tan, vaguely European, perhaps Spanish. He wore a purple tailcoat, dapper black vest, and orange pants. On his head a black flat cap, and on his feet pointed shoes. He seemed both exotically foreign and strangely familiar, the kindly uncle returning from far away with magnificent stories to enthrall nieces and nephews. There was no missing him, his face and name everywhere, on T-shirts, shopping bags. The banners hanging from above. SEBASTIAN LUNA'S CONTEST EXTRAORDINAIRE. He would crown her the winner.

But Tommy stood under Sebastian's arm, grinning from ear to ear.

The shock stopped Gillian cold. Even the water in the tank hadn't numbed her like this. Unreality enveloped her, as if she piloted her body from deep within her brain, a control center cut off from feeling. She pulled levers to stir her legs. She attempted to steer her head from side to side, to take in the cheers meant for someone else. She plodded toward Sebastian and Tommy and stood before them, waiting for Sebastian to notice her. He had eyes only for the victor.

"You did it, my boy!" The man lit up from within. When he looked at you, you believed he saw no one else in the world. "I knew you could do it."

A lavalier microphone cast his voice throughout the tent. Although the magic of Sebastian had you convinced his voice could carry unamplified for miles and miles.

Tommy was electric. He bounced in place. He could hardly believe his luck – or, more appropriately, his skill. Gillian knew exactly what Tommy was feeling. She'd imagined and practiced her reaction to winning the Contest for months.

She'd crafted the perfect version of what was to be and replayed the scenario in her mind every minute of every day until ten seconds ago.

Her lips parted but she didn't know what to say. She saw the jeans, the T-shirts, the Nikes – all Tommy's size. The giant million-dollar check. The lawyers holding photos and paperwork, talking new cars and residence in a five-bedroom house, today.

The other losers had disappeared, Sebastian's team artfully shuffling them offstage. Gillian was the only failure to stand front and center. Bathing in defeat.

At last Sebastian took notice. His eyes fell on her like she was a loose thread poking from one of his buttons. His mouth quirked. "And here's little Gillian."

Little Gillian. As if she was a bauble he'd all but forgotten.

"But," she said.

That was all she could say. *But.*

Sebastian's eyes twinkled. "But what?"

"I stopped to help Martin," her voice croaked. "He... He couldn't swim."

Sebastian squat on his heels. It was another of his trademarks. Bringing himself to eye level with children. Gillian had always appreciated the gesture.

"But that's not true," he said.

Deep in the recesses of her mind, deeper still than her imagined control center, something stirred. A dark suspicion. A truth she'd suspected but avoided because she hadn't wanted to face the ugliness. Gillian knew the words before Sebastian could say them.

"Martin can swim just fine."

The crowd had quieted. There were laughs. A few sympathetic groans. And then finally applause, rising from behind and growing in a wave until the stands were alive with sound.

Martin Ellsberg shuffled past Gillian and went to stand with Sebastian and Tommy.

Gillian's eyes burned. Anger and shame and disappointment coalesced and threatened to pour hot tears down her face. But she would not cry. She would not let them see.

Ellsberg wouldn't make eye contact. The little shit was too guilty.

"He was working for you," Gillian said.

Sebastian shook his head. "That's not the point, child. The point is you made two mistakes."

Two wrongs.

"The first was stopping. Never stop. Never stop chasing the prize when you know you are right. If you hesitate, if you second-guess, that's when you will lose."

He said it with such conviction. This man who had built himself and his empire from nothing. He knew what he was talking about. She wished she couldn't believe him.

"And your second mistake," he said, "was helping Martin."

"So I was supposed to let him drown?"

She hated the reckless anger in her voice. But the words washed over Sebastian and left him untouched. He set his hand on her shoulder in a tender expression that still managed to feel dismissive.

"You were supposed to chase your dream," he said. "And trust I would never let a child come to harm in my Contest."

Sebastian stood tall. "Conviction," he said, more to the crowd than her. "Strength of purpose." He released Gillian and again brought Tommy close, the boy lost in his realized dreams of wealth and privilege and access until the end of his days. "I saw these things in Tomas Kundojjala. And I knew he would win."

The crowd stormed to their feet, their cheers deafening. Pandemonium swelled the tent, the confines increasingly hot and close and threatening. Gillian didn't know what to do. This wasn't how it was supposed to be. Fury lit inside her chest. Passion fired her throat and a blast of words erupted.

"I could have won!" she said. "I could have won the whole thing."

But no one heard her, or if they did, they no longer cared. Subtly, Sebastian summoned his handlers: pleasant-looking people with strong hands who guided Gillian from the center ring, which was now meant only for Tommy. His family dashed in as the handlers escorted her out. They ran so very fast from their old life, confident they'd never have to return.

You did the right thing, Gillian told herself, the words firm, even as she was led back to the life she'd failed to escape. *Saving Ellsberg was the right thing to do.*

But it was the words she'd said out loud that haunted her.

I could have won.